Marianne,

INSURABLE
INTEREST

*Smooth
Sailing —*

Vint Nash

11·06·03

INSURABLE INTEREST

By Vincent Lash

Trimble & Durst, LLC

Publishers   Baltimore Maryland

Cover illustration by Murray.

INSURABLE INTEREST
Copyright © 2002 Vincent Lash

International Standard Book Number: 0-9718891-0-4

Library of Congress Cataloging-in-Publication Data
Available upon request

Manufactured in the United States of America

Dedicated to
Mary P. McDonald

And always for my wife, Babs

And our children,
Jacob, Christopher, Raechal, Addison

CONTENTS

INSURABLE
INTEREST

Prologue

"I disagree, Tom. There should be more curve in the hips."

"This isn't Rubens meets Warhol," Tom Padgett said, raising his voice to be heard over the hissing flame from the welding torch he held in his hand. He walked over to the acetylene and oxygen tanks and shut them off by screwing down on the valve of each bottle, one at a time. The excess fuel in the neoprene hoses connecting to the hand element cleared with an expected, resounding snap.

Both men removed their welding goggles and scrutinized their work. Eric Kinsley stepped back from the abstract iron sculpture to better examine it. Eleven feet tall and four feet wide, this was their largest creation yet. "Look—right here. There should definitely be more curve."

"I don't think so. It'll look like it's bending over."

"More curve in the hips and bulkier all the way around," Eric said. "It needs to be bolder—bigger than life—our pièce de résistance!"

"Why must you do this with every project?"

"What?"

"We agree on a design, we get into production, then you start making changes—it's the same thing every time," Tom said.

"Don't say 'in production.' This isn't a factory."

"At least factories finish what they start."

"It's got to be perfect."

"Come on, Eric. I'm exhausted."

"I'm tired too."

"Yeah well, I'd like to get home before Hope and the kids wake up."

"Can't help it. The artist in me speaks."

"Fine," Tom said, throwing his hands into the air. He walked over to a three-foot-high Corinthian column standing on the far side of the room. On it sat a clear glass dome over a gold coin—a 1907 twenty-dollar Saint-Gaudens. He raised the dome and snatched up the coin, something both men had done many times before. "Here's your speaking artist." He shook his clenched fist. "Heads it stays as is and we get home by three AM; tails and we work on it until sun-up or I drop over—whichever comes first." He tossed the coin into the air, caught it in one hand, and slapped it onto the back of his other wrist. Without hesitating he moved his hand away for both of them to see.

"Curves, it is!" Eric took the coin from Tom, kissed it, and returned it to its pedestal.

"Have it your way, but I'm getting horizontal for twenty minutes before I do anything else."

"What's the matter with you tonight, Thomas?"

"You really want to know? I'll tell you. I can't work every hour of every day. I'm tired, and I miss my family."

"I believe the word is *sacrifice*.

"Are you kidding? Try *divorce*."

"Don't tell me—Hope's pressuring you again."

"Can you blame her? I'm never home."

"Come on. She knew when we got involved with the Coterie there'd be a quota."

"Sure, we all did. But it's too much."

"Listen to me. No matter what it takes, we have to see this through. Everything depends on the next exhibition."

"So you keep reminding me."

"And I'm not going to stop until it sinks in. We've got a good thing going here. Let's not mess it up."

"I don't want to mess anything up, but be realistic, Eric.

We have no artistic control. What the Coterie say goes—and that's that."

"What do you call what we're doing here? I don't see anybody else in the studio. They didn't have a thing to say about this beauty's hips. We're doing it—you and me, partner."

"This is one job. I'm talking about our careers."

"We're playing major league. We don't have to worry about the incidentals. Our job is to be artists—end of story."

"It's not that simple, and you know it."

"Just go lie down, and I'll trace out the new hips for our lovely lady. Okay?"

Tom sighed. "I know we've been over this too many times these past weeks, but I mean it, Eric, I want us to get out of the contract with the Coterie."

"And I'm telling you we'd be crazy to leave such a sweet deal. You know, the only time you stress over this is when you're tired."

"I wish that were true." Tom walked to the door leading to a room behind the studio. "We'll regret ever getting in bed with them."

"Look, we're going to make a hell of a lot of money when we sell this stuff. If you still want to get rid of the Coterie after that, I'm game. Man, we'll be so popular we won't need them anyway. But we have to stay focused on the art, or we won't have anything worth selling. Now, go get some sleep, so we can get on with it."

Tom retreated to the back room and lay down on a cot. The partners had built the little inner sanctum without windows when they had remodeled the inside of the one-story shingle house. Alone in the darkness, it took little time before Tom drifted to sleep, undisturbed by the muffled sounds made by Eric as he worked in the studio.

Suddenly there was a crash as something broke through the studio window and struck the floor with a low-pitched pop. Startled, Eric instinctively turned toward the noise, but he never had a chance to realize what happened. One moment, he stood looking straight ahead, dumbfounded. The next moment, the studio became a raging inferno. Eric went into shock, and for an instant, did not comprehend that he too was ablaze. Finally, he saw the fire on his arms and hands, and in a panic, he flailed his limbs about wildly and screamed, until he fell to the floor unconscious.

The blaring sound of the studio's fire alarm and the roar of the fire as it quickly spread awakened Tom. He jumped up from his cot and reached for the doorknob, but it was unbearably hot and he cried out in pain. The noise and the heat intensified while choking smoke invaded the room from the opening under the door. Gasping for breath, he stepped backward and stumbled over the cot, landing hard on the floor. He shouted as loudly as he could, "Eric!"

Across an empty wooded lot, two hundred yards away, two men sat in a black Lincoln Continental, watching the building collapse inward as it burned to the ground. Convinced that no one had survived, the driver turned on the headlights of the car and headed down the lonely country road. As they distanced themselves from the blaze, the driver looked into the rearview mirror at the all-engulfing flames.

"Make the call," he said.

The man in the passenger seat pulled a cellular phone out from the inside pocket of his suit jacket. He pushed the send button and handed the phone to the driver.

"Baines here. There's been an accident."

Chapter One
Bone-in-Teeth

A forward-moving boat churns water at the bow causing a froth of white foam, referred to in olden times as a bone. A boat has a bone-in-teeth when she moves speedily through water creating an exceptionally large, spray-throwing bone.

Trustrum Crook moved bone-in-teeth toward achieving a lifetime dream.

~~~~~~~~

"I've known you for—what—close to twelve years now?" William Weinstein asked.

"Actually, thirteen and a half," Trustrum Crook responded. "I know because we met a year before I started working for myself."

"Okay, then in nearly fourteen years, why haven't you ever told me how you got the name *Trustrum*?"

"Maybe it's because we've never been together on a four-hour train ride before. Or maybe it's because you never asked me."

"Then, I'm officially asking."

"Well, let's see," Trustrum said. He paused, taking his time, as if giving the matter in-depth consideration. "I guess I had at least two things going against me before I was even born."

"Oh boy, here we go."

"Now, do you want to hear this or not?"

"My apologies, please, go on."

Trustrum looked straight at William. "The guilty parties are no longer with us."

"Really? I'm sorry to hear that."

"Thanks, but it was a long time ago, you know."

"Just the same, it must have been rough."

"It had its moments, I'll say that. Of course, it didn't help that I had a mother who idolized her grandfather—that would be great-grandfather Trustrum to me. Oh, and I can't forget dear father—Mr. Crook, if you knew what was good for you—with his odd sense of humor."

"So, your great-grandfather's name was *Trustrum*? I got to tell you, in sixty-three years I've never heard that name before."

"Victorians were always naming their children after virtues or anything positive like *Felicity* and *Justin* and *Patience*. Mom swore *Trustrum* was a fairly popular name in its day."

"Ah, yes, nothing like being on the cutting edge—of the nineteenth century. So, I guess you're going to make me ask to see the necklace, too?"

Trustrum turned his head and scanned the passenger car. "I'm surprised there aren't more people aboard today. I suppose it's safe enough."

William also glanced around. In his profession, being careful was second nature. He settled back in his chair. "Nobody's paying any attention to us," William said.

Trustrum reached into his leather satchel that he had placed on the seat between them and pulled out a twelve-inch square, three-inch deep, hard-sided case. He handed it to William. "That's the culmination of nearly twenty years of my life—my masterpiece."

William carefully opened the case. Trustrum watched his friend's eyes widen in wonderment when he saw what was inside. "I had no idea, Trustrum. Are you out of your mind showing me this now—here on the train?"

"Well then, give it back so I can put it away."

William laughed. "Calm yourself," he said. Then his expression turned serious. "Just look at this thing. What a stunning necklace. Platinum?"

"Only the best."

"What are the specs?"

"One hundred and sixty-seven assorted-shape diamonds with a total weight of about a hundred and sixty carats—above average clarity, color, and proportions," Trustrum said.

Reminiscent of Edwardian design, the necklace was a breathtaking piece—dazzling with thousands of sparkling facets. Throughout his career, Trustrum had collected one diamond at a time, except for the last thirty-eight, which he acquired in one consignment parcel from William. A diamond expert in his own right, William Weinstein had forty-one years in the wholesale trade.

Trustrum had found his calling—as he liked to think of it—for the jewelry industry at the age of seventeen. Over the past nineteen years, he had done just about everything there was to do in mastering the industry—from platinum and goldsmithing to clock and watchmaking, from studying gemology and metallurgy to hand engraving and managing a retail jewelry store. There was even a time, short as it was, when he carried a wholesale line of high fashion jewelry, selling to jewelers in Delaware, Maryland, and Virginia.

At one time or another, and often overlapping, he had succeeded in learning the heart of the business as well as the tricks of the trade. Throughout the past ten years, he had made a living specializing in the appraising of old and new jewelry of cultures from all parts of the world. He had always preferred appraising to other aspects of the jewelry business and had learned the additional skills only to hone his appraising ability. For it was early in his career, when he had realized that a proficient appraiser must have a well-rounded mastery of the business of jewels—and when it came to jewelry, Trustrum Crook knew what he was doing—most of the time.

"I could stare at this all day," William said. "I can't remember ever seeing anything quite like it." He seemed to take in as much as he could of the beautiful jewel as it sat in its open case before reluctantly handing it back.

Trustrum gazed at the necklace before closing the lid of the case and putting it safely away in the satchel. When he returned his attention to William, he could not stop from smiling. He chuckled and, with his elbow on the armrest, brought his hand to his chin, partially hiding his mouth.

"Look at you grinning. You can't help yourself, can you?"

"It's been a long time coming, William."

"I guess I'd be a happy man, too, selling a jewel like that. What do you expect to clear at auction?" William asked.

"Well, I estimate in the retail market it would list around seven hundred and fifty thousand. Based on that, I figure the auction reserve should be about three hundred thousand. Of course, I'm hoping that aggressive bidding will push the price up and that it'll sell for more. After paying you for the consignment, I'm shooting to walk away with a minimum of two twenty-five to two hundred and fifty thousand."

"Not a bad day's work," William said.

"More like a lifetime's. I mean, I have a little savings and some stocks, but for the most part, I've put my discretionary income into these stones."

"Always riding that edge, aren't you, Trustrum?"

"Believe me, I don't mean to. Things just seem to work out that way more times than not."

William stretched out his legs, folded his arms, and

closed his eyes to take a short nap. But before he dozed, he said, "It's the nature of our trade." He yawned, and then added, "You got to love this business, huh, kid?"

"There's no doubt about that," Trustrum said. He also closed his eyes and leaned his head back to rest, but only after pulling the satchel containing the necklace onto his lap and wrapping both arms around it.

The Amtrak train he and William were on headed for New York City. They had boarded in Washington, DC, but now the train had just left Newark, New Jersey. Manhattan's Penn Station, their final stop, was the next point of arrival and less than twenty minutes away. It was the same line Trustrum had ridden many times before out of Philadelphia during his school days at the Gemological Institute of America. And now, so many years later, he had come full circle. Trustrum Crook was unquestionably a happy man.

~~~~~~~~

Once the train came to a stop in Penn Station, Trustrum and William went their separate ways with plans to meet three hours later in one of the bars on the upper level. That would allow them enough time for a few drinks before catching the 5:09 PM for the return trip to Union Station in DC. William went to meet with a number of his usual diamond suppliers in the jewelry district on Forty-seventh Street, while Trustrum continued to Abernathy's, an auction house on the East Side.

Trustrum felt invigorated as he made his way through the crowds of people in Penn Station, but as he passed through the doorway leading outside onto the narrow side street next to Madison Square Garden, he resisted the urge to stroll along the busy sidewalks with his valuable possession. He feared he stood out from the local crowd for some reason—or was it just paranoia? He was not certain, but he was not going to wait around to find out. He hailed a

9

taxicab and off he went.

"You just arrive in town, yes?" the driver asked. He wore a blue turban on his head, matching the one he wore in the photograph on the displayed license. Trustrum noticed that his name was Suneel Singh.

"Now, how in the world did you know that?"

"I do not know. Perhaps it has something to do with walking out of the train station. Most times, people who get off trains come from somewhere else, yes?" Suneel said. He looked at Trustrum through the rearview mirror and smiled. Trustrum responded with a smile of his own and a nod.

The traffic was bumper to bumper. Trustrum looked out the window, taking in the sights of the busy city, as Suneel slowly maneuvered the taxicab onward. Thirty-five minutes later, the car came to a stop at Lexington Avenue and East Sixty-seventh Street.

"If you do not tell anybody you are a country boy, they will not know. Look at me—I am here just three years, and already I fit in with the other drivers, yes?" Suneel said.

Trustrum looked at him for a moment: the turban, his braided, scraggly beard, his loose-fitting polyester shirt with an oversize collar. "A regular old Joe, huh?" He handed Suneel a ten-dollar bill and climbed out of the cab. Standing on the sidewalk, he bent at the waist so that he could talk through the opened, front window of the passenger's side. "Keep the change—and thanks for the advice."

Trustrum stood up straight as he turned away from the street and headed for the front door of the building. Abernathy's was on the first three floors of a skyscraper. Its outer walls were finished with three-foot-square slabs of black-colored stone polished to a mirror finish. Before entering the building, Trustrum looked at his faint reflection in one of the slabs.

At thirty-six years of age, he was in the best shape of his

life. His charcoal-colored, double-breasted suit was tailor-fit to his five-eleven, muscular 170-pound frame. And few could deny he was a handsome man, with his strong jaw and high cheekbones, deep green eyes, and neatly trimmed light brown hair. He gazed at his reflection and smiled at the thought that he was on his way to having it all.

Just as he was feeling as though he were the consummate master of his profession, Trustrum hesitated. He suddenly realized that for all his expertise in stones, he did not know what kind had been used for the building's facade. "Granite, marble, I don't know," he said out loud, not caring if anyone heard him speaking to himself. Humbled, he pushed open one of the front doors of Abernathy's and went inside.

~~~~~~~~

A tall, slender man wearing a navy jacket, white shirt, tan slacks, and a yellow and blue striped bow-tie walked quickly into the cavernous lobby up to the young woman sitting behind the front desk. Trustrum had spoken to her minutes before. Now, she pointed him out, as he sat in an uncomfortable chair, attempting to appear as though he were patiently waiting. With rigid form that reminded Trustrum of a soldier's stride, the man marched up to him and extended his hand. Trustrum stood up to greet him.

"You must be Mr. Crook." He clasped hands with Trustrum. "My name is Ira Bernard. How was your trip from Washington?"

"Very nice, thank you."

"Let's find a private room where we can talk, shall we?" Mr. Bernard said. He led Trustrum down a hallway past rooms with paintings and sculptures and antique furniture and oriental rugs and silver services and just about anything of value imaginable. "As you can see, we're gearing up for a sale in three days. It gets a little hectic around here sometimes. Here we go." Mr. Bernard put out

11

his arm, directing Trustrum into a small room that had a scroll-legged, dark wood, rectangular table and matching chairs with padded chintz-covered seats. The walls were papered with red-paisley print; on one wall hung a pair of gilded sconces with a combined scroll and acanthus leaf motif. To Trustrum's surprise, the room had poor lighting— at least, for examining diamonds.

They sat down at the table opposite each other, and Mr. Bernard said, "Let's see what you've brought for me."

Trustrum gently pulled the jewel case out of the satchel and placed it onto the table. He waited just a moment before opening the lid, and then slowly raised it, revealing the diamond necklace in all its glory.

"Hello!" Mr. Bernard said, raising his eyebrows in surprise. He used both hands to pick up and support the necklace, being careful not to strain any of its many hinged-connections as he examined it from different angles. "Is there any provenance?" he asked, not bothering to look at Trustrum.

"No. Then again, I suppose at one time there were one hundred and sixty-seven of them, but they're long-lost in history."

Trustrum knew Mr. Bernard was searching for an exciting, marketable story; for instance, a famous past owner, such as the Duchess of Somewhere, who had last worn the thing while singing in her final performance at the internationally famous opera house in Austria just prior to its burning to the ground at the height of the Great War. But how could it have such a provenance? It was brand new.

"Everything about it says circa 1905 to me," Mr. Bernard said.

"I'm glad to hear you say that, but it's not that old. You see, I—"

"Mr. Crook, the design, the diamonds, the platinum base. Everything points to early twentieth century."

"Yes. That's exactly how I intended it to look when I designed it and made it," Trustrum said.

"You *made* this?"

"Hot out of the oven."

"Oh. Well, you certainly left no signs to give away that it's a reproduction," Mr. Bernard said. He gently placed the necklace back in its case.

"Edwardian influence, yes—but reproduction? How can you call a necklace like this a reproduction?" Trustrum asked.

Mr. Bernard did not respond. He was the auction's resident jewelry expert, but he had lowered his guard and misspoken twice in a matter of minutes. Trustrum grew more distressed with every moment Mr. Bernard remained silent, just staring at the necklace as if contemplating whether or not he would accept it for auction. Of course, Trustrum had not intended to alienate the man he hoped would take charge of his life's work. But it appeared that in the short time they had been together, Trustrum had succeeded only in making Mr. Bernard resent him. He wished he could think of something to say that would ease the tension between them, but his mind was blank.

Then, without warning, Mr. Bernard looked up and glared at Trustrum. "What did you intend for the reserve price?"

"Three hundred thousand dollars."

Trustrum closely watched Mr. Bernard for a reaction. However, the man simply looked down at the necklace. Finally, he said, "I can tell you right now that it won't be that much."

"How could you already know that?" Trustrum asked. His tone of voice was higher and his words came out more quickly than before. "You haven't properly appraised each diamond. The lighting in this room is horrendous."

"Nevertheless," Mr. Bernard responded, "I see our

taking it in at one hundred and fifty thousand. Having said that, let me point out that after my colleagues and I examine it, we might find it to be more, should the diamonds be as high quality as you apparently believe them to be. If that's the case, we can make the appropriate price adjustments at that time. Now, remember, whether we do or not, the reserve price only reflects the lowest amount you would accept for it in order to establish the *starting bid*. There's no reason why it won't sell for a much higher figure. But, in order for me to take it in for insurance purposes, one fifty is the best I can do."

Trustrum paused, trying to decide what to say. "Well…I think we both know it's worth far more than one fifty. Let me change tack and ask you this: What if it turns up missing before you and your colleagues get around to properly examining it and satisfying yourselves of its real value? I'm out hundreds of thousands of dollars."

Mr. Bernard straightened his back and slightly raised his chin. "Mr. Crook, Abernathy's was established in 1910. And from what I am to understand, in all that time, we have never lost a single item. Now, you have two options. One is to obtain additional insurance through your own source. The other is that you not leave it with us."

Trustrum took in a large breath and slowly exhaled. *Stay calm. It's just another deal. It's all part of the game.* Then he said, "How long before you can appraise it and confirm my numbers?"

"As I said earlier, we are currently overwhelmed by the upcoming auction. However, I would think it safe to say we'll get to it within two weeks. Then, if the price is as much as you believe it to be, we'll make the appropriate changes."

"At least insure it for two hundred thousand. Because I'm telling you, I will not agree to a reserve lower than two fifty," Trustrum said.

Mr. Bernard stared at the necklace without blinking, as if

in deep thought. Finally he said, "You shouldn't expect so much. You're in the trade. You ought to know better." He shook his head, seemingly disgusted. "Ordinarily, I'd hold my ground. But it just so happens that I know of two—maybe three—clients who would be interested in acquiring such a necklace. So, I'll meet you halfway and agree to the take-in amount of two hundred thousand. But I'll have to call you about the reserve price after we appraise it."

"Agreed," Trustrum said. "As long as it will be on the block in April."

"The deadline for the April auction was four weeks ago."

"I really need this to happen by April, Mr. Bernard. Isn't there anything you can do?"

"It is an exceptional necklace...I suppose it could still make it into the catalogue, if it was photographed by the end of the day."

"I would be very grateful."

"I'll see what I can do."

"Thank you. By the way, what is the date for the April auction?"

"Let's see, here," Mr. Bernard said. He pulled out an electronic organizer from his shirt breast pocket. "I'm thinking it's the seventeenth...oh no, I'm wrong. It's in the beginning of the month—April seventh. Hmm, that's only about six weeks away. That'll be on us before we know it."

"I'm sure it will seem that way to you, but I have a feeling it'll be the longest six weeks of my life," Trustrum said.

~~~~~~~~

With the empty satchel in hand, Trustrum walked out of the auction house in a daze. All around him were crowds of people, but he barely noticed them—the necklace weighed heavily on his mind. Glancing at his wristwatch, he saw that he had about an hour and a half before meeting William in the bar, so Trustrum decided to walk and try to enjoy the city. But with thirty minutes to spare, he found himself standing in front of Penn Station. He decided to go inside and get a head start.

The bar was nearly empty. Trustrum sat on a tall stool, drinking a beer and staring into space. William arrived as Trustrum started his second tall mug.

"Hey, how'd it go, Trustrum?"

"I'm not sure, really. How did you do?"

William sat on the stool next to Trustrum. "Oh, business as usual. Did the numbers work out like you hoped?"

"I had to twist his arm, and I still didn't get what I wanted."

The bartender approached them, "What can I get you, sir?"

"Pull me the same as my friend, here," William answered. He reached for a handful of complimentary nuts that were in a bowl in front of him and tossed them into his mouth. In between chewing, he turned to Trustrum and said, "Don't worry, there'll be some bites. You'll pull the numbers."

"The guy low-balled me. We definitely had a conflict of personalities."

The bartender had served the beer while they had been talking and now headed for the cash register at the opposite end of the bar to add it to their tab. "Thanks," William said loud enough for him to hear. Lowering his voice, he continued, "Of course you know, it's to their advantage to take it in as low as possible."

"You mean the insurance they have to pay on it?"

"That and the image of the auction house."

"Yes, we've all read that headline many times."

"What headline?" William asked.

"Abernathy's sales triple experts' predictions."

"Then, why are you surprised?"

"I don't know. I guess I expected a little professional courtesy."

"Eh, come on, what do you care?" William asked, appearing for the moment to pay less attention to the conversation than to the bloodstone and gold ring on his ring finger.

"I care because as it stands, the reserve is way too low. I'm not willing to take the chance of putting it on the block for so little—not after all I've put into it. Anyway, he's going to have his *experts* let me know if it can list for more. I think he's just sticking it to me."

"Sounds like it. Besides, if they don't increase it, just don't do it. Take it back and go somewhere else. It's not like they're the only auction house in the world."

Trustrum nodded thoughtfully.

William chuckled and said, "It'll work out just like you planned. And then, your real worries begin."

"What do you mean?"

"Well, it's one thing making money, but it's another thing keeping it. You, my friend, are going to need a whole slew of tax deductions—and fast."

~~~~~~~~

Chapter Two
Pinched

When a sailboat points too far into the eye of the wind her sails luff from backwind, slowing forward motion. When this occurs sails are described as pinched. This is sailing's equivalent to an uphill battle.

From the moment he awoke and rolled over in bed, Trustrum Crook had a terrible feeling that his day would be pinched and pinched again.

~~~~~~~~

"Doesn't anybody respect the sanctity of a holiday! What's happened to civility!" Trustrum shouted to no one, although his seal point Siamese cat, Marquise, raised her head with a yawn as if to agree and to sympathize. It was already after midday, Thursday, February 21, the day after Trustrum and William had traveled to New York City. The phone had been ringing off the hook for the past three and a half hours, but Trustrum had no intention of answering it. He had forgotten to turn the phone's ringer off the night before and was too tired to get out of bed to do anything about it. Besides, he considered the day a holiday, and if he could avoid work, he planned to simply enjoy a leisurely day. At the moment, Trustrum, like Marquise, longed for one thing—and that was sleep.

Trustrum was not a lazy man; in fact, his friends knew him as someone who would work twelve-hour days when necessary. But he also reasoned that with life as short as it was, every day should be a holiday, if at all financially possible. This was why, even though many people would have viewed his calendar as worrisomely empty, Trustrum saw just the opposite. The way it looked to him, he had enough appraisal appointments scheduled throughout the next two months to pay the bills and then some. By that time, the necklace would have sold—and how much money did a person really need anyway?

He was still in bed half-asleep, curled up with Marquise, as the early afternoon light shone through the window. The phone rang again, and the answering machine clicked on.

"Mr. Crook, this is Mike, over at the shop. Got some bad news for you. It's the engine block after all. Looks like we're going to have to rebuild the whole thing. I'm pretty sure I can get my hands on another one, and between the two, I can come up with one you can depend on. Let me know if you want me to go ahead with the job. I figure it'll cost around three grand to do it right."

Trustrum knew that Mike was one of the best boat mechanics in Annapolis and that his word could be trusted. But that did not lessen the agony caused by such a costly engine overhaul. He could just imagine his engine in hundreds of pieces on the workbench of Mike's repair shop.

"Three thousand dollars!" Trustrum exclaimed to Marquise. "Thank God for the Allen account. That'll pay the bills for the month, right girl? Oh, what do you care? You eat no matter what happens!"

The phone rang, yet again, but Trustrum was still not ready to talk with anyone. He listened to the message as he went to the large walk-in closet of his bedroom to choose what he would wear that day.

"Hello, Trustrum? This is John Allen, over at Allen and Associates. Look, we need to reschedule this appraisal program of yours. I want to do it, but right now, I'm swamped with all these claims. So, I won't be able to send out the advertisements to my clients. It's really been a busy month. Give me a call so we can reschedule. Thanks."

By the time Trustrum recovered from shock and ran to the phone, John Allen was gone. Allen and Associates was supposed to have been his financial lifeline for the month. "Now, what am I going to do?" he asked Marquise, who paid no attention and trotted down the stairs to the kitchen where she sat next to her bowl waiting to be fed.

~~~~~~

Trustrum found his wallet and the trade magazines he wanted to take with him, but he could not find his keys. He ran up and down the stairs and went from room to room looking everywhere he thought they could be. Finally, he found them wedged between two cushions of the living room sofa. "Ah, here they are…if I didn't know better, I'd say you hid these from me," he said to Marquise, who sat licking her mouth and paws the way cats do after gorging themselves. Trustrum had left her enough food to last until the next day, and she had enjoyed more than her usual fill. "I'm out of here, Marquise. Make yourself useful and catch a mouse or something."

Trustrum's house, in a waterside community, in Annapolis, Maryland, was a three-level contemporary with more glass than wood siding. Every window had a view of the Magothy River. It was a gated community, but Trustrum had discovered that the gate added little to security. From the pizza delivery girl to the garage door repairman, every delivery service he had ever used already knew the access code. Fortunately, crime had not yet been an issue at the end of the peninsula where the community stood. Still, the jewelry business had a way of making a person overly security-minded.

Now, Trustrum turned on the alarm system, using the keypad on the wall in the foyer, and stepped outside onto the brick stoop. He locked the three deadbolts and handle lock of the front door and immediately checked each of the four locks a second time. Then he cupped his hands against the glass door and gaped inside the house, noting that the red keypad light was blinking, which confirmed that the alarm was properly set. Finally, he checked a third time that each lock was properly engaged. Whether he had valuables in the house or not, Trustrum had made it a habit always to confirm that his home was tightly secured.

As he turned to leave, he heard the phone ring. *That could be business. I should answer it, now that I need more work this month.* He quickly started to undo the locks, then halfway through said, "To hell with it. I have to get out of here."

Trustrum locked the two deadbolts he had just unfastened and forced himself to turn away without checking all of the locks, yet again. He quickly walked to his steel-blue BMW convertible, sitting in the driveway in front of the closed garage door. He climbed in, tossed the items he had brought along onto the passenger's seat, started the car, and drove the half-mile to the marina where his sailboat lay waiting without her engine. As expected for a February weekday, there was little activity around the marina grounds.

Jack Foulkes, the marina caretaker, was working in the cockpit of a powerboat that stood in the far corner of the grounds. A short, stocky man in his sixties, he looked the part of an old—but still capable—man of the sea, complete with a raggedy navy peacoat, a worn, discolored captain's hat, and a limp. He lived alone aboard the tugboat, *Rebecca May*, which floated at the western side of the marina. And though she was his home, Jack continued to use her on the Chesapeake Bay for what she was originally designed, whenever the rare opportunity presented itself.

Sailboats and powerboats of all sizes and designs were dry-docked for winter storage, leaving only a crowded, winding path that led to a small parking area by the pier. Trustrum slowly drove up close to the water's edge and parked. He got out of the car, locked it, and headed toward the floating boats.

Along with a few other diehard sailors, Trustrum had left his sailboat in the water that year. They had gambled and won that the winter would be mild, and when the temperature rose to unseasonably warm levels, Trustrum had enjoyed a number of day sails and a few overnight outings. Now, more than ever, he needed to get away for a while to figure out what to do to raise some quick money. So, whatever the temperature, Trustrum was determined to spend the night on the water, hoping to clear his mind and find a solution to his predicament.

His sailboat was a thirty-two-foot sloop. Trustrum had named her *Tavernier*, after the seventeenth-century gemstone merchant, Jean Baptiste Tavernier, who was believed, among other things, to have carried the historic Hope Diamond from India to Europe.

He boarded *Tavernier*, unlocked the companionway door, and went below to prepare to leave. In minutes, he was topside raising the mainsail and jib. Since *Tavernier* was without her auxiliary engine, he untied the mooring lines, quickly jumped onto the pier, and leaned his weight into her so that she started to glide from the berth. Without hesitating, he leapt off the pier and, using the lifelines, pulled himself aboard.

There were no clouds in the sky, and the wind blew at a steady five to ten knots. Had it been gustier, the already difficult single-handed maneuver would have been nearly impossible; as it was, Trustrum made it look simple. A final push from the portside piling and *Tavernier* was free. He trimmed the sails for a broad reach and made the short distance down Mill Creek to the Magothy River.

As far as he could see, there were no other boaters around—the river was his as he sailed between the channel markers, making his way toward the Chesapeake Bay. As he sailed into the dark green waters of the great estuary, he watched giant supertankers power to and from

Baltimore, carrying tractor-trailer-size containers full of valuable cargo from all parts of the world. They followed a deep, narrow channel that centered the bay; his course would not take him near them. He was heading for White Hall, an enclosed body of water nestled south of the Magothy River and north of Annapolis's city dock. The two-hour sail cleared his head, and for a while he forgot his financial concerns.

Upon entering the cove that would be his place of residence for the night, Trustrum watched the depth finder count down as he passed into shallow water. At fifteen feet, he turned *Tavernier* into the wind to relieve pressure on the sails and dashed to the bow. He released the jib halyard and efficiently doused the jib before stuffing it into its storage bag. All the while, the main gently luffed in the wind and, like a weathervane, kept the boat pointing windward.

Still on the bow, he dropped anchor, releasing a total of seventy-five feet of rode, which is the rope or chain that tethers boats to their anchors. At the moment, the weather was calm, but Trustrum knew all too well just how quickly it could take a turn for the worse. And so, it was imperative to have the proper amount of scope in the securing rode if the anchor flutes were to set firmly into the soft, muddy bottom. It was one thing to be able to control a sailboat efficiently from point *A* to point *B*, but it was another thing altogether to confidently moor a sailboat in one place. In the end, his skills as a seaman made the task routine, and for the rest of the day and night, after he had downed the mainsail, Trustrum was successful in going nowhere.

So, as the sun went down, Trustrum sat in the cockpit, bundled in sweaters, a coat, and two blankets, watching the surrounding shores disappear in the darkness and the lights along the coastline turn on. When it became uncomfortably cold, he went below to the heated saloon. For hours into the night, he studied the magazines he had brought along. Gemologically, they were interesting—even educational—but they did not help him in finding a solution to his dilemma. *The necklace will sell and everything will be all right,* he thought. "Of course, I'll have to wait at least a month after the sale before I get the damn check," he said aloud. *Man, my creditors aren't going to be happy not getting paid.* He shook his head and said, "That'll be nothing compared to Michelle if I'm late with the child support." *So close to making it big, and now I barely have an income for the next two months.* "And that's if I'm lucky. Why does it always have to be so hard?"

Finally, Trustrum resigned himself to the fact that even though finances would be tight, he would simply have to make do. Somehow, he would squeak by with what few remaining scheduled appraisal appointments there were. He lay down in the starboard settee and started to drift to sleep, thinking of his five-year-old, auburn-haired daughter, Sarah. Suddenly, he startled awake and sat up. "Why didn't I think of it before? Time to pull a rabbit from a hat!"

~~~~~~~~~

Trustrum woke up early the next day, refreshed from his six-hour sleep and inspired by the plan he had thought of the night before. The sail back to *Tavernier's* marina on Mill Creek was beautiful, with light patches of fog wafting over the water. Holding a cup of coffee in his left hand, he controlled the tiller with his right. The little wind that there was pushed *Tavernier* along at a mere two to three knots. "Fast enough, old girl. We'll be there before we know it," he said to *Tavernier.* As enthusiastic as he was to begin the day's task, he could not resist savoring the quiet morning on the water.

Eventually, he arrived at the marina, furled the sails, and secured the companionway door. He had a habit of stealing quick glances at *Tavernier* as he walked along the pier toward land. He did this to assure himself that she was safely tied down, even though he had already double-checked each of her mooring lines. When he arrived at his car, he got inside and quickly drove away, forcing himself not to look at *Tavernier* one last time. "*Phobia* would have been a better name for her," he said aloud, and laughed at himself as he sped down the road to his home.

At ten o'clock, Trustrum started making phone calls. By noon, he had spoken with twelve different people scattered throughout the Washington and Baltimore metropolitan areas. Some were with pawnshops, some were with estate jewelry concerns, others were with traditional retail jewelry stores, but none of them had what he needed. He thought of one more person as a last hope and made the call. The phone rang seven times before Bob Harris answered it.

"Harris's Pawn and Curios."

"Hey, Bob. It's Trustrum Crook. How are you?"

"I'm fine, Trustrum. How about yourself?"

"I'm okay, thanks. Listen, Bob, I'm looking for a diamond. Something over a carat. Got anything you want to turnover?"

"Sure. Got a lot of rocks I want to turnover—but for retail prices. What's the matter, aren't appraisals treating you right?"

"Lost a big account at the last minute," Trustrum said. "Thought I might hustle up some cash flow if you have something you're tired of looking at."

"Stones I've got. But nothing I'm desperate enough to sell at liquidation price."

"Now, think about it, Bob. This is your chance to get rid of a rock you don't have a market for. You know, statistics show that if a stock item hasn't sold within a year, chances are it's not going to sell for a while—if at all. And there your money sits, doing you no good."

"I hear what you're saying. Wish I could help, Trustrum. But I don't have anything like that now, and nobody's been coming in to sell, lately. Business has been slow that way for weeks. If anything, I need some fresh inventory. I'll tell you what, though. If something does turn up that fits the bill, you'll be the first person I call."

"Thanks, Bob. I'd appreciate it."

"No problem, Trustrum. Good luck."

Trustrum hung up the phone and looked at Marquise, who sat at his feet staring at him. "Forget the rabbits, I can't even come up with a hat." He looked at his watch and saw that it was half past noon. A wave of anxiety overcame him, and he felt a knot develop in his stomach. He hated to think he would have to withdraw from his savings—or worse yet, sell some of his stocks. *The plan was to improve my finances, not deplete them.* He studied his calendar and saw that his next scheduled opportunity to make money— a twelve-item jewelry appraisal—was five days away. After that, the calendar squares were blank for two full weeks. His stomach tightened.

"Oh well, at least there's more time for Sarah."

Chapter Three
All-a-Taut

Shipshape, cargo and gear properly secure, ready to venture forth and face what sea and weather may bring.

Finally, after years of unrelenting perseverance, Trustrum Crook's life was nearly all-a-taut...if he could just make it through the next several weeks.

~~~~~~~~~

Large cumulonimbus clouds darkened the late afternoon sky. There was a moderate breeze blowing twelve to fifteen knots, causing the Magothy River to have long waves with white caps. Trustrum wore a blue and green windbreaker. He was barefoot, and his pants were rolled up above his ankles. Jacqueline Hurlock, also barefoot and wearing a floral print dress, a long string of pearls, and a navy-blue blazer, held onto his arm as they slowly strolled along the sandy beach in sight of Trustrum's home. Sarah was warmly dressed in two layers of brightly colored sweaters over a white turtleneck shirt. It was much too cool for her to go barefoot this windy, overcast day. She wore two pairs of white socks with her pink sneakers, which left tiny hourglass-shaped impressions in the sand with each step.

While Trustrum and Jacqueline talked, they watched Sarah, who was determined to stay ahead of them, sometimes disappearing behind tall patches of swaying brown sea grass as she searched for driftwood to add to her collection. It was April 15, eight days after the necklace had sold.

"Do you want counsel as your lawyer or a suggestion from your *loving* girlfriend?"

"Sounds expensive either way," Trustrum said, grinning.

"I was thinking…two weeks in Bermuda," she said.

"I hope that's the loving girlfriend talking."

Sarah ran up to an eight-foot-long branch that had washed onto the beach from the last high tide. She wrapped both her arms around its smooth, water-worn surface as if she were holding it. "Daddy, look at this one!"

"Throw it back, it's too small," Trustrum shouted. Sarah giggled and resumed her search, leaving behind her large catch. Trustrum looked at Jacqueline and said, "You'd think after all those years of sweating over that necklace, I'd be elated to see it go for a profit of three hundred and fifty thousand dollars—but I'm not. I feel as if I sold a piece of myself."

"Hmm? Think any other part of your anatomy warrants a four-hundred-and-twenty-thousand-dollar bid?"

"Considering that supply and demand dictates price, you tell me." Before Jacqueline could respond, Sarah ran back and pushed between them. She grasped one of each of their hands as they headed to the road that led home.

"Are you talking about that necklace again?"

"Honey, I have a feeling I'll be talking about *that necklace* for the rest of my life."

"I thought you made it for me, Daddy," Sarah said. "Now, what am I going to wear at my tea parties?"

"Your tea parties?" Jacqueline asked.

"We've been entertaining some of the neighborhood girls for tea every once in a while," Trustrum said.

"I see. What *is* a girl to do?"

"A new ring would be nice," Sarah said.

"I'll *ring* you, little girl." Trustrum laughed and lifted Sarah up onto his shoulders. As the three of them made their way around a cluster of evergreen trees growing between the beach and the road, they saw John and Delores Reynolds, two longtime residents of the community. Since they were both retired, it was not unusual to see them out walking or riding their bicycles. This afternoon, however, they stood still, holding hands and staring up at the sky.

"Impressive cloud formations, aren't they?" Trustrum asked.

Mrs. Reynolds turned and looked at them. "Look who it is."

Mr. Reynolds glanced at them and quickly returned his attention toward the sky. "We were just noticing that one, there," Mr. Reynolds said, pointing to a great dark cloud with its top significantly larger than its bottom. "It's called an anvil head when it's shaped like that."

"It's moving our way quite quickly, too," Mrs. Reynolds said.

"Ooh, see the flashes, Jacqueline?" Sarah asked.

"Yes. We'd better get inside," Jacqueline said.

"It's still a ways off. But it'll be a nasty one when it gets here," Mr. Reynolds said.

"Storms scare me, Daddy!"

"Oh, but it won't last long, Sarah," Mr. Reynolds added.

"How do you know for sure?"

"The same way old-time sailors knew—and they remembered it as a rhyme." Mr. Reynolds said. "The sharper the blast, the sooner it's past."

~~~~~~~~~

They were home eating dinner by the time the storm reached its peak with near gale winds, constant thunder and lightning, and torrential rainfall. As they were in the kitchen, cleaning up after the meal, the electricity went out. Trustrum found matches in one of the cutlery drawers he used as a catchall, while Jacqueline carefully felt her way through the darkness into the dining room and returned with a pair of candlesticks. All the while, at Trustrum's suggestion, Sarah loudly sang "My Country 'Tis of Thee." They finished the dishes under candlelight, singing "This Land is Your Land," with much laughter and no attempts at harmony.

They blew out the candles after Trustrum built up a large enough fire in the living room fireplace, and for almost an hour, Trustrum and Jacqueline took turns reading children's books to Sarah. With Marquise in her lap, Jacqueline was nearly finished reading the *Tailor of Gloucester* when—

"I think she's asleep," Trustrum whispered, looking down at Sarah, who was curled up in his lap. "You're staying, aren't you?"

"I should go. I have an early morning tomorrow," Jacqueline said in a soft voice.

"But tomorrow's a holiday. You should stay."

"Tomorrow is *not* a holiday, Trustrum."

"It's an official holiday, I'm telling you. Every year, in Austin, Nevada, the town celebrates April 16 as the day the first auction occurred in 1864. Now, that might not be important to some people, but to me—to us—well, I need not tell you, there'd be little chance of our getting to Bermuda if there was no such thing as an auction. Stay."

Jacqueline shook her head and smiled. "Where do you come up with these things?"

"Holidays are important to me," Trustrum said, still whispering.

"So, when did you say the auction house pays you?" Jacqueline asked.

"Don't change the subject, this kid is getting heavy."

"When do you get paid?" she insisted.

"In a month or two. Why?"

"It's no problem if you need to borrow some money to see you through," she said.

"That's really nice of you, Jacqueline, but I'm far from destitute." Without warning, the power was restored. Lights throughout the house went on, the microwave beeped, and the refrigerator started humming. "There, you see, even the electric company knows I can pay my bills. Truth is, I'm sort of enjoying playing the struggling artist."

"Okay, but it's there if you decide you need it."

"Thanks."

"Come to think of it, maybe I'll take that offer back."

"Take it back? Why?"

"Suddenly I'm finding the struggling artist concept appealing…Yes, I do believe I can work with that."

"Is that right? Then give me five minutes to situate Sarah and close up the house for the night. I'll meet you in my chamber."

After tucking Sarah into bed in her room on the second floor and turning on her night-light, Trustrum returned to the first floor. He turned off the lights that had come on with the electricity and set the alarm system. Then he went downstairs to the family room on the lower terrace level and confirmed that the door leading outside to the brick and mortar patio was locked. It was dark, except for what little light came in through the glass doors. Turning to walk back, he stubbed his toe on the heavy doorstop—an antique deadeye, a round wooden disc about the size of a big man's fist drilled with three holes through which lines would pass and fasten to the shrouds of a boat. Framed by a thick metal collar clamped tight by a large nut and bolt, the deadeye weighed about ten pounds. He fell to the floor and lay there for a few minutes, holding his aching left big toe.

Eventually, he got back to his feet and limped toward the stairway. But before heading up, he tried the doorknob to the entrance of his studio, confirming that it too was secure for the night. Then, he went back upstairs, at first stepping gingerly with his left foot until the pain wore off. He peeked into Sarah's room and saw that she was still asleep, then quietly pulled her door shut. He walked across the hallway to his bedroom and gently pushed open both French doors, to find his room aglow with soft lighting. He saw that Jacqueline had lit the three candles in his sterling-silver candelabrum, which sat on a dresser. *Nothing like instant atmosphere,* he thought.

Then, Jacqueline stepped through the bathroom doorway. Wearing only her opera-length string of pearls, she gracefully walked toward the bed. As always, Trustrum was in awe of her. He gazed at her lovely body as she playfully made a full turn, allowing him to see her from every angle.

When she neared the bed, she seductively crawled onto it and lifted herself up with one arm so that she lay nearly on her side. Trustrum noticed how her long, dark brown hair reached past her delicate shoulders and how her raised, outstretched position accentuated her curving hips and long legs.

"Do you like my pearls?" she whispered.

"Pearls always were my favorite clothing." Trustrum raised his arm and placed his index finger on the light switch. "On or off?" he asked.

Jacqueline pouted her full lips, though not from displeasure, and said, "On."

~~~~~~~~

It had been four days since Trustrum had taken Sarah home to her mother in the town of Cambridge on Maryland's Eastern Shore. When she was not staying with him, Trustrum made it a point to call her on the phone at least every other day, and Sarah had called him once, using his toll-free business line, so that already, they had spoken with each other three times.

The frequency with which Trustrum and Jacqueline stayed in touch was quite the opposite, however. He had learned early in their relationship not to expect to hear from her for days or weeks at a time. And though subtle about it, she let him know if his call came too soon for her liking. At first, her need for distance had been disconcerting, but ultimately, he became accustomed to it. So, as unusual as Trustrum and Jacqueline's erratic bond was, it worked for them.

Now, Trustrum sat in a corner of a jewelry store in Rockville, Maryland, behind a card table covered with a white-colored cloth. Most of his portable gemological equipment, including his notepad computer and travel printer, was spread out on the table. He wore his usual work clothes: a dark, double-breasted suit with a white shirt and a colorful tie.

Since he started working for himself, Trustrum had performed appraisals for this store for one day nearly every month. The relationships he had developed with the people who worked at the store were such that they felt more like family. So, even though he would have just been grateful for any work, on this day, he was also glad to be among friends.

It had been a profitable day: eight customers with a total of forty-three items. It would not cure his financial problems, but at thirty-five dollars apiece, his circumstances were improving.

Mrs. Tam, a Chinese-American woman in her mid-sixties, was Trustrum's last customer of the day; she approached his corner of the store with a cheerful smile. Well dressed and heavily clad in jewels, she shook hands with Trustrum and exchanged pleasantries before he started the appraisal examination. She had brought with her an expensive jade and diamond brooch in eighteen-karat yellow gold and a rare thirty-two-inch length South Sea pearl necklace with a diamond and platinum clasp. By the end of the appraisal, Trustrum would appraise the ring at fifteen thousand dollars and the necklace at fifty-three thousand. Using his solid-gold loupe with its ten-power magnifying glass, he inspected the jade and diamond brooch first.

"Have you heard the legend of jade?" she asked.

"Which one do you mean?"

"There's more than one?"

"Most gemstones have several. I think of it as ancestral marketing at its best."

"Well, the one I was raised on is that it's believed that jade turns a darker shade of green with the improved health of the wearer. So, the healthier the wearer, the darker green the jade becomes."

"As a matter of fact, I have heard that one," he replied, finishing with the brooch and picking up the pearl necklace. "Did you know that pearls only have a life-span of about one hundred to one hundred and fifty years? Being organic, they eventually dry out and crack and lose their luster and, of course, their value."

"Really, that's true?"

"Yes. That's why there aren't many natural-pearl necklaces floating around any more. The industry had been pretty well over-fished by the 1890s, which is about the time cultured pearls hit the scene and took over in the marketplace. The 1930s Great Depression was the final blow to what little interest buyers had in what was left of the natural-pearl supply."

"So what happened to all the natural-pearl necklaces that people had already owned? They didn't just disappear right out of their owner's jewelry boxes, did they?"

"In a way they did. You see, my theory is that great-grandmother buys a lovely string of natural pearls about a hundred years ago and wears them for much of her lifetime. Ever so slowly they age, losing just a little of their perfection—not even great-grandmother realizes the lesser nuance in quality. Then grandmother inherits the pearls—they're nice but they're no longer extra-fine quality. After losing still more of their beauty with yet another generation of wear, mother inherits the sort of dull-yellow beads, never realizing that they had started out as such high-quality gems—and of course, great-grandmother is long gone, and grandmother vaguely remembers that they were supposed to be top notch. By the time daughter finds the string tucked under the back earring tray of mom's jewelry box, they've become nothing more than a bunch of ugly beads that nobody's really sure where they came from. I see it all the time."

Mrs. Tam's shocked expression revealed her surprise. She had no way of knowing how long the pearls had existed before she had acquired them nearly thirty-five years earlier. Distressed, she hesitated for a moment, then asked, "How long do you think I have left to enjoy my pearls?"

Trustrum smiled and said, "I suppose that would depend on how dark your jade gets, don't you think?"

She frowned, and then realizing that he was teasing her, burst into bubbly laughter.

"And still, pearls remain my favorite gemstone," Trustrum stated.

"Even though they don't last forever?"

"Forever, huh? That's a tall order to ask of anything."

"I own diamonds that will last forever."

"I see lots of century-old diamonds chipped to oblivion."

"Diamonds chip?"

"Sure. You see, when we call diamonds the hardest natural substance known to mankind, we're referring to their resistance to scratching. But it's another thing altogether when it comes to being struck."

"I wasn't aware of that."

"Hey, whether you're talking about diamonds, pearls, or your life—believe me, nothing lasts forever, so you better savor it while you can. Just one more example of why it's so important to have your jewelry properly appraised and insured."

Mrs. Tam chuckled. "Why do I get the feeling you try to see reasons for having jewelry appraised in every conversation?"

"You found me out, Mrs. Tam." Trustrum handed her the appraisal, which she immediately began to inspect. She took her time reading the three-page document. When she finished, she asked, "I couldn't sell them for this much, could I?"

"Of course not. If you read the appraisal again, you'll see that it states the amount shown reflects the retail replacement value. In other words, what it would cost on average for you to go out and replace them new through traditional jewelry stores. Think about it, what *can* you buy from a retail store, then turn around and sell at a profit? It doesn't work like that."

"Well, what would they sell for?"

"Now you're talking liquidation value, and that would depend on how you sold them. The easiest way would be to sell them to a jeweler who deals in estate jewelry, which, of course, is just a pretty way of saying, used jewelry. In most cases, they offer ten to twenty-five percent of the retail replacement value. Auctions are the next place you could go. On one hand they claim to liquidate jewelry for more—like thirty to forty percent of retail, but on the other hand, I've found that they want you to offer them at a much lower reserve price, which means if the item is not bid up by at least two competing parties, there's the risk of it selling for less; plus, the auction house takes a percentage off the top, and there are usually additional costs for listing the item in their auction catalogue. Oh, and if it doesn't sell, the auction house still charges something."

"So, with the higher stakes comes more risk."

"True of most things in life, isn't it?"

Mrs. Tam shrugged her shoulders and shook her head. "Any other way to sell them?"

"You could try consignment at a jewelry store. Usually, professionals dealing this way agree to pay from twenty-five to fifty percent of the item's retail value. But now, your problem is that you don't get paid until it sells. And let me tell you, if it comes down to a jeweler selling a piece from his inventory that he has money tied up in, or selling yours, he's going to push his own piece every time. So, there's no telling how long it might take for someone to buy it and you to get paid."

"But I had always heard that jewelry was a good investment."

"It depends on how you use the word *investment*. First you have to realize that there are basically only two things in this world: real estate and personal property. Real estate is the only thing a layperson can venture into and hope to make a financial go of it. That's because real estate deals in fair market value—meaning what something is worth in its present condition. With personal property—which is just about everything that's not real estate—the retailer incurs expenses: rent, electricity, insurance, shipping, displays, a work staff, advertising, taxes, and on and on. All these expenses have to be paid just so that thing—whether it's jewelry or a stuffed teddy bear or a set of dishes—can sit in a showcase or on a shelf, waiting for you to buy it. You just can't buy something from a retail store and expect it to be a financial investment like stocks and bonds, because as soon as you buy that new thing and take it out of the store, it becomes in essence a used thing of lesser value."

"So when *does* jewelry become a good investment?"

"Ah," Trustrum said, pointing his index finger upward for a moment. "Historically, it's often been jewelry that has allowed people to regroup financially once some kind of catastrophe has overwhelmed them. Look at World War II, when so many had to quickly leave Europe. Imagine how many Steinways were left sitting in parlors useless to their owners because they couldn't be carried. But with a pocketful of jewels, people were able to begin new lives in other countries—even though the items would have sold for only a fraction of their original purchase price."

"So when all else fails, that's when jewelry is good to fall back on."

"And that's how personal property—tangibles—work for the most part. It's just that jewelry is the easiest to transport. Now, in a lot of third world countries, where labor costs are miniscule to none, gold jewelry is strictly based on weight alone against the spot gold price. That makes a big difference in the equation when it comes to getting as much of the original purchase price back out of a piece of jewelry when selling—but that's not the same kind of jewelry you have in mind, I'm sure."

"Oh my," Mrs. Tam said. "What if I sell it myself?"

"You mean, to somebody not in the trade, who would be buying it for herself?"

"Yes."

"Sure. That would be the ideal situation. People are willing to pay anywhere from twenty-five to over fifty percent of retail. But now you're playing jeweler, and you have to find someone to buy it. That's not always so easy to do. Listen, when you're thinking about buying a piece of jewelry, it should be bought with one thing in mind, and that's the pleasure of adornment; because with few exceptions, jewelry is only an investment to jewelers."

On his return trip home to Annapolis, as he sped along the Capital Beltway, Trustrum thought about his successful day. He would deposit the check first thing in the morning.

Suddenly he frowned. "Where did I put the check?" he wondered aloud. He remembered the store's owner handing it to him, but he could not recall what he had done with it. And it would not be the first time he had absentmindedly left a check sitting on a showcase counter.

The convertible top was down as he traveled at sixty miles an hour in the middle lane of the three-lane highway. As soon as the first lane was clear, he put on his right turn signal and moved over. His plan was to take the first exit ramp he saw, find a safe place to park, and search his equipment bags for the check.

Looking in his rearview mirror, he noticed something alarming: a black Lincoln Continental, which had been three cars behind him in the fast lane, had quickly swerved to the right, crossing the entire three-lane highway, as if mirroring his actions.

As an appraiser, Trustrum used specialized equipment—enough to fill two large suitcases. Carrying such bags in and out of jewelry stores, all appraisers were aware that they appeared, even to a casual observer, as though they were jewelry wholesalers, who might be transporting valuable jewels. Unfortunately, it was not uncommon for thieves to make the same mistake. So, whenever he was working, Trustrum instinctively kept a close eye on his surroundings. He took note of the people around him in the different jewelry stores as well as out on the street. And of course, he watched for cars that might be following him.

Seeing an exit ramp, Trustrum took it. He sped south on New Hampshire Avenue. If he left the car behind, he would know it was simply another driver going in the same direction—a coincidence he could laugh off. He prayed that it would be so—but as he could plainly see in his rearview mirror, the car had stayed with him. Trustrum changed lanes and veered around slower moving vehicles. Still the Lincoln followed—now, only two car-lengths behind.

As he approached the intersection, Trustrum slowed down. He could see that there were two men in the car. Feeling desperate, he made a sharp U-turn and cut in front of an oncoming car, whose driver slammed on his brakes, narrowly avoiding a collision. Trustrum floored the accelerator pedal and sped back toward the Capital Beltway. As his car passed by his pursuers, Trustrum's eyes met with the driver's. It all happened quickly, and yet, Trustrum could clearly see the driver. The expression on the man's face was more than anger or frustration, Trustrum thought. His face was contorted in a smirk that Trustrum could only describe as pure evil.

The Continental was forced to stop at the light, unable to copy the U-turn because of the now heavy flow of oncoming traffic. Shaking with a kind of fear he had never known, Trustrum shuddered. He continued well above the speed limit as he followed the entrance ramp back onto the Capital Beltway heading east or south or whatever direction it was labeled at that section of the loop. What did it matter? All Trustrum cared about was that it led home.

~~~~~~~~~

Chapter Four

Shanghaied

In the romantic days of tall square-rigged ships, men were kidnapped and forced to volunteer as crew. Stolen from their family and friends, plucked from their chosen lives, they were coerced into signing onto ships sailing the China trade route after having been made insensible by a blow on the head or drugged unconscious by too much drink.

Trustrum Crook discovered first-hand that romance had little to do with it.

~~~~~~

It had been three days since the incident with the "highway bandits," as Trustrum had started referring to it. And even though he acted nonchalant when telling friends the details of what had happened, he felt uneasy now that he was on the road for the first time since the frightening experience. Despite the fact that it was a warm, sunny day, he had decided to drive with the Beemer's black convertible top up.

For the past fifteen minutes, he had noticed a dark-green Cadillac Sedan Deville following behind him. But he refused to allow himself to panic. *Thousands of decent, law-abiding people travel everyday on this road,* he thought. He forced himself to remain calm, remembering that he was prone to paranoia.

He was on his way to Brookeville, Maryland, to the home of his dear friend and mentor, Sebastiao Silva. In his early days in the trade, Trustrum had apprenticed as a bench jeweler with Silva—as he preferred to be called by his friends—learning the skills of the old-school craftsman. For this, along with years of friendship, Trustrum would forever be indebted to the old man. So, when Silva had called Trustrum on the phone the day before, stating that he must speak to him in person as soon as possible, Trustrum did not hesitate. He sensed the urgency—as well as the slight but definite underlying tremor—in Silva's voice.

As he was about to turn off Georgia Avenue onto a secondary road, Trustrum saw that the Deville was still behind him. Not wanting to overreact, Trustrum put on his left turn signal well in advance and cautiously slowed to a stop in the middle of the intersection, while he waited for a safe gap in the flow of oncoming vehicles.

The Deville approached his car from behind and continued past. As it did, Trustrum turned and looked at the driver. *No!* Trustrum thought. *It can't be!* Behind the wheel of the Deville was the same man who had been driving the Lincoln Continental.

Startled and in shock, Trustrum jerked. His right foot slipped off the brake and snagged the side of the accelerator pedal, while his right hand lost hold of the steering wheel. His car lurched forward out of control into the lane of oncoming traffic. Horns blared and tires screeched all around him as he strained to regain his senses. In a panic, he stomped on the brake with all his might, and his car abruptly stopped in the middle of the road.

For a moment, he sat there, shaking, looking at the cars he had unintentionally forced to a stop. Some of the people stuck their heads out their car windows and yelled obscenities at him. He tried to start the engine, but he could tell from the gurgling sound it made that he had flooded it. All around him people continued to shout and blow car horns. He tried his engine again, then again. Finally, it started, and he slowly continued through the intersection.

Trustrum decided it was not safe to go straight to Silva's home. Whatever was going on, he did not want to involve his friend. So, he turned onto a number of side roads, randomly heading left or right in an effort to make certain that he had not been followed. Every few seconds he glanced in the rearview mirror and eventually, not seeing the dark-green car, regained his composure and headed for Sebastiao Silva's house. Still, as a last precaution, he parked two blocks away from Silva's property.

Cutting through neighboring yards, he walked the distance from his car to the privacy fence that surrounded Silva's backyard. Trustrum was clumsily pulling himself over the wooden fence, when Silva came out of the house onto the wooden deck, holding a glass of iced tea.

"What are you doing, Trustrum?" he called.

"I'll be right up." Trustrum crossed the well-manicured lawn, marched up the short flight of steps onto the deck, and slumped into a lawn chair.

"Would you like some tea?" Silva asked, as if Trustrum always arrived by climbing over the fence

"Sure…that would be great."

Silva went into the house. He returned minutes later and handed a glass to Trustrum. He quickly gulped down most of the tea, crunched an ice cube, and then told the story of his two incidents with the highway bandits.

Silva listened intently, looking at Trustrum over a pair of brown, horn-rimmed glasses he had purchased at the corner drugstore. After a thoughtful pause, he said, "This is not good."

"I know."

"You're sure they did not follow you here?"

"All I can tell you is that I don't *think* they did."

Since the deck was one story above ground, Silva could easily see over the privacy fence into the surrounding yards—and anyone hiding in those yards could see the deck. He scanned the area, and then said, "Let's go inside."

"Good idea."

They walked into the house, carrying their empty glasses, which they put into the kitchen sink.

"Is Adriana home?" Trustrum asked.

"No, she's out. Always running errands."

Silva led the way to his basement studio. It looked just as it had the last time he was there and the time before that and every other time he had visited his friend since starting his apprenticeship with him fifteen years ago, Trustrum thought.

It was a little room paneled with pressed-wood boards. Large, industrial-sized machinery, including a drill press and a lathe, filled the area along with two jewelry workbenches, a large side table, and three tall, gray storage bins.

"It's nice to be here," Trustrum said. "It's hard to believe how long it's been since I apprenticed with you."

"Time and tide wait for nobody…that's not right, is it?" Silva asked.

"Time and tide wait for no man."

"That's it," Silva said, then punctuated his words with a quiet sigh. He picked up a fourteen-karat gold bangle and using a scribe marked off an evenly spaced, straight row of five pinpoint dimples where he would drill and file holes in order to bead-set stone enhancements.

"So, what's wrong, Silva? Why did you want to see me?"

"Hand me that briefca," he said, pointing to the paper parcel sitting on the side wooden table. Trustrum picked up the three-inch by one-inch folded paper and handed it to him. Silva carefully unfolded it and spread it gently on the top of his workbench, revealing five round, brilliant-cut diamonds, about thirty points each. Using specially adapted tweezers, he picked up one of the diamonds and held it over the bangle in the spot where it would be set. "Nice, huh?"

"Yes," Trustrum answered.

Silva tossed the loose diamond back with the others onto the open briefca, and began drilling where he had just marked on the top half of the rigid bracelet. He leaned against his workbench for support as he pressured down on the drill bit. Trustrum sat in a chair behind him yet slightly off to the side so that he could watch what Silva was doing by looking over his shoulder.

"I asked you here so we could be eye to eye. I need you to promise me something." Silva looked up with a serious expression and without blinking said, "I need you to promise to take care of Adriana if something happens to me."

"What are you telling me—somebody's following you, too?"

"No."

"Then what is wrong?"

"Nothing is wrong. But I am an old man, Trustrum. And we have no family here in the States. I've been bothered by this for some time. Adriana is eleven years younger than I am, you know?"

"Yeah."

"If something happens to me, she wants to return to Brazil."

"I thought the place was an economic mess?"

"Not like it used to be when we left in seventy-eight. Now, the fighting is mostly far away in the south. Anyway, home is home. It is where our family lives."

"What's happened to make you think about this all of a sudden?"

"Nothing. But if something *did* happen, I need to know I can count on you."

Before Trustrum could answer him, they heard Adriana returning home. "Sebastiao, it's me," she called.

Trustrum started to his feet, but Silva firmly took hold of his forearm with one hand and held his finger up to his mouth with the other. Eyebrows raised, he stared at Trustrum. "Yes?" he quietly pleaded.

Trustrum relaxed back into his seat and stared at Silva's face before answering. He patted Silva's hand and whispered, "Of course I will. You have my word."

Just then, Adriana came halfway down the steps. Trustrum and Silva looked up when they heard her shoes click against the wooden boards. "Sebastiao, you're back already?"

"I did not go yet."

"You'd better get a move on if you want to get back before dinner."

"Look who's here, Adriana," he exclaimed

"Trustrum! When did you get here?"

"Just a little bit ago. How are you, Adriana?"

"I'm fine, everything's fine. Come upstairs and talk to me. Sebastiao, you need to hurry."

The two men left the studio and headed up the stairwell. "I have to run to Four Corners before the supply shop there closes—running low on gold solder. Come with me, Trustrum."

As they entered the kitchen, where Adriana had already started to prepare dinner, she said, "No, Sebastiao. My turn with Trustrum. He doesn't want to go to Four Corners anyway. Right?" Trustrum smiled without answering her. "You will stay for dinner?"

"That'd be great," Trustrum said. He approached the counter next to the sink where there were six large potatoes and a peeler. "I can earn my meal. Do you mind, Silva?"

Silva chuckled as he snatched up his keys and headed for the door. "Now you are in for it. She will have you washing the dishes next." He stopped before stepping through the doorway. Adriana and he kissed and off he went, promising to return within the hour.

Trustrum washed his hands, then picked up the peeler and started his first potato, while Adriana prepared a roast for the oven. Adriana asked about Sarah, then Jacqueline. Trustrum inquired about her work at the flower shop. When he finished with the potatoes, he washed his hands again. His eyes wandered to the far end of the counter on the other side of the kitchen. There was a stack of photographs and what appeared to be a large scrapbook. On the top of the pile was a picture of Silva as a young man, working at a jeweler's bench. "What's this?" Trustrum asked, having walked over.

Adriana turned to see what Trustrum meant. "Oh, things about Sebastiao and his work." Trustrum leafed through the collection of photographs, certificates of accreditation, and newspaper articles, which were from both Brazil and the United States. "Fascinating. What does it span—forty years?"

"Closer to fifty."

"Wow, he's really had some career," Trustrum said.

Just then, there was a knock at the kitchen door. Trustrum froze, his eyes wide open.

"What's wrong, Trustrum?"

"Don't answer the door!"

"Why not?"

"Someone's been following me."

The curtain on the door window prevented them from seeing who was there. They could only make out a human form from the chest up. Adriana laughed. "You're being ridiculous." She marched over to the door and pulled the curtain off to the side. "Look, it's my next-door neighbor."

Adriana opened the door. "Hi, Claire. Come in."

"Hello, Adriana," she said, stepping through the doorway. "Oh, you have company."

"You remember Trustrum, don't you?"

"For heaven sakes, yes. How are you, young man?" Claire was in her seventies. Her hair was gray, and age spots and wrinkles were visible on her face and hands, but she had a warm, sincere smile and a youthful spunk about her.

"Fine. Thank you. It's nice to see you again."

"Oh, you don't remember me, do you?"

"I could never forget you, Mrs. Koenig."

"Oops, wrong neighbor. Mrs. Koenig lives on the other side of the Silva's. I'm Claire Perkins. I live over here," she said pointing over her shoulder.

"I'm sorry Mrs. Perkins. I do remember you. I just got the names twisted around."

"It's been a long time, hasn't it? Are you still in the jewelry business?"

"Yes. Appraising."

"Don't like getting your hands dirty, eh?"

"In the jewelry business, people who have talent work on the stuff, like Silva, and people without talent become appraisers." All three laughed.

"You're pulling my leg," Mrs. Perkins said.

"Claire, you should have seen the necklace Trustrum recently finished. It is unbelievable," Adriana said.

"Is that right? So you learned a thing or two from Silva."

"He's the master."

"You spent enough time hanging around. I remember you were always here working away."

"I was lucky to have such an opportunity. It's been an important part of my skills as an appraiser."

"Oh, sure, I can imagine," Mrs. Perkins said. Then she turned to Adriana. "Listen, hon. I was hoping you could give me a ride to the grocery store tomorrow afternoon."

"After two I could," Adriana said.

"Wonderful. I'll come over then. Is Silva in?"

"No, he stepped out. Did you need him for something?"

Mrs. Perkins took a gold band off one of her fingers and held it out to Adriana. "I found this in with some old junk. I was hoping he could tell me if it's real or not."

Adriana took it from her, glanced at it, and then turned to Trustrum. "Mind taking a look?"

"It would be my pleasure," Trustrum said. He took the ring from her and turned it from side to side a few times. Then he held it up to his nose and sniffed it. "Fourteen-karat gold, turn of the last century."

Both women laughed. Mrs. Perkins said, "You're right about it's age. I believe it belonged to my grandmother, and she would have been married around 1899. But how can you know that from a simple band?"

"If it were anyone else, I wouldn't owe up. But since it's you, Mrs. Perkins, I'll tell you the secret. See how the yellow metal has a strong pink undertone?"

"Yes."

"Turn of the century gold contained a higher amount of copper than what is used today. Plus, just the way the band is shaped is something I see a lot from that era."

"If they added more copper to it, how is it still fourteen karat?"

"Think of karat gold as a pie with twenty-four pieces. If gold is pure, all twenty-four pieces of the pie are gold—so it's twenty-four karat. If gold is fourteen karat, then fourteen of the twenty-four parts are gold, and the remaining ten parts are some sort of an alloy mixture. It doesn't matter what combination those ten parts are, as long as fourteen of the twenty-four parts are gold, then it's fourteen karat. So using more copper and less silver gives yellow gold a red tone. Throw in a little nickel and it comes out slightly blue-green. White gold consists of copper, nickel, and zinc. Mix gold with nothing other than aluminum and it appears purple. So, whatever ten-part alloy mixture is used to make whatever color, as long as fourteen parts are gold, it's fourteen karat.

"But how do you know for sure that it's fourteen karat. Don't tell me you can really smell it—can you?"

Trustrum smiled. "Ah, Mrs. Perkins, it takes years of experience to be able to perceive such slight telltales…oh, and it's marked on the inside of the band. See?"

The women laughed again. Both of them leaned forward to view where Trustrum was indicating.

"Looks like a pit in the gold to me," Mrs. Perkins said.

"How can you read that?" asked Adriana.

Trustrum chuckled. "It helps to know what you're looking for. Here you go," he said, and handed the ring back to Mrs. Perkins.

"Thank you, sir." She looked at Adriana and said, "Boy, he's in the right business, huh?" Then she looked back to Trustrum. "So what'd you use, rhinestones?"

"Pardon—oh, you mean the necklace?"

"Yes."

"Pretty little diamonds."

Mrs. Perkins reached toward Trustrum and squeezed his forearm in a friendly gesture. "Nice to see you, Trustrum. Maybe next time we can chat longer."

"I look forward to it."

Mrs. Perkins walked out the door and Adriana followed. The storm door with its spring-loaded hinge closed behind her. Trustrum could see that the two ladies were talking, so he turned his attention back to the photographs and articles about Silva.

Trustrum was reading one of the news clippings that had been written about his mentor when he had first come to America over twenty years ago—new jeweler comes to small town sort of thing—when Adriana came back into the house. She picked up their conversation as if Mrs. Perkins had not interrupted them.

"What did he tell you, Trustrum?"

Trustrum look up. "Huh?"

"What did Sebastiao say?"

"Actually, Adriana, he didn't say much. What's going on?"

Adriana gave a half-smile in a vain attempt to hide her concern. Her long, dark hair with a touch of gray was pulled back into a ponytail, emphasizing her big, round, dark eyes. Her complexion was smooth, but the crows-feet around her eyes revealed her fifty-seven years. Trustrum thought she was beautiful.

"It's his heart, Trustrum. He's not well," she blurted out. She adjusted her dark blue cardigan sweater, pulling it higher up around her shoulders and neck, as if for comfort, and softly began to cry. "The doctor wants to put him on an organ transplant list, but Sebastiao will not allow it. He says he does not believe in such things…Ah! He is a stubborn man."

"I didn't know, Adriana. Do you want me to try to talk some sense into him?"

"He would be furious if he knew I told you, Trustrum."

"He did say something about your wanting to return to Brazil."

"It is where the only family I have lives. But they do not have much. I could not expect them to support me, and I do not have to tell you how things have been for Sebastiao and me these past years."

Trustrum nodded and continued sifting through the pile of pictures. Over the course of his apprenticeship, he had listened to Silva tell his story many times, so Trustrum knew exactly what she meant.

More than thirty-five years ago, Silva had been a successful and prominent jeweler in Brazil. In his early twenties, he had started a small jewelry manufacturing company in Rio de Janeiro, eventually building it to factory-size and employing over forty craftsmen. But after a coup d'état by a military regime in 1964, everything had changed. Because Silva had not supported the new government, his factory had been raided—everything from his inventory of gold and precious stones to his hand tools and heavy equipment had been confiscated. Hoping for a better life, he and Adriana had immigrated to America, but with little more than a modest handful of diamonds he had had stashed away in his home.

Silva had prospered over the next twenty years, as did many in the jewelry business. He had wisely used his little diamond inventory to start another business in the States, and by the early eighties had been positioned to benefit from the skyrocketing prices of diamonds and gold, which eventually soared to over eight hundred dollars per ounce.

Unlike *memorandum*, which means an item can be returned to the supplier should it not sell, *terms* means that although an item can be taken before making payment, it is nonetheless a sale, and returning it to the supplier is not an option. And if the market should suddenly change in any way, it had no bearing on the previously agreed to price.

Unfortunately, as it turned out, like so many others in the industry lured by big profits, Silva had overextended himself, purchasing a large supply of diamonds on terms at inflated prices. Then, the bottom had dropped out, and by the mid-eighties, Silva had been left holding diamonds on which he had owed many times more than what they had been worth. Although many wholesalers and jewelry manufacturers had gone bankrupt, Silva had held on and had spent the next ten years paying off his debts. To put it simply, he had little to show for years of highly skilled, hard work.

Trustrum put down the picture he was holding and touched Adriana's hand. "Everything will be all right. He's too ornery to die. You know that."

Adriana forced a smile. "I'm so worried."

"Hey, listen. Whatever happens, you can count on me. All right?"

"Yes…thank you, Trustrum," Adriana said with tears in her eyes.

$$\sim\sim\sim\sim\sim\sim$$

Trustrum left the Silva's home soon after dinner. Between the bad news about Silva and the fear of being followed, he found the return trip to Annapolis extremely stressful. At least, the highway was well lit, so he could see that no one was pursuing him.

The gate to his community was chained open, something done when it malfunctioned, which seemed nearly a weekly occurrence. As he drove past the gateway, Trustrum shook his head in disgust over the lack of security. When he neared his home, he activated the garage door opener by pushing the button of the remote. As the door rose, he looked up and down the street in search of anything out of the ordinary, but from where he sat in the car, everything appeared fine.

Safely inside the garage bay, Trustrum pushed the remote button again before getting out of the car. The door banged closed and he sighed. He was exhausted—physically and emotionally—and the only thing he wanted to do was go to bed. He used his key to unlock the door leading from the garage into the house. Marquise cried out at him as she did every time he came home and frantically rubbed her head against his leg, while he punched in the code in the keypad, disarming the alarm system. She stayed close to his feet as he climbed the stairs to the kitchen on the second level. Wearily, he opened a can of cat food, dumped some on a plate, and gave it to her, then refilled her water bowl. Marquise attacked her late-night snack, ignoring Trustrum as he climbed another flight of stairs to his bedroom and fell facedown onto his bed. He had intended to lie there for only a moment, but it was nearly an hour later when he awoke with Marquise curled in a tight ball, soundly sleeping in the small of his back.

The house was dark except for moonlight that shone through a semicircular window, which was positioned above two wide, rectangular-shaped windows covered with designer Phoenician blinds. He considered getting up to brush his teeth, maybe even to take a quick shower, but his muscles were heavy and weak.

He remained still with Marquise on his back and listened to the gentle sounds of the Magothy River, no less than fifty feet away, as it washed against the sandy shore. His thoughts drifted to Sarah, then to a memory of sailing *Tavernier* one sunny day on the bay. Slowly, Trustrum succumbed to sleep once again.

Hours later he heard a singular, soft creak. Generally, he was a heavy sleeper and would not have noticed the slight noise, but he had just had Sarah staying with him. A paternal switch clicked on when she was in the house, causing Trustrum to be on the alert. And even though he had just returned her to her mother's, he must still have been in mode. *It's nothing,* he thought and rolled over onto his side. Marquise was disrupted and forced to reposition herself. She stretched and yawned, then sprawled out by his side. Although he could not hear a sound, Trustrum could not shake the feeling that something was wrong. He opened his eyes to total darkness, the moon having disappeared behind the clouds, and remained perfectly still. *Is the house perimeter alarm set?* He could not remember. *Damn it,* he thought. Then, wishing not to get out of bed and using the logic of a half-asleep man, he proceeded to rationalize that everything was as it should be and that he should just drift back to sleep.

Of all the houses around here, why would mine be the one hit—especially with the alarm system…did I turn that thing back on or not?

Just then, the image of the smirking highway bandit came to mind, and though he did not move, the thought shocked Trustrum awake. He lay on his bed and listened. He could have sworn he had heard a sound, but he could not really say what it was. He strained to listen. *There! A creak!*

Trustrum remained motionless as a rush of fear overwhelmed him. *What if it is somebody!* Finally, building up his courage, he pulled himself together and thought, *Enough is enough!* He quickly sprang high out of the bed, startling Marquise into flight with a shriek. Now standing, he concentrated on finding the light switch in the darkness. As he blindly reached toward the wall, he felt the presence of someone in the room. But before he could react, Trustrum was struck on the head by a skull-crushing force, and he collapsed to the floor, unconscious.

～～～～～～～

Chapter Five
Mayday

In the year 1948, mayday became the official international radio distress call used by vessels in danger at sea. Anglicized French m'aidez, it means, "help me!"

Trustrum Crook suddenly found himself in very deep and perilous waters.

~~~~~~~~

Because he was in a room completely devoid of light, it took Trustrum a long while before realizing that he was returning to consciousness. He struggled to sit up, trying to shake off the heavy sensation he felt in his chest. He groaned from the effort and fell back onto the cold, hard floor, shivering. He realized he was naked. He began gasping for breath, and the shivering increased. Whether it was chemically induced or from nerves he didn't know…his mind whirled in a blur of thoughts. The only thing he was certain of was that he needed fresh air…and some light.

"Hello? Hey! Is anybody there?" he shouted, deciding to remain perfectly still, since he had no idea if he was injured or not.

Without warning, the door swung open and a bright light shot into the room; he had never appreciated the forceful impact light could have. He tried to protect his eyes with his hands and arms, but the overwhelming light was relentless and made it impossible for him to see.

"Mr. Crook, allow me to introduce myself. I am Mr. Baines." His voice was deep and gruff, and he spoke slowly. "I will be your guide during the next few weeks. I hope that we can get along and be friends."

Trustrum tried to get up, but he felt as though he were pinned to the floor. He tried shielding his eyes from the blinding light. "Who are you?"

At that, Baines snapped his fingers and two men charged past him into the room. Without hesitating they began kicking Trustrum again and again. He curled into a ball with his arms wrapped around his head and neck.

Finally, they stopped their attack and left, while Baines remained standing near the door. "Having to repeat oneself wastes time. And frankly, I find it annoying. Friends shouldn't annoy one another, don't you agree? So hear me and remember—the name is Mr. Baines."

Trustrum could not respond. He just lay there in pain, until he passed out.

~~~~~~~~~

When Trustrum awoke, he was back in complete darkness—this time he feared he was near death. Every joint, every muscle, every nerve ending screamed out in agonizing pain. Delirious, he did not recognize the sound of the door opening. The glaring light struck him again without warning.

"Crook. Crook, can you hear me?" Then louder, "Trustrum Crook, can you hear me?"

"Yes," he garbled, forcing the words to come out while choking on blood.

"It seems that you have come into an unusual situation, haven't you? You must be very confused. So, I will simplify it for you. Join us. Become one in our organization and do everything that is asked of you, and you will have happiness and pleasure. Refuse me—now or ever—and you will severely suffer."

"No more, please. Whatever you want," he blurted out,

57

still attempting to protect his eyes from the drilling light.

"Whatever I want what?"

"Whatever you want, Mr. Baines." The door slammed shut, and the room returned to a state of blissful silence and darkness.

~~~~~~

"Mr. Crook…Mr. Crook, are you feeling better today?" asked what sounded to Trustrum as the sweetest little voice in the whole world. It belonged to a lovely woman with an angelic face wearing what appeared to be a nurse's uniform. His eyes were swollen, drastically hindering his vision; his lips felt five times their normal size; and the rest of his body was numb from combined beatings and shots of the painkiller Demerol, of which he had been given an overly generous supply.

"What's…happened…to me?" he asked, slurring his words. He was aware that he was lying in a hospital bed, but he had no idea how he had gotten there.

"You had an accident, but you're fine. You'll be sore for quite a while, I'm afraid. When you feel up to it, you have a visitor waiting to see you," the nurse said.

"Was it a car accident?" he pressed.

"Just relax, Mr. Crook. Everything is fine now," she said.

"I had bad nightmares. Was anybody else hurt?" he asked.

Without answering his questions, she walked out of the room. He noticed that the door was left unlocked.

He lay in bed, trying to recall what had happened. Slowly he realized that he had not been in a car accident at all, that he had been kicked and beaten and that some man named Baines was in some way involved. None of it made any sense. The way he felt, he reasoned, he should simply be glad that he was alive. Then, with a jolt, he thought of

Sarah and panicked.

"Oh, no! Where's Sarah?"

Adrenaline alone gave him the strength to get out of bed and cross the room to the door—he had to know if Sarah was safe. He swung the door open and dashed into what he expected would be a hospital hallway. Instead, he found himself in a large room that looked like it was part of a warehouse. Two men stood on either side of the door.

Although the two men appeared surprised at Trustrum's ability to move, it took little effort for them to overwhelm him, and they easily forced him back into the smaller room. Trustrum now knew that he was not in a hospital, and the two men posted at the door were not policemen.

"What's going on here? Where's my daughter!" he screamed, though his energy level quickly diminished and was replaced with excruciating pain.

The men easily pushed him onto the bed where Trustrum, defeated by exhaustion, lay still. The two men took their places on either side of the bed, just as a tall, broad man wearing a dark suit walked into the room.

"Crook, you have a higher tolerance for pain than I would have expected you to have."

First the sight of him, then his words caused Trustrum to become petrified with fear: it was the face of the driver who had stalked him—it was the voice from his nightmare—it was Baines.

"Who are you, Baines?" Trustrum asked, as if he were empowered by having recognized him.

Baines laughed tauntingly. "Your recognizing me is no great feat, I assure you, Crook. I would have been surprised had you not. I am unhappy to hear that you have forgotten the correct manner to address me. Do we need to revisit that area of your training?"

"What training? What's going on here? Why have you kidnapped me?" Trustrum struggled to get up, but the two guards held him down as Baines stood by the foot of the bed. The nurse returned to the room and without hesitating injected Trustrum in his left thigh. He felt a sharp stinging prick, the burning pressure as the medication surged into his muscle. He quickly felt an overwhelming sense of exhaustion.

"Where's my…daughter?" Trustrum barely forced out, fighting to stay conscious.

"I would expect that your daughter is doing just fine with her mother. We haven't touched her, and we don't intend to—as long as you cooperate."

Hearing that Sarah had not been dragged into this madness, that she was safe, Trustrum succumbed to the drug.

~~~~~~~~

Over the following week during his recuperation, only the nurse entered the room. She would bring him food three times a day and help him eat, redress his cuts, and inject him with enough painkillers and who knew what else to keep him passive.

There were no windows in the rectangular-shaped room, which seemed to be about fourteen feet long by ten feet wide. The walls were painted white, matching the white-tiled floor. The ceiling consisted of large rectangular, bark-textured, white boards and three matching, large fluorescent light fixtures. If it wasn't a hospital room, Trustrum thought, someone had gone to a lot of trouble to make it look like one.

The consistent drugging made him so that he could barely move his arms or lift his head. Except for when one of the guards and the nurse would help him into the bathroom, he stayed in bed. There was not a television or radio in the room, but Trustrum did not miss them. His thoughts were blurred at best, and usually he slept and suffered from disturbing dreams. Finally, Baines visited him again.

"Before we go any further, Crook, we need to go over some things. I realize that you've been through a lot during the past week, so I will allow you some slack where otherwise I wouldn't. But I do expect you to listen and follow instructions. Fall in line and things will start to look up, I promise." He stood near Trustrum's bed with his arms clasped behind his back, while the two guards stood at attention by the doorway. "Foremost, it's important that you show respect at all times for me and for my associates, which includes *everyone* affiliated with this organization. You will not ask questions of any kind unless you are offered the opportunity. You will be submissive to our every request at all times, or you shall suffer the consequences, on that you can be assured. Now, that's plain enough, isn't it?"

"Yes, Mr. Baines."

"Do you anticipate any problems following these few, simple guidelines?"

"No, sir."

"Good. Then, I think we can move along to the next level of our program," he said, smiling with his final statement as one does to a friend. Trustrum resisted asking or saying anything. The nurse entered the room carrying a bundle of casual street clothes and shoes in one hand and a sport coat on a hanger in the other. She laid them on the bed and began helping Trustrum out of his white gown.

"When you're ready, I'll be outside. It's a beautiful day," Baines said. As he left the room, the bigger of the two guards came in. Trustrum ached everywhere and moved slowly. But finally, with the nurse's help, he managed to get dressed, and the guard helped him to shuffle out of his room and through the empty warehouse. As he walked across the doorway, Trustrum was surprised to see a waiting black limousine. The door was open, and Mr.

Baines, standing next to it, beckoned him to climb inside.

Trustrum could only take small half-steps as he slowly moved along. Climbing into the car was exhausting, and Baines had to help him swing his legs inside and close the door. Baines walked around and entered from the opposite side. The driver, having remained in his position behind the wheel, drove off.

The first thing Trustrum noticed about the inside of the car was that the windows had been blacked out.

"Crook, you're about to be offered the opportunity of a lifetime. I've told my superior that you're ready. I expect that you don't let me down. No, you won't let me down—I know it. Just remember our protocol, and you'll be fine. Okay?"

"Yes, sir, Mr. Baines," Trustrum said.

"Good, Crook. Very good."

At first, the limousine moved along at a swift pace, but twenty minutes later, Trustrum perceived that they were caught in a traffic jam. Eventually their speed seemed to pick up again, and once for a short interval, he noticed a muffled or humming sound—as if the car were moving through a tunnel or passing over a long bridge with its road surface constructed of metal grating. Trustrum tried to keep track of the passing time, but when the limousine finally came to a stop, he was not sure if it had been two hours or three.

The driver opened the door and remained standing at attention, until it was apparent that Trustrum needed assistance out of the car. He put his arm under Trustrum's and continued to hold on until he had managed to get to his feet. Baines had left the car from his side and was already standing by the doors to an elevator. Trustrum recognized that they were in an underground parking lot in a city high-rise—but which city, he had no way of knowing.

They took the elevator to the forty-third floor, which appeared to be the highest level. Baines directed Trustrum down a long, wide corridor and into a grand office. Trustrum was disappointed to find that the expansive room had had its window blinds closed, for he had hoped to discover what city they had taken him to. Four expansive murals enhanced the high walls; each painting was of a different city: Paris, New York, London, Rome. The room was so immense that Trustrum felt as though he had shrunk.

"Please, come in, Mr. Crook. It's a pleasure to meet you. I hope that things have not been too unpleasant?" said the man who sat behind a large, oval, bleached-wood desk. Across from him sat a woman in business attire. She finished typing on a notepad computer, closed it, and took it with her when she left the room, giving the new arrivals a quick greeting.

From the lavish décor of the office and the way Baines stiffened to attention, it was apparent to Trustrum that this was the man in charge. Trustrum knew that he was not expected to respond honestly to the man's question, so he gave a half-smile and remained silent.

"Let's not waste any time and get right down to it," he continued, as if this were just a regular business meeting. "I have a busy schedule today, and I'm sure you're excited to begin the program."

"What *program* are you talking about?" Trustrum blurted out, then instantly regretted his words. This was undoubtedly the man, Trustrum thought, who had been responsible for his kidnapping and his beatings. The man hesitated and frowned, then gave Baines an incredulous glare.

"First of all," the man said as he stood up and slowly walked around the room with his hands clasped behind his back, "my name is Max Coulbourne. I am the CEO of the organization. It is I who have final say over all decisions related to your program. Mr. Baines, with whom you are already acquainted, works for me." Up to this point, Coulbourne had been cordial and polite. He looked as though he could be someone's loving grandfather: late sixties to earlier seventies, slightly stooped but still standing nearly six feet of height, thinning white hair, and an apparently expensive, hand-stitched, gray herringbone suit. Had Trustrum's head and body not ached from all the abuse he had recently suffered, he might have forgotten that Coulbourne was not his friend. Continuing, he said, "The program, Mr. Crook, will make you famous and a very wealthy man. What do you think about that?"

Noting how the last time he had spoken had been a mistake, he did not respond to Coulbourne's question until he looked at Baines, who nodded his head. Whatever this was, Trustrum did not want any of it. Still, he thought he would fare better if he played along.

"Who wouldn't want fame and wealth?" Trustrum said.

"Precisely. Who wouldn't? And that's exactly why we have gone ahead and pressed you into service. Imagine realizing your greatest dreams: fame, prosperity, unbound success…you'll live like a king, Mr. Crook. We call our exclusive group the Coterie."

"Coterie?"

"Yes. It's a bit of a play on words, really. You see, some time between the ninth and early sixteenth centuries—in what is referred to as Old French—the word *coterie* stood for a fraternity of peasants who were tenants under the same lord. But in our fraternity, Mr. Crook, the *peasants* are some of the wealthiest and most powerful people in the world."

"I see. I suppose that makes you lord."

Coulbourne laughed and then said, "That is correct. And as lord of the Coterie, I have the pleasure of informing you that we have chosen *you* as our next artist. Welcome, Mr. Crook. Welcome to the Coterie."

"With all due respect, Mr. Coulbourne, I'm not an artist."

"But you are, Mr. Crook, and a very good one at that," Coulbourne said as he directed Trustrum's attention to a closed wooden box sitting off to the side of the desk. Trustrum immediately recognized it as the box he had made for his necklace, which had recently been sold but for which he had yet to be paid by the auction house. Coulbourne opened the lid, disclosing the necklace as it sparkled and shone as if alive and saying: Hello, how are things going?

"You see, Mr. Crook, we at the Coterie are already fans of yours. How long did it take you to craft such a lovely jewel?"

"I was listed as an anonymous seller. How did you get my name?"

"We rely on experts for many things, Mr. Crook. As I'm sure you know, with the right tools, difficult tasks become elementary. Please, don't keep me in suspense. I really must know. How long did it take you?"

Trustrum hesitated, and then said, "My entire career."

Coulbourne obviously found his answer humorous, for he chuckled. "Well, you will have to work more quickly from now on. Please, sit down. Allow me to explain to you just how we will all benefit from your God-given skill," he said, proffering Trustrum one of the two, burgundy-colored leather chairs standing in front of his desk and Baines the other. Coulbourne sat down behind his desk, then continued, "The Coterie is a unique investment group. We find struggling, unknown artists and assist them in achieving their goals, both artistically and financially. As long as the chosen artist subscribes and adheres to our instructions, he is destined to succeed. I'm pleased to tell you, Mr. Crook, that we have performed this *service* for no less than forty-six artists over the past twenty-three years. And we are diverse; let me say that right from the start. Our artisans work in virtually every medium you can imagine: stone, wood, metal, glass, paint—we've even ventured once into the music industry. The items range from specialty doors to traditional sculptures and tapestries.

Anything and everything that collectors crave made by artistic people just like you."

"This sounds wonderful, Mr. Coulbourne, but—" He was interrupted by Baines's hand grasping his shoulder, reminding Trustrum of the Coterie's protocol, which he had recently, and painfully, learned.

"I'm sure you realize that our motives, though genuinely philanthropic, also include our financial betterment—as it should. For the Coterie to continue to exist and help today's struggling artist, it must be able to entice investors. Everyone involved in a business relationship must benefit in order for that relationship to flourish. Don't you agree?"

"Yes, of course," Trustrum said.

"Trustrum—if I may call you Trustrum—let me tell you how happy I am that you will be joining our family."

"Thank you, sir. But I'm afraid I'm not clear on how I would fit in as one of the Coterie's artists."

"Don't you see, Trustrum? Your medium will be precious metals and rare gemstones, and you will create marvelous objets d'art. You, my friend, will fashion works of art the likes few would even dream of owning."

"But who would buy such things?"

Both Coulbourne and Baines laughed. "That's the beauty of the Coterie, Trustrum," Coulbourne said. "We will give you the specifications for your creations. Then, you will make them, and the members of the Coterie will buy them during special exhibitions. We do it all. From the agent who will represent you, to a first-rate publicity network that will develop your image in the media. You'll be famous, and the Coterie will own your work."

"I'm afraid I don't get it, Mr. Coulbourne. If the Coterie is financially backing me in the first place, what's the benefit of buying back my work at a higher price? It'd be buying what it already owns?"

"Why, to develop your reputation as an artist-in-demand,

of course. Let me explain. Let's say, according to our specifications, you create a large, solid-gold water pitcher encrusted with rubies and diamonds, which intrinsically is valued at one hundred thousand dollars. Because it is an artistic piece by the up-and-coming artisan, Trustrum Crook, it is purchased at exhibition for half a million. But the money that is paid for the piece conveniently recycles back to the same syndicate member through the Coterie. Now, they own a rare piece of art, which is documented to have been purchased for five times its intrinsic value. Then, as your popularity grows, the value of that piece will grow likewise. There is no limit to how much it could turn into in five, ten, or fifteen years. And that's when we sell, Trustrum. After repeating this simple formula with a number of artists…well, the financial benefits are obvious. You, of course, will be well paid for your efforts, and I need not tell you the benefits you will have from the fame. The world will want the napkin you wipe your mouth with, Trustrum. Think of it—think of the power you will have."

Trustrum was bewildered. "Is this legal?" he asked.

"That is the supreme beauty of it all. It is most definitely legal," Coulbourne said. "There is absolutely nothing illegal with investing in an artist and then buying his work. Why, even van Gogh received support from his brother in just the same way. This sort of thing goes on every day. Granted, we push it to the edge. Still, everything is legal, I assure you."

"Except for one thing," Trustrum said.

"What's that?" Coulbourne asked.

"You and your goons kidnapped me and nearly beat me to death!"

"Oh, yes. Well, that is unfortunate, but we've been having problems lately with participants. You artists seem to think you're required to be non-compliant in everything you do. And, you see, in order for such a venture to survive, the Coterie must remain a complete secret to outsiders, mustn't it?"

"Quite a neat little package you're selling, Mr. Coulbourne. But there's a hitch."

"How do you mean?"

"Look at it from my point of view. Here you are expecting me to become one of your *artists* and that I should feel good about it. But by doing so, I must stick to a set of guidelines the Coterie dishes out concerning—"

"Watch yourself, Crook," Baines interrupted.

"—concerning what I make, how much I make, and when I make it. In other words, call it what you will, you'd be enslaving me."

"Mr. Crook," Coulbourne said, making light of the growing tension, "we are all slaves to something. What matters is how we are compensated for it—and the Coterie does compensate very well. But, it is imperative that you clearly understand what it is you commit yourself to."

"What are you saying? You're giving me a choice, here?"

"Of course you have a choice. There's always a choice, Mr. Crook."

"Then I choose: no!" Trustrum exclaimed, he stood up as quickly as his aching body would allow him to. Baines responded by also jumping to his feet.

Coulbourne remained seated and said, "If you're certain there's no changing your mind, then—"

"Oh, I'm certain," Trustrum said, as he started for the door to leave, "What gives you the right to do this to me or anybody else!"

"*Poetic license?*" Coulbourne said.

"We'll see who's making jokes tomorrow, Max!" Trustrum shouted.

"Mr. Baines, see to our disapproving guest, if you please."

"Right away, sir," Baines said. He walked past Trustrum,

opened the door, and bade him to pass through. As Trustrum hobbled out into the hallway, his heart sank. Standing there were the two guards from the warehouse. Since they had not traveled with them on the way over, it had not occurred to Trustrum that they might meet them there. They accosted Baines and Trustrum in the hallway outside the office, which now had its door closed.

"Crook, I neglected earlier to properly introduce you to my associates," Baines said. He shoved Trustrum toward the waiting strongmen. Mr. Steeg, Mr. Abrams meet Mr. Crook."

Trustrum suddenly realized he had made the wrong choice.

~~~~~~~~

Steeg easily overpowered Trustrum, restraining him in an arm lock. Instead of beating him again, Abrams, the smaller of the two associates, injected Trustrum with something that made him unconscious. In less than two minutes, his eyes became glazed and his vision blurred. He was aware that he was taken on the elevator, and he knew he was pushed into the waiting limousine. Then he again entered an uncomfortable, drug-induced world. He had no concept of time: could have been an hour, a day, or weeks. When he finally came to, he found that he was again lying naked on the cold, tiled floor of the room he thought of as the torture chamber.

He had been stripped naked again, and he shivered violently. He thought that his brain must have been withering away from all the drugs and the beatings, which had commenced again on a regular basis. His head and his body throbbed painfully from all the abuse.

Without warning, the door was thrown open. Trustrum looked up to see Baines standing over him. "You embarrassed me, Crook." Then, a large bucket of ice-cold water was thrown over him. "I warned you of our protocol—

69

that we require strict adherence."

"I'm freezing to death," Trustrum protested.

"Don't worry. We won't let you freeze. It takes too long. We'll crush your skull long before that," he said, then gave a light-hearted chuckle. Next, a large bucket of near scolding-hot water struck Trustrum with full force.

"Ah! I'll do it! I'll do whatever you want me to do! Listen to me—" His words were interrupted by yet another bucket of ice cold water smacking him square in the face and covering most of his body. "—I'll do it, I swear!"

"How do I know you're telling the truth this time? You agreed to behave before. Now, I'm suddenly expected to believe you?"

"Please, I promise. I give you my word. Please, stop this. You're killing me!"

"Yes, Trustrum. We are," Baines said, and he slammed the heavy door of the room closed and bolted the lock, leaving Trustrum shivering uncontrollably in the darkness.

~~~~~~~~

When Trustrum awoke again, he was wearing a hospital gown and was lying in the impromptu recovery room. The associate named Steeg sat in a plastic and chrome chair, leaning back against the door, reading a magazine.

"Where's Mr. Baines?" Trustrum asked, weak from his ordeal. The man said nothing; he rose to his feet and left the room. Baines entered moments later, carrying Trustrum's clothes and shoes.

"Good timing, Crook. Mr. Coulbourne has an opening in his schedule that we can fit you in. Do you need help getting out of bed?" His manner was as if he were helping a loved one who had befallen a terrible accident. It was as though he had nothing to do with Trustrum's present ill condition.

Trustrum attempted to leave the bed of his own volition, but he quickly realized he did not have the strength. Baines, observing the way Trustrum struggled, appeared genuinely pleased with the results of his labor. He helped Trustrum change. Then, they slowly walked through the doorway into the old warehouse and climbed into the waiting limousine.

Upon arriving in the underground parking lot, they got out of the car and entered the elevator, which took them to the top floor. When they entered the impressive office, Coulbourne was just hanging up the phone.

"Trustrum, my boy, I'm so glad you've changed your mind and decided to come aboard," he said, sounding pleased with himself.

"I appreciate the opportunity you're giving me," Trustrum said.

Smiling, Coulbourne stood, walked around to the front of his desk, and leaned on it. "It really is, Trustrum. I would think there would be hundreds—thousands—of artists the world over, like yourself, who would jump at a chance like this. And you're the lucky one. Be pleased for yourself."

"I am...very pleased."

Coulbourne smiled and looked deeply into Trustrum's eyes. Then, he said, "Good. Cigar?" He held open a box filled with illegal Cuban Cohibas. "You see, Trustrum, from now on, nothing but the best."

For whatever reason, an image of Sarah flashed into Trustrum's mind. It seemed like a lifetime since he had seen his little girl. He desperately longed to see and to hold her, and he longed to be rid of the nightmare in which he had somehow become entrapped.

"Thank you," he said, taking one of the cigars. From his desk, Coulbourne picked up a cigar cutter and handed it to Trustrum. He tried to hold it so that he could snip off one of the cigar ends, but his sore, swollen hands lost their grip, and it fell to the floor.

"Let me help you with that, my boy," Coulbourne said, who prepared the cigar. Once Trustrum had it in his mouth, Coulbourne held the lighter for him.

"Now let's discuss the topic that brings us together—your program. Trustrum, I want to review your schedule. Normally, I would expect you to have a presentation ready for the Coterie's approval within a month's time. But in light of your present physical condition, I'm going to allow two months. Nevertheless, I expect that you start to organize your objectives—slow as it may come at first. Even if your sketches are simply notes to work from later, I want to see some designs by the end of the week. There must be progress every day—every week—every month. You must continually move forward to remain in the Coterie's good graces. Is that clear?"

"Yes, Mr. Coulbourne. What I'm not clear on is exactly what you want me to make?"

"Well, I've already told you, haven't I? Objets d'art. It doesn't matter exactly what it is: large figurines, urns, clocks, boxes—or better yet, chests perhaps. I don't care because it doesn't really matter. Just don't do the egg thing, Faberge wrapped that one up long ago. What does matter, Trustrum, is that you pick a theme and stick with it. The Coterie gives you the space you need to be creative—our approval withstanding, of course."

"Of course," Trustrum said.

"The rest of the details are here in this file. In addition, you will be assigned a personal agent who can answer incidental questions you'll no doubt have. What we ask of you is really quite simple, Trustrum. Using gemstones and precious metal, focus your creations so that their intrinsic values are in the realm of fifty to one hundred thousand dollars. Besides that, follow your artistic whimsy wherever it may lead you. I will be anxious to see your proposals. You are required to have forty-eight designs finished for submission by the end of two months. The Coterie will choose up to twenty-four from that. You'll then have twelve months to make them, at which point, you will have your exhibition. Can you imagine that? The Coterie's publicist, along with our media network, will have done their magic by then—thrusting you into the limelight. Trustrum…in less than a year and a half, you'll be a star!"

"That's it?" Trustrum asked, believing there had to be something missing.

"You surprise me, Trustrum. Usually after hearing the schedule demands, our artists tell us it can't be done so quickly," Coulbourne said.

"Thought I'd wait to address that concern, sir. I suppose what I want to know now is whether any artists have been rejected? I mean, what if my work doesn't cut it with the Coterie?"

"There are always those who will not make the standard, Trustrum. That's a fact of life. The key is not to allow yourself to be one of those people. I have faith in your abilities—positive thinking and persistence, that's what gets the job done every time."

Trustrum got the message. Should he not live up to Coulbourne's or the Coterie's expectations, he would be erased from the equation. It would be as simple as that. "Thank you for this opportunity, Mr. Coulbourne," he said.

"Now, I must attend to other matters. I leave you in the capable hands of Mr. Baines. He will introduce you to your agent, Mr. Pritchard. Trustrum, your agent is your lifeline. Your success depends on him as his success depends on you. Trust him. Use him. He is there for you—for your success—for the success of the Coterie." Coulbourne took a deep breath and sighed. Then, he continued, "There is one last thing that needs to be said. On this point, there are no second chances. Should you speak of the Coterie to anyone outside of the syndicate, that person must be killed and will be killed. Should you breathe a mere hint of the

Coterie to anyone *ever*, that person *shall…be…killed*. Secrecy is everything—not just for your success, but also for all of those affiliated with us in the past, at present, and in the future. This needs to be absolutely clear. Do you understand what I'm telling you?"

"Yes, I understand," Trustrum said, then, following Baines's lead, he departed from the office as Coulbourne picked up the phone to make another call.

~~~~~~~~~~

"You're about to become a legend in you own time, Crook," Baines said. He laughed out loud at his words as they walked down the corridor. Although his was a casual stroll, Trustrum had to struggle to keep up. Steeg and Abrams, who had appeared from nowhere the first time Trustrum had met with Coulbourne, did not seem to be around. Trustrum did not focus on Baines's words; his thoughts were on his location. Since having been abducted from his home—from his very bed, no less—he had only one weak clue as to where they had taken him: it was a place with at least one skyscraper with forty-three stories, as the elevator control panel indicated. *Well,* thought Trustrum, *that limits it to just about any big city on the planet Earth.* Since he had been unconscious during his capture and had no concept of the time spent traveling, he could not begin to determine where in the world he was being held. He realized that for all he knew, he could be in Baltimore or the outskirts of Washington DC or Philadelphia or…right up the street from his home for that matter. For some reason, he felt a twinge of comfort at the possibility of not having been taken far from home.

The two men reached the end of the hallway, where Baines directed Trustrum away from the elevator and into another room, less extravagantly decorated than Coulbourne's had been. There was a man seated on a beige-colored leather couch, apparently waiting for them to arrive. He stood up when they entered the room.

"This is Mr. Pritchard. He will act as your agent," Baines said to Trustrum, who nodded his head at the man. Baines looked at Pritchard and said, "This is your new boy, Mr. Pritchard. Mr. Coulbourne has a good feeling about him. But do let me know if you require any more of my assistance." He turned and left the room, closing the door. Neither Trustrum nor Pritchard spoke as they listened to the sound of the door's deadbolt being locked.

"Are we both trapped in here, or just me?" Trustrum asked.

"Nobody's trapped. That's just his way of saying he's rid of you. You're my responsibility now, Mr. Crook. It's going to be okay, and we'll be good friends. You'll see."

"Anything but friends, please."

"Why do you say that?"

"Because every time one of you tells me we'll be good friends, I get the living daylights beat out of me."

Pritchard laughed and said, "Not this time, friend." He was an average man: average build, average looks, conservative hair cut and clothes. Trustrum thought that his soft facial features made him look more like a kindergarten teacher than a goon employed with an underworld syndicate in the business of kidnapping and enslaving people for profit.

"Delightful. We're already sharing a bonding moment," Trustrum said. "But if you really want to be my friend, you could answer some questions for me. You know, I don't even know how long I've been with you guys. I do have a daughter to think about."

"Mr. Crook—Trustrum—we know everything about you. We're well aware of Sarah, and that you participate in her life on a regular basis. Your ex-wife, Michelle, has already been contacted, and she knows not to expect you around for a while."

75

"What? What did you say to her?"

"Just that you had to travel overseas for business and that you'll be in contact with her and Sarah as soon as your work allows you to."

"She knows I don't do overseas business trips. She's not going to fall for this nonsense."

"Trustrum, she accepted what I had to tell her quite well. It was my impression that she would be just as glad if you never returned, I'm sorry to say."

"Then you, yourself, actually talked with her?"

"Yes, but there's nothing else to tell. I called, told her I was an associate of yours and that you asked me to make the call because you were too consumed with work and had to leave the country suddenly. I told her you were representing me on a large gemstone purchase in Ida Oberstein."

"And she didn't doubt your story?"

"No, Trustrum, she didn't. For God's sakes, you're divorced. What does she care?"

Trustrum shook his bowed head. When he looked up, he asked, "So…just how long have I been your prisoner?"

"It's important, right from the start, that you lose the attitude. Otherwise, our friend, Mr. Baines, will need to be called in again. I don't like threatening you, Trustrum, but you need to know up front what we're both facing."

"What we're facing? You're as much a part of this as Baines and Coulbourne."

"I have to answer to my superiors just as you do. If my performance with you is inadequate…well, let's just say that penalties come in all forms."

"Fine. Then, let me put it to you this way. How long have I had the privilege of being part of the Coterie?"

"About two weeks."

"Two weeks! My cat will have starved to death! And I've

got bills to pay, and—"

"Relax, Trustrum. We're attending to all of your needs, including the cat. You no longer need to be concerned with daily, trivial matters. Your only concern from now on is your art."

Trustrum stared blankly at the wall. "I can't believe this is happening to me."

"Well, it is happening, and you need to come to terms with it. Fit in and you'll be fine. Buck the system, and there'll be trouble. It's as simple as that. Just give us what we want over the next fourteen months and you're a free man."

"He said one year."

"Now listen. Two months building your portfolio of designs, then one year creating the chosen twenty-four objets d'art."

Trustrum bowed his head, closed his eyelids tightly, and rubbed them with the heels of both hands. "This is a nightmare. It's got to be a nightmare."

"Come on, it's a walk in the park. Remember, Trustrum, you're not alone in this. I'm on your side—you should be on my side. If you fail, then I fail, and we both will have to pay a price. Let's aim not just to survive, but to succeed. This is a chance of a lifetime. Let's do something with it."

Before continuing, Pritchard leaned forward and whispered, "And if you think they aren't listening to every word either of us is saying, then you're a fool. I would advise you to accept your fate and proceed ahead—with enthusiasm."

Trustrum considered Pritchard's words and realized that he was right. There was nothing he could do—at least for now—and the last thing he needed was another thrashing from Baines and crew. "So, what's next?" he asked.

Pritchard walked over to the door and knocked on it with his hand. The deadbolt unlatched with a loud click. The sound it made suggested that it was electronically controlled, perhaps from a central control area. He opened the door and indicated to Trustrum that he should follow.

As Trustrum stepped out of the room into the corridor, he said, "In this together, huh? I bet I couldn't have done that, friend."

~~~~~~~

Trustrum was relieved to see that the hallway was empty. They entered the elevator, and Pritchard pushed the button for the lower garage level. Neither man spoke as the elevator car descended. Then Trustrum had an idea. Without moving his head, he scanned the walls in search of the elevator's certificate of registration and inspection; he hoped the address—certainly the state—would be listed on it. But the notice had been removed.

When the elevator doors opened, Trustrum and Pritchard climbed back into the waiting limousine. The car pulled away with Steeg at the wheel. Trustrum assumed that they were returning to the warehouse—he was nearly correct. One and a half hours later, the car came to a stop. When Trustrum and Pritchard climbed out, Trustrum realized, although in a warehouse, it was not the same one.

Pritchard directed Trustrum up a flight of metal stairs and into a windowless room. The décor surprised Trustrum, for it was an eclectic combination of antique furniture and cutting-edge appliances.

"Now, this isn't so bad, is it?" Pritchard said.

"I suppose not, but you guys sure have a problem with windows."

Pritchard ignored Trustrum's remark and continued, "This is your work area, of course." He indicated by pointing to an area of the room that appeared to be fitted with everything a jeweler could wish for—Trustrum thought how envious Silva would be of such a studio. "Your bedroom is here and the bathroom is over there," he said, directing

Trustrum's attention to each room's doorway. Then he walked quickly to the other side of the room. "Here is your living room area, complete with a full collection of reading material, as you can see."

"No television or phone, I suppose?" Trustrum asked.

"No phone, Trustrum. No TV, either. It's a waste—sucks the time right out of your life. And we need productivity, right? Right," he answered for Trustrum, as though he were a hopped-up cheerleader. "Your food will be from the finest restaurants the city has to offer."

"And what city is that, may I ask?"

Pritchard smiled and looked directly into Trustrum's eyes, "You may not. Now listen, while you stay with us, you'll be treated like royalty. Just name it: supplies for your art, luxuries of any kind for your comfort. You'll have everything necessary to get the job done. But you must be ready to submit your work proposal within sixty days. Understand?"

"I trust when you say 'treated like royalty,' you're not referring to the Czar of Russia or Marie Antoinette or...gee...how many other blue-bloods ended life the hard way?"

Grinning, Pritchard said, "Clever. Sorry to disappoint you, but we seem to have misplaced our guillotine."

"The Czar and his family were *shot*, Pritchard," Trustrum said grimly.

<center>~~~~~~</center>

Chapter Six
Neaped

Neap tides vary slightly from their highest to their lowest depths. Neaped is the ship that runs aground during such tides and cannot break away.

Trustrum Crook realized that he was neaped. He would have to bide his time and play the Coterie's game if he hoped to survive.

～～～～～～

Three weeks slowly passed by. Trustrum, having no other choice but to cooperate, worked diligently to complete his drawings and clay models. The first four items he designed were large urns, each with a differently shaped body, supporting pedestal, and gemstone enhancements. As he put the finishing touches on his fifth drawing, Pritchard, sitting on a stool off to the side, looked on.

"You're going to be big—a phenomenon, Trustrum."

"I'll be a phony, that's what I'll be."

"Why would you say that?"

"It's all a sham. I'm a sham."

"Get real, Trustrum. You don't really think that most of the people you see at the top are there because they're talented and deserving of it, do you? Talent is passé. I don't care if we're talking about actors or painters or writers. It doesn't matter. If it's not nepotism, it's money: how much you're worth to the guy who's pulling the strings. That's just the way it is, my friend. That's life and that's why you should be happy. It's your turn. You get to play artist."

"You're one cynical bastard, Pritchard."

"Look at these drawings you're putting together. I can tell you—now, there's real talent here. The Coterie scored when you came aboard." Pritchard smiled and slapped Trustrum on the back. "Keep up the good work, Crook," he said. He laughed as he walked out of the room, locking the door behind him.

"Talented stooge, more like," Trustrum muttered under his breath.

~~~~~~~~

He continued working for the rest of that day and the following seven days straight, breaking only to sleep or to eat a light meal. He figured the sooner he finished, the sooner he could return home and see Sarah—he missed her so. His portfolio grew to include, along with the urns: gigantic picture frames, massive centerpieces with multiple tiers and extending arms, a tea and coffee service, and ornate containers of assorted shapes, which he called reliquaries. The reliquaries caught Trustrum's imagination the most. *This*, he thought, *the Coterie could appreciate as a theme—an empty box*. In the middle of his fifth week of captivity, Trustrum had a visit from all three men: Pritchard, Baines, and Coulbourne. It was the first time he had seen both Baines and Coulbourne since having been indoctrinated into the syndicate.

With a pleased expression, Mr. Coulbourne said, "Trustrum, you really have come the distance. These are magnificent, simply magnificent. I especially like these receptacles."

"I call them reliquaries," Trustrum stated.

"Nice touch," Mr. Coulbourne said. "I like the sound of that. Stick with it. Are you're thinking of making them your specialty?"

"Yes. They're comparatively easy to make, I believe they'll meet the Coterie's requirements, and the design possibilities are endless."

"Excellent, Trustrum. Excellent," Coulbourne said, as if he were talking about an accomplishment of one of his grandchildren. Baines looked on with reserved emotions; he seemed to enjoy playing the part of the silent enforcer. Pritchard shared Coulbourne's excitement and was smiling with apparent relief.

"Sir," Trustrum said, "I've been here a long time. I've never gone a week without at least speaking to my daughter on the telephone. Is there any way that I might persuade you to allow me to call her—for her sake?"

Coulbourne considered Trustrum's words, then asked, "What will you say when she asks why you haven't seen her?"

"Just that my job's keeping me away, but that I hope to be home soon. She's just a child, and my ex-wife apparently doesn't care that I'm not in the picture. It won't be difficult to get around."

"What about your girlfriend? I suppose you want to call her as well."

"I haven't figured out what I'm going to say to her yet."

"I believe it's important that you call your daughter—as you put it—for her sake. In fact, I think that it's time for you to call some of your friends, as well as your girlfriend. It's important for it to get around in your normal circle that you're well. We don't want anybody getting the wrong idea about things, do we?"

"No, sir," Trustrum said.

Coulbourne turned to Pritchard and said, "See that Trustrum is given access to a phone today to call his daughter. As long as things go smoothly with that call, he may call his girlfriend and a few others." He turned back to

Trustrum and put his hand on his shoulder. "I'm sure Mr. Pritchard and you can come up with something plausible."

"Thank you, Mr. Coulbourne," Trustrum said.

"Not at all. In fact, I am so pleased with your progress, I believe it's time to meet with the publicist. In just a few weeks, I want to present you to the Coterie membership. With their approval, which I am confident you will receive as long as you stay on this path, we can begin the creation of your persona."

~~~~~~~~

Steeg was the driver of the car that day, while Abrams sat next to him in the front passenger's seat. In the back compartment sat Trustrum next to Pritchard; both of whom faced Baines, who sat in the opposite seat. They had collected Trustrum from his studio earlier and were heading to the publicist's office—where that was, Trustrum had no way of knowing—in the same limousine they had always used with its blackened windows.

At first, the men sat without speaking. Trustrum had his eyes closed and his head against the back of the seat. He was daydreaming about sailing on the Chesapeake when Baines interrupted his thoughts. "I'm sure that I don't have to remind you, Crook, but I will anyway. Unless you cooperate fully during this outing, you're a dead man. Is that clear?"

With his eyes still closed, Trustrum answered in an exasperated tone, "Yes, dead man, man with no life, man who does not breathe. Yes. I am clear on the death thing."

Trustrum had responded without thinking, but soon after realized he had misspoken. He opened his right eyelid slightly, and while cringing more than squinting, saw that Baines, who was silent and looking at something he held in his hands, had not noticed the remark. Trustrum turned his head to the side as little as possible and looked at

Pritchard, whose surprised expression was obvious. Baines went out of his way for an excuse to hurt people. But there it was—nothing. Trustrum gently shrugged at Pritchard and returned to his original position, resting with both eyes closed.

Baines's attention was on a ring he wore on his finger. Finally, he took it off and held it out toward Trustrum and asked, "What do you think of this, hot shot?"

Trustrum opened his eyes, expecting to see the muzzle of a gun pointing at him. Instead, he saw Baines's outstretched hand. In the instant before his eyes had a chance to focus, he thought Baines was about to hit him. Trustrum quickly ducked his head to the side in reaction and nearly hit it against the door window.

"What's your problem, Crook? Take this and tell me what you think," he said, snickering.

Trustrum realized that Baines was holding a ring in his hand. Relieved, he took the monstrosity and stared at it. "It looks surprisingly new for something from the seventies," he said.

"What do you mean seventies? I just got it! It was at a mall jewelry store, at one of those while-you-wait things…they even used gold wedding rings that had belonged to my parents. The jeweler melted them down and made this one-of-a-kind design for me. The diamonds are from my mother's engagement ring."

Trustrum raised his eyebrows and looked at Pritchard, whose startled expression had not faded.

"I never would have pegged you to be the sentimental type," Trustrum said, then seeing an opportunity to torment his torturer, continued, "Shame they took you."

"What do you mean, took me?"

"They might have told you they used gold from mommy and daddy's rings, but they most likely didn't."

"How do you know?"

"Well, it's impractical for one thing. The alloys mixed with gold vary considerably in jewelry, and they don't usually mix well, which causes the gold to become brittle. Plus, there's so much gold loss during shrinkage and filing and buffing, you wouldn't have had enough gold from just two or three rings to make this thing." Trustrum held up the oversized, rectangular-shaped, nugget design to examine it better and shuddered inside. *Hideous when they were fashionable in the seventies and altogether frightening now,* he thought.

"I can't believe they lied to me," Baines said. "Are you sure about that?"

Trustrum was amazed at what Baines, of all people, had just said. Seeing another opportunity to torment him, he said, "Well, maybe they did use your gold, but I doubt it. Oh, and as far as that one-of-a-kind thing goes…sorry."

"What do you mean?"

"It's all been done many times before. Man, I know of one particular company that has encyclopedia-size volumes for all of their designs. Each page has two hundred styles. Each volume has five hundred plus pages, and they have no less than thirty or forty volumes." Trustrum chuckled. "There are thousands of companies like that just in New York City—forget the rest of the world. I'm telling you, there is no such thing as a one-of-a-kind. It doesn't work that way in the jewelry business. The economics of it prevent it—not in the price-range you paid."

"Okay then, how much *did* I pay for it—since you think you know so much?" Baines asked.

Trustrum hefted the mounting in his hand. "You say you had it made in a mall store, at a so-called special while-you-wait promotion. Hmm. Then, I say you overpaid for this grotesque thing—which, by the way, looks nothing like a real gold nugget—hmm. Well, I'd say twelve fifty, including labor."

"Huh. Shows what you know, Crook. It cost close to

two grand."

"Ouch. They really got you. You paid about three times what you could have gotten it for."

"You're riding me, Crook."

"Afraid not," Trustrum said, his tone serious. Inside, he was grinning. "Think about it. The remount company that actually does the one-day event is a separate company. It has high overhead being on the road and carrying a complete inventory of merchandise—not to mention covering losses from robberies the company faces each year. The jewelry store that sponsors the remount event has to make its cut. And don't forget, whether directly or indirectly, the mall gets its piece of the pie, right off the top. Basically, Mr. Baines, they saw you coming and overcharged for an ugly, outdated design and one more thing—"

"What?" Baines asked.

Trustrum glanced at Pritchard, who appeared to be holding his breath so as not to burst out laughing. "As is usually the case with those on-the-road jewelers, since they're pressured to get a tremendous amount of work done in a short time, the stones might as well have been pounded in there—it's a sloppy job. Let me guess, you've been catching the prongs on your clothes, haven't you?"

"I *have* snagged some things. Damn!" Then he reached out his right arm so that his jacket sleeve pulled back, exposing a two-tone gold, curb-link bracelet on his wrist. "What about this?"

"What about it?"

"I got it at a fifty-percent discount."

"Fifty percent of what?"

"Of what it usually sells for, what else?"

"No you didn't."

"Now, you really don't know what you're talking about,

86

Crook. It was listed at fifteen hundred, and I walked out with it for seven fifty."

"Do you really think that people usually buy similar bracelets for fifteen hundred? Come on, the price was jacked up so that you'd think you were getting a discount."

"Really?"

"Listen to me carefully: the retail replacement value for that bracelet is what it costs on average to *buy* it new. I don't care if the price tag was marked fifteen hundred dollars or fifteen million, if it's selling at jewelry stores on average for seven fifty—I'm talking the out-the-door price—then its retail replacement value is seven fifty or something close to it. Think about it this way, if you called that same jewelry store right now and said that you wanted another bracelet identical to this one—the one you *just* bought from them a day or two ago—how much do you think they would charge you?"

"I guess seven fifty," Baines said.

"Exactly."

"But they gave me an appraisal that says fifteen hundred."

"If you bought it for seven fifty and they say the *average* price for that bracelet is fifteen hundred, then that means there have to be people out there paying more than twenty-two hundred for it? I don't think so."

"I see your point. There's no way that fifteen hundred could be the average selling price. How can stores get away with giving false discounts? I mean, you'd think the law would shut them down."

"Ah, because they walk a fine line. Look closely, the signs don't say what you think they're saying."

"What's your point?"

"Fifty percent off gold chains—half-price diamond sale—customers are led to believe the store means fifty percent off the average market price—in other words, half-price off the normal industry price. Instead, what they really are saying is: fifty percent off the store's ridiculously inflated prices."

"They really took advantage of me—bunch of liars."

"An equivocation to some, clever marketing to others."

"So without the discount, I'd be paying way over the normal selling price."

"Correct."

"Since I got the discount, I at least paid the going price, right?"

"You paid just a little on the high side. I can give you a long list of mom-and-pop-owned jewelry stores that would have sold it for less, and they wouldn't have needed to mislead you into believing that you were getting a steal. Remember, in the end, it's not the discount, it's what you pay. You just have to be sure to compare apples with apples."

"This burns me up," Baines said.

"Don't take it so hard, you're not alone. Those big jewelry store chains are infamous for playing this same game every day. They take a piece of jewelry that costs them one thousand bucks, mark it up to five thousand, then advertise it with a fifty-percent discount, selling it at twenty-five hundred. A typical mom-and-pop shop would sell the same thing for fifteen hundred to two thousand and not have to discount it. It's called ethics."

Baines made a grunting sound and snatched his ring out of Trustrum's hand.

"Nevertheless, they're still handsome pieces of jewelry, Mr. Baines."

"Don't patronize me, Crook," Baines quickly responded. He pouted like a spoiled little boy for the rest of the day. It was the best day Trustrum Crook had had in weeks.

The limousine pulled over alongside the curb. Abrams hopped out and hurried to open the back passenger door nearest the sidewalk. First, Baines stepped out—next, Trustrum—last, Pritchard.

When Trustrum stepped out, he quickly looked around, turning his body in a full circle. "This is New York City!" he declared. Few people on the noisy, crowded street noticed him or heard his words.

"Shut up and keep moving," Abrams ordered, closing the door after everyone had moved away from the car. He walked up to Trustrum and took hold of his arm, just above the elbow, and led him into a four-story brick building.

"We'll have no more of that, Crook," Baines said.

They marched in procession into the lobby of the building and filed up the stairway and through a doorway leading into a narrow hallway on the third floor. The building looked as though it had been there for half a century, and it appeared not to have been painted—or cleaned for that matter—for just as long. There was no seeing into the offices. The hallway was nothing but wall and door.

Baines stopped in front of the door at the farthest end of the hallway. It was a wooden door with a main panel of privacy glass on which was painted: Peter C. Underwood and Associates, Publicists.

Baines gave Trustrum a stern look and said, "Now, watch yourself and keep in line." Then, he proceeded inside. It was not much of an office in size or décor. And like the lobby and hallway, it appeared not to have been modernized since the fifties.

"Hello, Mr. Baines—Mr. Pritchard. How are you today?" greeted a woman sitting at the front reception desk.

"I'm just fine, Carolyn. How about yourself?" Pritchard greeted.

"Great, but busy—the phones are ringing off the hook today. Mr. Underwood is expecting you, if you'd like to have a seat," she said.

Neither Pritchard nor Baines sat, so Trustrum remained standing as well.

Carolyn, a slim, attractive woman in her late forties, got up and opened the door behind her. She whispered something—probably to Mr. Paul C. Underwood, Trustrum thought—then closed the door.

"Mr. Underwood is just getting off the phone. It'll be a few moments more." She smiled sweetly.

Is this lady in on this or is she really as sweet as she seems? Trustrum thought.

Finally, the door opened and out walked a fat, half-bald man. He was smiling and walked straight to Baines. "Mr. Baines, how nice to see you again." The two men shook hands, then he shook Mr. Pritchard's hand, noting that it was "just wonderful" to see him so soon since the last time, and finally, he introduced himself to Trustrum.

"I've heard many exciting things about you, Mr. Crook. It's good to finally meet you. Come, gentlemen, let's move into my office."

Fortunately, Abrams stayed in the reception room with Carolyn, since Underwood's office was small and cramped with just the four men. Pritchard closed the door behind him so that they could talk privately.

"Yes, indeed. Yes, indeed. Well, Mr. Crook, Mr. Baines has shown me some of your drawings. I can tell you here and now that we are going to be very successful with your art."

"Thank you," Trustrum said.

"For someone who's about to become the next big talk of the art world, you certainly don't seem too excited," Underwood said.

"I prefer to keep my feet on the ground."

"I never thought I'd hear that out of an artist's mouth." He laughed, as if amused by his own words, and then continued, "Well now, the purpose of this gathering is simply for the two of us to meet and to review what I've put together as a possible publicity campaign. The first thing we'll do is get you into some collector, art, and fine living magazines. I have the necessary connections to proceed with that. We'll want to have you interviewed by them over the course of the next year—long before your first exhibition. Next, we'll hit the AP news wire and see if we can tag a few newspapers around the country. We're not going to worry about the smaller papers, but they still might pick up a story or two—never can tell with these things. Then, we'll want to come out with a book of your work: one of those oversize, coffee-table jobs with more pictures than words. We'll want that out and ready to go about a month before the exhibition. Now, the beauty with the book is that we self-publish it—real high quality printing, of course—and mail it gratis to prospective bigwig collectors. That alone will shake the tree. Of course, I'll start the rumors going that there's a new player on the field who's destined to do some big things. With all that, well, I'm sure we'll reach our goals."

Pritchard spoke up. "It sounds as though you have it well mapped out, Mr. Underwood."

"Thank you for your vote of confidence, Mr. Pritchard. Mr. Baines, it was great to see you again, as always. And, Mr. Crook, I look forward to working with you in the future." He shook everyone's hand, then escorted them out of his office into the reception room. Abrams stood up from his chair where he had been waiting. Carolyn smiled as all of the men walked by her desk as they left.

The next and last stop was the tailor's. The same routine was followed getting out of the car and into the tailor's for a fitting. Four dark suits and one charcoal tuxedo were ordered with all the accessories. On the return trip to the warehouse, which Trustrum now knew was located somewhere near New York City, Baines said, "I guess you'll need some jewelry, as well. If you're going to play a jewelry artist, you need to be wearing the right stuff. Will it be enough to have your personal jewelry box delivered to you from your home?"

"That'll be fine," Trustrum said, "But if you don't mind my asking: why did you take *me* to them? I mean, Mr. Underwood works for you guys, doesn't he?"

"Of course he's one of us," Pritchard said.

"Then, why not just have him come to me? You wouldn't have needed to risk bringing me out in public that way. And even if the tailor wasn't in on it, he could have come to us for the right price."

"This is true," Baines said, "But sooner or later, you'll be on your own. Not to mention, had you not conducted yourself according to protocol, we'd then know you weren't ready to be presented to the Coterie membership. We won't tolerate an embarrassing scene at the board meeting."

"So, how did I do?"

For the first time, Baines seemed to warm up to Trustrum and replied, "You did just fine. In fact, I'm going to suggest that you return to your home in Maryland as soon as the presentation is over—as long as everything goes as it should."

Trustrum had to fight to contain himself. Could this terrible ordeal nearly be over?

~~~~~~~

Chapter Seven
By Guess and by God

When relying on experience and instinct—rather than charts—a skipper is said to be navigating by guess and by god.

Trustrum Crook prayed that he could make his way home—alive.

~~~~~~~~

Baines, Pritchard, and Trustrum Crook stood in the elevator as it lifted them to the forty-second floor. Although all three men wore tuxedos, it was Trustrum who looked a cut above the others, for he obviously wore by far the most expensive outfit among them, accented with choice selections from his personal jewelry collection.

He took advantage of the plastic wall panels of the elevator after noticing that they were reflective. He thought he looked exceptionally well for a man in his predicament—besides having lost five or ten pounds during his captivity.

He looked over at Baines and said, "I would have preferred a rented tux, you know."

"Why is that?" Baines asked in a coarse tone.

"You wouldn't shoot me in a rented tux—even if I did make a mess of things tonight, would you?" Trustrum asked. Pritchard smiled.

"Let's be sure we don't have to concern ourselves with such ugly images," Baines said, "because, as luck has it, we do own your threads."

Pritchard stepped in. "Trustrum, focus on tonight. The

way you carry yourself, the things you'll say, your overall attitude—all these things are just as important as the drawings and models of the objets d'art themselves. Unless you are highly marketable to these people, you're worthless to them, and all of our time and energy has been for nothing. It's your job to sell yourself as much as your art. Assure each and every one of the Coterie's members that you can handle yourself in formal surroundings as well as with reporters when you're in front of cameras. Trustrum, collectively, they will be investing millions of dollars in you. Show them that their money is safe."

As the elevator doors slid open, Baines added with a soft chuckle, "Do or die, Crook."

The three men stepped into what seemed to Trustrum to be another world. *If this is a board meeting, then how do these folks celebrate?* he asked himself. Everyone was stunningly dressed: women wore beautiful gowns, men wore hand-sewn tuxedos. It was definitely a jewelry crowd; Trustrum saw pieces the likes of which museums would be envious. They slowly walked across the room toward the place where Coulbourne stood talking with two couples.

Trustrum gazed through a doorway and saw an elaborate dining room where staff was cleaning up after an apparently lavish feast. On the far side of the room, a string quartet played soft baroque concertos. Trustrum noticed that his drawings had been enlarged and handsomely framed and hung on the walls, which the Coterie membership scrutinized along with his three-dimensional clay models, displayed on columns in the center of the room. Coulbourne interrupted his conversation when he saw the approaching three men.

"And here he is now, our man of the hour. Hello, Trustrum. What a night it is," Coulbourne said, reaching out and shaking Trustrum's hand. "You'll be glad to know that at least the five of us think your talent is just what the Coterie needs."

"Thank you. I'm thrilled to be a part of the organization."

One woman extended her right hand, and Trustrum shook it. "Hello. It's a pleasure meeting you," he said.

"The pleasure is ours, Mr. Crook. It's not every day that we're fortunate enough to meet such a skilled artist as yourself."

"Thank you." He noticed that she had not given her name nor properly introduced the others in their circle.

"Mr. Coulbourne was telling us that you've spent much of your professional career as a jewelry appraiser," she said.

"That is true."

"Which do you prefer, appraising or creating?"

"I've often wondered that myself. I must admit, up until recently, I've thought of myself as more of an appraiser."

She held out her left hand and asked, "What can you tell me about this, Mr. Appraiser?" On her hand was a white-gold ring with a diamond that had to be at least six carats. Realizing she was attempting to catch him off balance, Trustrum responded by taking her hand, slightly lowering his head, and examining the jewel. For a moment, he did not speak, then, without looking up he asked, "Can you guess what I like the most about the jewelry business?"

"No, tell us," she said.

Trustrum looked up and said, "I get to hold hands with lovely women." Everyone in the circle, including the woman, laughed. Then Trustrum released her hand and said, "I must say, whether I'm appraising or creating, it's a pleasure working with such beautiful things as this."

"I already know it's beautiful, Mr. Crook. You'll have to do better than that if you want to impress us with your skills."

Trustrum smiled. Without another word, he began, "The diamond in your ring originally belonged to your grandmother or someone near her age who received it in the mid to late thirties."

"It *was* my grandmother's, and it was 1937, if I'm not mistaken," she said.

"She passed on suddenly and unexpectedly in the mid-fifties, maybe early sixties, when your mother inherited it and had it reset into this mounting."

"That's right!" she exclaimed.

"Your mother is still alive, but she decided she'd rather you have it. I'd say that she gave it to you about five years ago."

"Very good. It was about four years ago when mother handed it down to me."

"You had it sized smaller to fit, and the day you picked it up from the jeweler…it was raining."

For a moment, she did not say a thing; she was stunned by his accuracy. Then, she said, "Right again! Well, at least about the sizing down…I can't remember if it was raining. How could you know all this, Sherlock Holmes, or is it Houdini?"

"It's Trustrum Crook.

"Okay, Trustrum Crook, tell us how you know all that from one diamond ring."

"You see, your diamond is what we call a transitional round brilliant cut. That means it has some of the characteristics of a modern round and an old European cut, which was prominent from about the turn of the century to 1919. The twenties and thirties saw the dominance of the transitional round brilliant before today's modern round really became popular in about the early forties. Since you would be too young to have a mother from that generation, it had to have belonged to your grandmother….It had obviously been reset because during the thirties, platinum was the white metal of choice. Since it's in fourteen-karat white gold, which didn't become fashionable until the fifties, it had to have been reset. Now, I've found that few woman

96

are willing to give away their diamonds when they're in their forties or fifties—even to their loving daughters—so the odds were that she had died. That might seem a bit of a stretch to assume, until you consider the fact that few woman from the era of platinum would have opted to reset their diamonds into what they would have considered the inferior white gold. Therefore, it's only logical that her daughter, your mother, was the one who had it reset."

"How can you tell that it's white gold and not platinum?" she asked.

"Platinum is a silver-gray metal, whereas white gold still has a slight yellow undertone, as does yours."

"But how could you possibly know grandmother suffered an unexpected death?"

"As far as I'm concerned, if I die in my forties or fifties, I'll consider it sudden and unexpected," he said. The group laughed.

"I would have to agree with you on that, Mr. Crook. But, how did you know my mother didn't have it reset in the seventies?"

"She could have, but white gold wasn't as trendy by then—yellow gold had become the rage again. So, that would put your mother somewhere in her late twenties to early thirties when she inherited it back in the fifties or early sixties, making her now...in her sixties or seventies. Medicine what it is today, chances are that even if she's ill, she's still with us. Either way, she's probably like so many other elderly people I speak with and is afraid that she'll absentmindedly misplace it, or perhaps it's simply a matter that she's lost her interest in shiny baubles—especially when knowing you would enjoy it."

"Could you see where I had it sized down though? Wait, you didn't turn my hand over, did you?" she asked, looking at the bottom of the ring's shank.

"No, I didn't. And to answer your first question, no...if

sizing is done properly—and this obviously was—the sizing mark isn't visible."

"Then how did you know I had it sized at all—not to mention, made smaller?"

"Actually, that had nothing to do with jewelry. As you probably know, more than sixty percent of Americans are overweight. Again the odds say that certainly a lady who is in her sixties or seventies is going to be one of those overweight Americans—and if not overweight, she probably has problems with her knuckles, which is often the case with the elderly. Since you are obviously not overweight or suffering from enlarged finger joints, you would have had to size it smaller."

"All right, I'll bite. How do you know it was raining the day I picked it up from the jeweler who resized it?"

"To tell you the truth, I haven't a clue, but I figured you probably wouldn't either, since it would have been at least a few years ago. And since I was correct on every other point concerning your ring's family history, how could you challenge me on a little rain?"

Again, the little group of people who had listened to his explanation broke into laughter. The woman with whom Trustrum had been talking looked at the evening's host and said, "This one will do very well, Mr. Coulbourne."

"Yes, he will indeed," Coulbourne responded, then loud enough to catch the attention of all in the room, he said, "Ladies and gentlemen, if I can have your attention, please. Thank you. Allow me to introduce the artist of these fine drawings and models. Mr. Trustrum Crook."

The room filled with applause. Trustrum nodded and allowed a modest smile to form on his face. Coulbourne continued in a loud voice, "Trustrum, I think I speak for everyone when I say how excited we are to have you with our organization." With that, he stopped talking and waited for a response.

Trustrum was caught off guard, but he recovered gracefully. "It's a great honor to be given the opportunity to develop my creations. I *will* make each one a special treasure and a sound investment. I hope you enjoy yourselves this evening. Thank you." The crowd again applauded and returned to what they had been doing.

"Well done, lad," whispered Coulbourne after the two couples he and Trustrum had been speaking with had moved on. "I will see you in the morning."

Trustrum looked at Baines and Pritchard, who had been standing behind him all this time. With an outstretched arm, Baines indicated the direction back to the elevator. For Trustrum Crook, the long awaited moment on which his life so depended appeared to be over before it had barely begun.

~~~~~~~~~

"I'm sure Mr. Pritchard has already mentioned it to you, but let me say again that I thought last night was a stellar success. They loved your work, and they loved you."

"I didn't do much."

"Ah, but you did what was required of you. Come over here and have a seat; I need you to do something for me," Coulbourne said. He walked around to the back of his desk. Baines sat in a chair off to the side; Pritchard in the chair next to Trustrum's. "Mr. Baines thinks Trustrum, here, is ready to spread his wings. What do you say about that, Mr. Pritchard?"

Pritchard nodded his head and said, "I would agree with that assessment."

"Good. Then, it shall be so. The hard part is over, Trustrum. You've made it through. Now, look at how much better off you are. Mr. Pritchard will return with you temporarily and get you reacquainted with your Maryland home life, as well as see that you have everything you need to perform your duties for the Coterie. Surely, by now you realize the importance of punctuality. Do you feel that you can keep to our schedule?"

"Yes, sir, Mr. Coulbourne. I'm ready," Trustrum said.

"I believe that you are," Coulbourne agreed. "Mr. Underwood needs Mr. Pritchard and you to stop by his office today to review some publicity concerns. You can do that on the way out of town." Both Pritchard and Trustrum nodded their heads in approval. "That leaves one last issue that needs to be attended to before you're off to Maryland."

"Yes, sir?"

Coulbourne pushed a pile of bound documents at Trustrum and handed a pen to him. "I need not tell you the Coterie has already invested quite a lot of money and time in you, Trustrum. The future will, no doubt, necessitate more of an investment in both areas before there is a financial return. You would have to agree that we have quite an insurable interest in you. Therefore, it is standard procedure that a life insurance policy be taken out on all artists. The pages and lines requiring your signature are indicated with a red mark."

Trustrum took a moment to look over the papers. The amount of coverage stood out immediately: one million dollars. "That's quite a chunk of change," he said.

"We have invested *quite a chunk of change* in you," Baines said.

Trustrum did not protest. There was no sense to. He signed the documents where marked, making the Coterie the beneficiary.

~~~~~~~~

It quickly became clear to Trustrum that the motivation for one last stop at the publicity office of Peter C. Underwood and Associates was to reinforce one more time exactly what was at stake. Underwood sat behind his desk, rambling on about the latest success he had had in sparking the interest of one of the national collector magazines in the talented Trustrum Crook when the subject took a turn.

On his desk was a newspaper article with the headline: *Artists Killed in Explosion*. Baines pointed at the paper, "Is this the article about Tom and Eric?"

"Yes. Tragic thing. Terrible loss. Go ahead and read the article if you like," Underwood said. Then, he said nothing more as if on cue. Pritchard stared at the floor without blinking or saying a word. Baines picked up the paper and began reading the article aloud. "A freak explosion caused the studio of Tom Padgett and Eric Kinsley to burn to the ground. At first, firefighters hoped that no one was in the wood-frame building when the inferno erupted around three AM The two bodies of the artists were discovered hours later. Dental records were required for a positive identification of the two men. Mr. Padgett and Mr. Kinsley were known for their sculptures in iron and bronze. Signing their work with the first letter of each artist's last name, PK has come to represent the highest standards in quality to many in certain circles. Their creations have sold for thousands of dollars and have been exhibited in galleries around the world. Mr. Padgett is survived by..." He put down the newspaper. "Well, no need reading all that. Burning, damn, that's got to be a tough way to go."

When Baines finished, Underwood looked up, straight into Trustrum's eyes, and said, "I hope that we don't have friction in our relationship. As long as you don't give us trouble, there won't be a need for anything to happen to you. Right?"

Trustrum felt nauseated and could not gather his thoughts to reply.

"Right?" Underwood repeated.

"Right," Trustrum finally said.

"Well then, we're off to Annapolis. Gentlemen, it's been

a pleasure," Pritchard said.

The limousine waited out front of Underwood's office building, as did a different limousine with clear glass windows. Baines climbed into the back of the first car without saying a word more, and the driver headed off. Trustrum followed Pritchard's lead and got into the back of the new car.

"Looks like I've been promoted," Trustrum said.

"How's that?" Pritchard asked.

"Clear windows," he mocked.

"You'll need to know how to get to Mr. Underwood's office in the future. You'll find that in many ways your life will return to how it was originally—but it'll be better. Now, instead of your appraisal business, you'll create works of valuable art. You've got it made, Trustrum."

"It depends on how you look at it, I'm sure."

"Is there a problem I'm unaware of?"

"The Coterie gave me an unrealistic schedule."

"How so?"

"Are you kidding? It has me working nonstop. I don't live to work; I work to live. I've never needed to be rich to be happy. Except for a few seasonal slow periods, jewelry appraising has more than paid the bills in the past, and that's working less than one-third of the year, when totaled together."

"Well then, allow me to welcome you to the real world of the working man, because you're one of us now: six to seven days a week, ten to fifteen hours a day," Pritchard said and laughed.

But Trustrum did not hear him. As the car headed south on Interstate 95, he was too excited to think of anything other than that soon he would be with his little girl. *I'm coming home, Sarah. I'm coming home.*

Chapter Eight
Jolly Roger

The sight of a flag bearing the skull-and-crossed bones caused many a good, brave sailor to tremble in fear of losing his life. Like the pirates of past times who used the Jolly Roger as their banner, the rogues of the Coterie—Coulbourne, Baines, even Pritchard—were many things, but not jolly.

Trustrum Crook knew that he was in over his head.

~~~~~~~~

Marquise burst into loud screams and high-pitched wails, unique to the Siamese breed, when Trustrum arrived at home. It took over two hours for her to settle down, and when she was not vocally scolding him for having stayed away so long, she displayed her consternation by racing through the house, bounding over furniture, and bolting up and down the stairs.

"Man, that cat's crazy," Pritchard said. "Is she dangerous?"

"It's a cat. What do you think she could really do to you?"

"I don't know; she looks pretty ferocious."

"You guys! Between Baines's sentimental lapse with his parents' wedding rings and you scared of a little cat...well, I just don't know."

Trustrum noticed that Marquise looked a little thin even for her usual sleek build. But she was alive—so, even though he could tell that she had not been fed as frequently as he would have liked, he was still grateful that she was unharmed.

The first thing Trustrum did was to walk through the entire house. He wanted to be certain it was empty, except for Pritchard and him. "Looks like just the two of us," he said, having finished searching every room on all three floors, including the studio and the garage, and returned to the living room.

"Who else did you expect?" Pritchard asked, awkwardly hopping from one foot to the other, each bent knee in turn raised high off the floor, as Marquise charged past. "What's with that cat?"

"She's telling me off. She's more possessive of me than you guys are of your bank accounts."

"What the hell kind of name is *Marquise* anyway?"

"Not Marquis—Marquise—there's a silent *e* at the end, and the *s* is pronounced."

"The word is Marquis. There's no *e*."

"You're wrong. Without the *e* is masculine French—that's the car. In the jewelry trade, the brilliant cut with the double-pointed ends is *marquise*. It's feminine French—silent *e*, say the *s*."

"I've never heard that before."

"That doesn't make it untrue," Trustrum said, and he went to the kitchen. He did not see what he was looking for on the counters, so he started opening and slamming drawers and cabinet doors searching.

"What are you doing?" Pritchard yelled.

Trustrum stormed to the living room where Pritchard had seated himself in a chair.

"Where's my mail?" Trustrum demanded.

"We take care of those things now. We've already been over this."

"But my check from the auction house. I want my check, damn it!"

Pritchard laughed. "You just don't get it, do you? Listen, that check was recovered weeks ago. It's already been returned to the Coterie investor."

"I deserve something from it. It's mine...I earned it!"

"Settle down, Trustrum, or Baines and company will be banging at the front door. If I were you, I'd just be glad to be breathing. You pushed Mr. Coulbourne further than he's used to being pushed. If Baines had his way, you'd have been deep-sixed long ago."

Trustrum flung himself onto the couch and stared out the window at the churning waters of the Magothy River. It was a beautiful spring day, and he was finally at home—and yet, he was numb to any comfort he once would have felt by being there. It was as if he were a stranger and did not belong.

"You know, you really have something in this place." Pritchard stretched out his legs and raised his arms to support his head. "I could get used to this. It's so peaceful and serene."

Just then, with a startling burst, Marquise ripped down the stairs, still in a rage over Trustrum's long absence. With outstretched claws, she bounded over Pritchard's lap, who jumped high out of his seat.

~~~~~~~~

It was a warm, sunny day cooled by southerly winds that blew in from the Chesapeake Bay and up the Magothy River. Trustrum had been at home for three days and was overjoyed at seeing Sarah. He had arranged the day before to have her spend the weekend with him, choosing to stay on *Tavernier* instead of at the house where Pritchard would be.

Sarah was well accustomed to life aboard a sailing vessel; she had been exposed to wind and water since she was two years old. Now, with three years of experience, she knew the names and functions of most of the instruments and equipment aboard, and she moved about with more ease and assurance than most sailors who had had their sea legs for a far longer time. Her young, undeveloped muscles prevented her from performing most of the tasks required to sail a boat. Still, if the winds were low enough, she could man the helm, which she thought of as the most important and fun thing to do on a boat—short of playing with her dolls in the forward V-berth.

As soon as they boarded, Trustrum unlocked and opened the starboard lazarette. The cockpit compartment's opening was narrow, but it broadened below deck to a large storage area and held the bulk of the vessel's gear. He reached inside, searching through the pile of sailing supplies stashed there. He pushed aside the bagged storm jib and as many of the adult-size lifejackets one hand could gather in a single swoop. He was looking for the one and only child-size lifejacket that belonged to Sarah. He struggled with the weight of the pile with one hand while supporting the lazarette door with the other. Sarah sat on the port side of the cockpit and watched as he struggled with the cumbersome mass. Finally, he gave up and carefully closed the heavy seat.

"Isn't it there?" Sarah asked.

Trustrum chuckled and said, "I know it is. I just can't find it. I'm going to have to climb in."

"I'll do it! Let me, please!" she begged, as if not allowing her would keep her from a great adventure.

Trustrum did not see any harm in letting her climb below, but he also did not believe she would be able to do much good since many of the items were heavy or simply large and difficult to maneuver. Still, he did not wish to disappoint her, so he lifted open the door and helped her down.

"This is neat in here. It's wet! Daddy, we're sinking!" she screamed.

"Calm yourself. We're not sinking."

"But there's water down here!"

"Baby, it's just like the bilge. There's always some amount of water down below. That water's probably run off from the propeller shaft. It's designed to use the water as a lubricant. So, we actually want a little dripping going on."

"I want to come out, Daddy."

"Come on, sweetheart, don't be scared. Move over a little, so I can climb down and help you." He slid through the rectangular-shaped opening, having used one of the companionway door slats to prop open the lazarette door. He sorted through the mess of things while Sarah pulled herself through to the port side of the boat.

"Here it is!" Trustrum exclaimed, holding up the missing lifejacket, but Sarah paid no attention to him.

"What's this, Daddy?" she asked, pointing to an unfamiliar rectangular container that was attached to a bulkhead.

Trustrum examined the small device but refrained from touching it. He had crawled through every inch of *Tavernier* many times but had never seen that container before. *What is that thing?* he wondered. For a moment, he considered the possibility that his mechanic, Mike, had put it in with the rebuilt engine—that maybe it had something to do with new pollution control requirements or something.

The size and shape of a chalkboard eraser, it had a wire, about eight feet long, running out of it. The wire was tacked to the walls, coiling twice around the perimeter of the inside of the hold leading to...nowhere. But if not connected to anything, what would it be for? Certainly not the engine— unless it was an antenna! Then he realized what the whole thing was and thought himself foolish for not having expected something like this: *it's a bug, it has to be!* The Coterie had bugged their own offices and the studio in which he had been held prisoner for weeks. What was to prevent them from planting bugs to keep tabs on him in Maryland? *If they've bugged my boat, then surely they've bugged my house, my phones, my car,* he thought in a panic. He continued to study it, noticing that it was awfully large for modern technology. *Either they used obsolete electronics or…man,* he thought, *this thing must be for tracking, too!*

"What is it, Daddy?" Sarah asked again.

"Huh? Oh, I'm sorry, honey. It's something to do with the engine, I guess," he said looking her straight in the eyes— he hated lying but knew it was for the best. "Mr. Mike must have done it."

"Who?"

"Remember the man who fixed the engine?" Sarah had a look of uncertainty as she tried to place the mechanic's face. "Remember? You sat on the pier and watched him take the engine out of the boat."

"Oh, yeah. I forgot I did that."

"It must have to do with the exhaust system or something….Hey," he said with newfound energy in his voice, "we're wasting a beautiful day in this hole. Let's go catch some air!"

"Yeah!" Sarah shouted and out of the lazarette they climbed. He did his best to put his problems out of mind, but even as they sailed around the lighthouse at the mouth of the Magothy River, his thoughts were of the Coterie.

〰〰〰〰

Pritchard stayed on for a few weeks and oversaw that Trustrum had everything he needed to create the objets d'art. During Pritchard's stay, Trustrum had to keep reminding himself that the man was one of them and could not be trusted. He wondered if Pritchard knew about the bug and tracking device in *Tavernier*. He probably did, and he assumed the Coterie had heard Sarah and his conversation about it. He was glad that he had not given them any hint that he suspected what it was.

Trustrum had been given many new pieces of specialized equipment that he had never needed before having worked in the past strictly in jewelry and spent countless hours organizing his studio. Since only he knew where the new equipment would best go, Trustrum performed most of the labor while Pritchard watched and talked. But after three days of endless rambling, boredom overwhelmed the Coterie associate and he joined in the work, helping to clean and assemble the industrial-size drill press that Trustrum had yet to start working on. In no time, Pritchard was covered with oil and grime.

"Mr. Baines is concerned with the amount of time it's taking us to set everything up. If it takes much longer, you'll need to produce three a month instead of just two."

"Two a month is too many. I'm not making toys for bubble gum machines. These things are intricate and ornate. One a month is pushing it."

"Well, you'll just have to put in the hours. It sounds to me like you've made it pretty easy for yourself over the years, and now, you're just plain spoiled. Look at me, I put in sixty hours a week easy, and sometimes…"

Trustrum stepped out of the studio and headed for the kitchen as Pritchard spoke. He picked up the phone and called Jacqueline at her office. As he had hoped, she answered the phone.

"Jacqueline Hurlock."

"Answering your own phone these days?"

"Trustrum?"

"Are you still talking to me?"

"I shouldn't be. Where have you been?"

"Didn't you get my message?"

"If I remember correctly, you said you had left town suddenly on business, and you'd call when you got back. Could you have been any more vague, Trustrum?"

"So, here I am calling."

"How nice of you."

"Look, I'm sorry. I should have kept calling until I got through to you. But things were really hectic. The job didn't leave a lot of free time."

"You're telling me that in over two and a half months you couldn't make a few three-minute calls?"

"I'm telling you if I had had my way, I would have been *with* you—forget the calls."

"In a way, I suppose I deserve it. I'm the one who usually keeps the distance."

"It's not about that. I swear I wasn't trying to make a point. Come on now. We can talk about this later. I need to see you about Sarah, right away. Can I come over?"

"Right now?" she asked.

"Yeah. Right now."

"If you hurry, my secretary won't be back from lunch for another forty-five minutes."

"I'll be there in fifteen," he said and hung up the phone. He looked at his watch and hurried back to the studio and to Pritchard, who was in the throes of his mechanical puzzle.

"Where'd you get to? You're as bad as my wife, leaving me talking to myself."

"I didn't know you were married," Trustrum said, intentionally not answering his question.

"Believe it or not, I also have two kids."

"And what do they think of daddy's career choice?"

Pritchard responded to Trustrum's question by asking his own. "Where did you go when you left?" His tone was serious and firm.

"I went to the kitchen and called my lawyer, not that it's any of your business."

"You mean that girlfriend of yours?"

"She's my lawyer!" Trustrum snapped back.

Pritchard stopped working and looked up with a disgusted expression. "Who do you think you're kidding? We know everything about you."

"I said she's my lawyer, and this has nothing to do with the Coterie. It's about Sarah."

"And what would that be?"

"Same old thing, Pritchard. Time. My ex-wife doesn't want me to have Sarah for as much time as a father should have with his daughter."

"You're going to be too busy this summer for extended visits—you know that. Why are you doing this?"

"It's not just how much. It's also when. Look, Pritchard, it's not a big deal. You're going to be leaving in a week or two, aren't you? What's to stop me from seeing whomever I want, then? I know the rules. I'm playing ball with you guys. I'm not stirring up trouble. Just let me see the lady, so I can see my kid, okay?"

<hr />

"And this guy, Pritchard, is in your house, right now?" Jacqueline asked after Trustrum finished telling her about his experiences with the Coterie.

"As we speak."

"Have you found bugs in your house?"

"No, but then, I haven't been able to look for them, either. If it hadn't been for Sarah, I'm sure I wouldn't have noticed the electronics they put in the boat."

"Do you really think they've bugged my office, too?"

"It's highly likely. They've known about you from the beginning."

Jacqueline was silent for a short time as she tried to

think of what to do. Finally, she said, "Go to the police. You have no choice. Trustrum, you have to go to the police."

"I can't take that kind of risk, Jacqueline. By the time they get around to investigating, it'd be long over for me. These guys are professionals."

"What about the FBI? Isn't this the kind of thing they handle?"

"I don't know. For God's sakes, I'm just a jewelry appraiser. I'm not cut out for this."

"I think you should contact the FBI, Trustrum."

"Jackie, these guys are on me so thick, I'd be surprised if they weren't under that rock," he said, referring to a piece of macadam that had broken away from the alley surface.

"Really? Then how did you get away to come here?"

"I said I was coming to see you about Sarah. Now that I think of it, you'd better type up a letter for Michelle's lawyer about my requesting more time with Sarah—just in case."

"Sure. Just watch your step. That's all I'm saying." Pritchard went back to assembling the drill press, and Trustrum went to his bedroom and quickly cleaned himself up. Five minutes later he was in his car with the top down driving to downtown Annapolis to see Jacqueline.

~~~~~~~~~

Jacqueline's office was in a small, renovated colonial-style building on a side road only three blocks away from the city dock. He walked inside and, hearing Jacqueline speaking on the phone, quietly moved in front of the doorway to her office and waved to her. She signaled for him to sit down and quickly finished her conversation. After she hung up the phone, she said, "Just so you know, you're still on my list, so start explaining…Trustrum, you look terrible!" She walked around her desk toward him, and he stood up to meet her. They embraced.

"Thanks. You look great."

"What's wrong?"

"Nothing's wrong. In fact, I've stumbled into a great opportunity. Let's take a stroll, and I'll tell you the good news."

"I can't leave. Somebody has to answer the phone."

"I miss Annapolis. Come on, just a short walk. You do have an answering machine, don't you?" Trustrum held his finger up to his mouth signaling for Jacqueline to be quiet. "You're going to be very proud of me, Jacqueline. I'm on my way in a new career." As he spoke, Trustrum took Jacqueline by the arm and escorted her out the back door of the house, crossed the little yard, which was enclosed by tall brick walls, and exited through the back gate into the alley. When he felt it was safe to speak candidly, he said, "I don't have much time. I have to get back home. I need you to say nothing and listen to me...Jackie, I'm in big trouble."

"Trustrum, this couldn't be worse."

"I know I've put you at risk, but I can't come up with a way out of this. Lord knows I've tried to think of something."

"Will they come after me?"

"They shouldn't—as long as they believe my reason for coming here."

"Right. We have to focus and not become paranoid. But I think you're right about a letter. I'll throw something together when we go back to the office."

"I'm really scared, Jackie. I'm scared for Sarah, for you, for me. By the time the police or FBI or whoever takes me seriously, I'll already be dead. I know these people. They wouldn't hesitate to kill all of us if it would get them a better parking space downtown."

"I guess running isn't the answer."

"They know about Sarah."

"Of course. That was stupid. I can't think straight. Let's

see…I don't know what to say, Trustrum. We both need to just slow down and think this out."

"It's a nightmare," Trustrum said.

"You need to get back, so I need to get you that letter."

"You're panicking again. Think about it. You wouldn't drop everything to write me a letter. Just put something together, mail it off to Michelle's lawyer, and send me a copy."

"You're right. So all we talked about is this time thing with Sarah and your new wonderful life."

"Right." They walked back through the gate into the yard toward the house. "Just be careful, Jacqueline. I guarantee you that if Pritchard didn't follow me, another one of the goons did."

"I thought only Pritchard was here with you?"

"He may be, but as far as I know, they've got back-up everywhere. I'm telling you, this is a big organization."

When they reached the backdoor of the office, Trustrum hesitated before opening it. "Show time," he said, then he held the door open and Jacqueline walked in first. When they were both inside, Jacqueline walked quickly to the front of the office, locked the front door, and then came back to her office where Trustrum was waiting.

"Lauren's not back yet."

"Who?"

"Lauren, my secretary."

"Look, I have to get back to work. My art is calling me."

"We have one more thing to go over before you leave," Jacqueline said. She closed the door to her office and locked it. Trustrum was standing, leaning against her desk, as she walked up to him and wrapped her arms around his neck. They kissed passionately, until she moved so that she could ever so quietly whisper into his ear, "Show time."

"So, did you get it all worked out?" Pritchard asked as soon as Trustrum returned to the studio in his home.

"It went just fine, thank you. What's with the attitude?"

"No attitude, Trustrum, none at all."

Trustrum could not read him, and he grew nervous. He regretted telling Jacqueline and wished he could take it back. He looked around the studio surveying the work they had accomplished; all would be ready by tomorrow, and he could start on his first creation.

Two days later, a delivery car rolled up in front of Trustrum's waterfront home. It was not a commercial delivery service using an easily identifiable company vehicle as would be expected, however; the delivery was performed by two men, wearing expensive suits, driving a dark green Lincoln Continental. Before the delivery, Pritchard's pager had gone off. He activated the message; he was instructed to go to the front door and wait.

Five minutes later, he accepted an oversize briefcase from one of the men, while the second man stayed in the driver's seat of the car with the engine running. Trustrum, looking out a living room window, noticed that their car bore New York plates. When the delivery was completed, the man returned to the waiting car, having not spoken a word, and off they drove—Trustrum could only assume that they were heading for New York City, three and a half hours away.

"Don't you thugs ever need to use the bathroom?" Trustrum asked. Pritchard ignored him and set the black, hard-sided case on the dining-room table, then opened it.

"I'll take it from here, Pritchard," Trustrum said, casually pushing Pritchard out of the way. "I'm the one whose head will roll if something's missing. Since your people were in too much of a hurry to count out the goods as professionalism dictates, you need to oversee the inventory with me. If one of those jokers has decided to pocket a stone, they can be the ones responsible, not me."

"Fair enough," Pritchard said. "Whatever it is you think you need to do."

"Fine," Trustrum said. He slammed the case closed, snatched it up under his arm, and carried it to the studio. Once there, Trustrum handed the enclosed inventory list to Pritchard, then began to examine the gemstone packets, first confirming the weight of each stone on an electric digital scale and then viewing it through a microscope before returning it to the safety of the folded paper packet. The whole process took him—adept as he was—less than a minute with each stone.

When he finished with every gemstone as well as with the gold bullion, he turned to Pritchard, who had been checking everything off on the list.

"That's everything—just as expected," Pritchard said, as if his side had won a bet.

"In size and number, yes. But in quality, the syndicate was ripped off. This stuff might as well be borax."

"Borax? What are you talking about?"

"I can't believe you guys. You think because you have money and guns you can suddenly do as you please in whatever industry you decide to muscle in on. It might work with other businesses, but there's a lot more to the jewelry industry than just digging a rock out of the ground. I thought you guys used experts?" Trustrum spoke intentionally louder than normal.

"What's borax?" Pritchard asked again.

"Worthless garbage, as far as I'm concerned. These diamonds are inferior. I said nothing less than next to flawless and colorless. That means nothing under VVS clarity, D to F color."

"Are you saying these are fake?"

"No, but they might as well be. Listen, just be quiet and listen for once," Trustrum said. Exasperated, he sighed. Then with a louder voice, directed again at the eavesdropping Coterie, he yelled, "Pay attention! I can't start working until I have the correct supplies."

"Watch yourself," Pritchard said in a low but strained voice.

Trustrum ignored the warning. "You need to tell your supplier that we won't accept anything less than what we've asked for."

"I find it hard to believe our supplier would sell us the wrong stuff."

"Selling diamonds a color or clarity grade lower than what it's represented as goes on so much some of these guys think it's just part of doing business. Listen, I could run you through the grading systems, and you'll think you understand them, but you really won't. The only way to truly learn diamonds is to study and compare hundreds of stones. The subtleties are impossible to explain—they have to be experienced."

"I've bought diamonds for my wife. It wasn't that hard to figure out, Trustrum."

"And let me guess. When you examined the stones for clarity, the jeweler gave you a hand loupe to use, right?"

"Yeah, so what?"

Trustrum burst out laughing. "They give you a hand loupe because they know, unless you're a professional, you won't see half of what's really in the stone. This isn't third grade science. Use your head! The slightest nuance in either one clarity or color grade can mean a difference of hundreds, even thousands of dollars per carat."

"Trustrum, you need to stop—"

"Just wait a minute, I have an idea. Come here." Trustrum took Pritchard by the arm and escorted him to a window with a view of the Magothy River outlined by distant trees on the far side. "See those trees on the other side of the river?"

"Of course."

"Do you see all of them? How about the trees standing behind those along the beach?"

"How could I see them?"

"All right, then of the trees you can see, how many leaves are on each one? Can you tell me that?"

"Of course not."

"That's right. Not from here, you can't. And that's exactly what it's like when an untrained eye uses a loupe. Yeah, you see a magnified diamond, but you don't begin to see what's really going on."

"So, if I won't be able to see with a loupe, then how do I know what I'm buying?"

"In this day and age, you should question any jewelry store that doesn't use a microscope to show what's really going on inside a diamond. After that, you should have an expert appraiser confirm everything—and that's me. So, take these diamonds, give them back to your supplier, and tell him that he's dealing with a professional. If you want me to create something special, then give me what I need to do it!"

~~~~~~~~

Not everything was returned. Fortunately, Trustrum was able to use the eighteen-karat gold bullion. From the globular-shaped nodules, he milled his own gold sheet and drew his own gold wire. This Trustrum used to make the basic components that he would later combine together with a variety of precious metals and gemstones to create wonderful works of art.

Pritchard returned to New York City, leaving Trustrum alone in his home where he spent most of his waking hours in the studio. One day, nearly two weeks later Baines and Pritchard surprised Trustrum with an unannounced visit. He was working in the studio and heard someone unlock the deadbolts on the front door and enter his home. They wasted no time walking in on him.

"Can't you guys at least knock?" Trustrum asked.

"Special delivery, Crook," Baines said. He held up the briefcase he was carrying. Trustrum noticed Pritchard said nothing, which was not entirely unusual. He generally remained in the background when Baines was present, but today his mood seemed different somehow.

Baines handed the briefcase to Trustrum, who perfunctorily weighed and examined the stones and additional metals.

"You'll find them to be just what you ordered," Baines said. "I'm positive we won't have anymore problems with our supply of diamonds."

"Worked him over good, huh?" Trustrum asked.

"A man should love his work. Don't you think, Trustrum?"

Trustrum continued to review and check off the supply of goods. Pritchard sat on one of the workbenches on the far side of the room, out of the way, Trustrum observed. *Something's up,* he thought, barely containing his anxiety. Baines took a newspaper from where he carried it under his arm, leaned against the wall on the opposite side of the room from Trustrum, and began to read aloud various headlines.

"Another bank was held up, I see. Hmm, another accident on route two. This certainly is a busy place around here. Do you find it overwhelming, Crook?"

"Never really noticed...I've been stuck in this studio a long time, I guess."

Yes, you have, haven't you? Hmm, what's this here. Area lawyer found dead along roadside."

Trustrum stopped working with some diamonds and looked up. He had turned pale at hearing Baines's words.

"Gun-shot wounds to the head....Where's Deep Creek Road, Trustrum?"

But Trustrum could barely breathe, let alone speak. He grew sick to his stomach and lightheaded.

"Sounds suspicious to me. What do you think, Mr. Pritchard?" Baines asked. Pritchard refrained from speaking. He merely nodded his head.

"Hey, Crook, isn't this Jacqueline Hurlock your lawyer or something?" Baines asked.

Trustrum was horrified. He felt as if the room had collapsed in on him; he could not move.

Then Baines chuckled and said, "Goes to show, people just aren't safe in their own neighborhoods anymore…or their homes, for that matter—"

"You son of a bitch!" Trustrum suddenly shouted. He jumped to his feet and charged across the room. He dove at Baines and grabbed him with both hands around the neck, choking him with all his might. Baines fell back against the wall, and the newspaper he had been holding flew into the air, sheets scattering everywhere. "I'm…going…to…kill…you…Baines!" Trustrum screamed. With each word he slammed Baines's head against the wall.

"Stop it, stop it, Trustrum!" Pritchard yelled, while trying unsuccessfully to pull him off Baines. In a panic, Pritchard snatched up Trustrum's latest creation sitting on the workbench, then raised the solid gold, cylindrical reliquary over his head and swung it down, striking Trustrum with full force on the crown of his head. But Trustrum was still insane with rage, and the blow had little effect. Pritchard struck him again—then again. The fourth blow was enough to knock Trustrum to the floor. He held his head with both arms and wept. Baines recovered quickly. He used a workbench to pull himself to his feet, then began kicking and stomping on Trustrum.

"I'm going to kill *you,* Crook!"

"Enough! Stop!" Pritchard shouted. After fifteen, maybe

twenty blows, Pritchard finally was able to pull Baines away.

Trustrum could only lie on the wooden floor and cry.

Chapter Nine
Plimsoll Mark

Since 1876, ocean-going ships have been marked on the outside hull to indicate safe cargo-loading depths for certain weather conditions.

Trustrum Crook's plimsoll marks were gravely disregarded.

~~~~~~~~

Over the months that followed, Trustrum refused to allow Sarah to visit him. He talked with her on the phone nearly every day, but he was firm with his conviction that she stay as far away from Pritchard or any other of the Coterie people as possible. It was simply a matter that he did not want her exposed to them. Still, he knew that if the Coterie wanted to hurt her, there was no place Sarah was safe.

His resentment had long turned into hatred for everyone who had anything at all to do with the syndicate. He despised his demanding work schedule, which prevented him from visiting his daughter at her mother's house. In his misery, Trustrum began drinking—during the day, while working, and even more so at night.

One evening, only four weeks away from the exhibition that would introduce his objets d'art to the world, Trustrum, finished with all the work he could do for the day, decided to spend the rest of his evening—yet again—at the neighborhood bar. He had worked for fourteen hours straight, and his hands were sore from tightly gripping the graver, as he had delicately carved intricate designs on the inside lid of an irregularly-shaped gold box.

He entered the dimly lit bar and was engulfed by the deafening music and shouts of patrons trying to talk over the music.

"There he is—Annapolis's own self-admitted crook," greeted Chip, the bartender.

"Now that's original."

"Sorry, I guess you've heard them all, huh?"

"To this day, I still wonder what my parents were thinking."

Chip smiled. "What'll you have, Mr. Crook?"

"Just pull me the usual amber draft, there," Trustrum said. He sat down on a tall stool at the bar and looked over his shoulder at the crowd. The small room, with its genuine wood paneling and nautical theme, was packed with patrons of all ages—a few of whom, as Trustrum noted, appeared just under what was legal.

He quickly downed two pints, having already consumed a fair amount of Southern Comfort back at the studio, and slowed his pace on the third. He savored the glowing buzz that seemed to wash away his sorrow.

Trustrum was content to sit alone, though no one really sits alone at a crowded bar. Still, no one bothered with him, nor did he try to strike up a conversation with anybody either. Over the past year that Trustrum had regularly visited the bar, he had made it clear to Chip that he preferred to be left to himself. And in that year, Trustrum had consumed a little more alcohol with each visit, until his habit had neared dangerous levels of abuse. Trustrum knew what he was doing to himself, but his misery only increased his loss of will.

At the moment, Trustrum simply wanted to be left alone and enjoy feeling warm inside for a little while. He had become an expert at achieving what he referred to as a manageable level of inebriation. To Trustrum, this meant he was still capable of speaking, although his speech was slurred, and still able to walk the one-mile trek home at night's end without falling to the ground flat on his face more than three times. From an outsider's point of view, he knew he was a pitiful sight, but he did not care.

He was afraid to speak to people—afraid that he might slip and tell them of the Coterie and his wretched plight. His thoughts were jumbled and unrelated as he sat on the stool; the room whirled in a collage of festive sounds and movements, transporting him into euphoria. To the few people who noticed him, Trustrum appeared dazed, staring straight-ahead seeing nothing but his drug-altered thoughts.

~~~~~~~~~

It took little time for every male in the room to notice her when she glided into the bar. Her hair was long and dark, her lips were full and moist with bright red lipstick, her features were stunningly chiseled yet smooth. With her three-inch heels, she stood nearly six feet tall, and her voluptuous figure was accented by a fire-engine-red dress, which molded to her every curve and stopped well above the knees.

She stood still momentarily, as if to feel the watchful eyes of all in the room. It was not dramatic, but the brief cessation of sound was noticeable, even to the blindly intoxicated Trustrum Crook. He watched the woman as she confidently crossed the room, then smiled and stopped behind the man who sat next to him at the bar.

"I'll have a glass of your house white, please," she said to Chip. The man beside Trustrum turned when he heard her giving the order.

"Hello. Can I offer you my seat?" he asked.

"Thank you. I've been standing all day. My feet are screaming," she said. Her smile was captivating.

"Long work day, huh?" he asked, trying to keep the conversation going as he changed places with her and she gracefully slid onto the tall stool. She nodded but said nothing. Chip served her the glass of wine, which she thanked him for, then opened her handbag, obviously looking for her wallet.

"Don't bother, miss. Chip, put that on my tab, will you," the man said.

"Well, aren't you nice: first your seat, now my drink. Thank you," she said. Then, she turned her back to him and picked up her glass, obviously snubbing him. The man stood there uncertainly for a minute, then gave an embarrassed shrug, and drifted away from the bar.

Along with everyone else in the room, Trustrum had watched the femme fatale at work. Having no interest in being her next victim, he was careful not to make eye contact with her. It did not take long before another man accosted her, but she abruptly turned him away too.

"What's does it take for a girl to meet a nice guy?" she asked, directing her question at Trustrum, who glanced at her, making eye contact for just a moment, and smiled. Both men she had gone out of her way to embarrass had seemed fine to Trustrum. Both were around her age, well dressed, relatively handsome, polite, and showed signs of being prosperous. On the other hand, Trustrum realized that he had not taken the time to clean himself up after a long, tiring day of work. He had not cordially responded to her when she had spoken to him, and he was obviously quite drunk.

"How are you tonight?" she asked.

"I suppose I'm doing all right. How are you?" He spoke slowly, trying hard not to slur his words.

"What brings you here?"

"The AA meeting was full up. What's your excuse?"

"I'm new to the area, and I was hoping I could meet

somebody."

"Then I'd say your technique needs a little refining."

Just then, another respectable-looking man approached and started speaking to her, but the noise in the room prevented Trustrum from hearing what he said. He was casually dressed and sported too much jewelry. *Why do men insist on wearing the ugliest jewelry that's out there,* Trustrum wondered, having noticed the man wore a hideously-designed, fluted gold ring with a centered, bezel-set, dyed black onyx—he knew it was dyed because they all were.

The mystery woman barely acknowledged him. Instead, she turned back to face Trustrum. "My name is Susan. What's yours?"

"Any name will do…your choice," he said.

She looked him up and down for a moment and then said, "Well, you sort of have a Clark Kent look about you, but a little more rugged."

"Who could be more…*rugged*…than Superman?" Trustrum slowly asked.

"Hey, Mr. Crook, you all right?" Chip the bartender interrupted.

"Huh? Oh, yeah…sure, Chip," Trustrum responded.

"What do you say you call it a night, Mr. Crook."

"That is…an…ex…cellent…sug...ges...tion," Trustrum replied, climbing off the stool and nearly falling on the floor in the process.

"I've had my fill here. Let me see you home," Susan quickly offered.

"I'm fine…really."

"You're not going to drive, I hope," Susan stated

"Nope. I'm walking, thank…you very—"

"You can't leave me to fend for myself against all these

wolves. You'd be doing me a favor of escorting me to my car," she insisted.

Finally giving in, Trustrum said, "Since you put it that way, it would be...my pleasure."

He paid his tab, struggled into his jacket, and raised his arm toward the door, offering her the courtesy of leading the way. As he stumbled through the room behind her, he looked over his shoulder to see many of the patrons watching with open-mouthed expressions of astonishment.

Outside, Trustrum followed Susan to a white Mercedes 450SL. As he poured himself into the passenger's seat, he concentrated as hard as he could on focusing his unclear thoughts. Even drunk as he was, Trustrum realized that something was amiss.

Along the way, he decided to act more intoxicated than he really was. He wanted his actions to indicate that he would probably remember nothing tomorrow. But Trustrum would remember. Over the past months, he had developed a surprisingly high tolerance for the poison.

Having given her the barest of instructions to where he lived, he pretended to pass out. When they neared the street that led down to the end of the peninsula where his home stood, she somehow knew enough to shake him and ask which way to turn.

"Right," he mumbled, as she made the correct left turn, fueling his suspicions that the Coterie had something to do with this woman. Finally, she went through the gate and followed the correct road to his home, where she parked in his driveway.

Trustrum stayed in the front seat of her car, feigning to be asleep. Susan got out, walked around the back of the car, and opened his door. She had to practically bear all of Trustrum's weight in order to get him out and carry him to the front door. Still supporting him, Susan felt through his pockets until she found his keys.

"I've about had enough of this, lover boy," Susan said. She allowed Trustrum to slump down on the front porch and made certain that he was still passed out by squeezing his cheeks together, using one hand in a pinching grip. Then, she unlocked all of the door locks and stepped inside. She went to the alarm keypad and pushed the correct sequence of numbers that deactivated the system. Trustrum was enraged by her effrontery—by the Coterie's—but he forced himself to remain silent and continue with the charade.

Susan nearly carried him up the three stories of stairs to his bedroom. "Let's get you to bed. There you go," she said, helping him to lie down. She tugged and pulled at his clothes until he lay naked and asleep on the bed. She threw a sheet over him, then walked to the other side of the bed, leaving a trail of her own clothes on the floor before joining him.

~~~~~~~

"Good morning, sleepyhead," Susan seductively whispered in his ear, but Trustrum stayed in bed, trying to keep the bright sunlight out of his eyes—away from his pounding head. "Last night was wonderful," she said, moments later. Having known the correct code to deactivate the alarm system the night before was enough to confirm to Trustrum that Susan was affiliated with the Coterie, her last statement merely emphasized the fact. *Now, the question is,* he asked himself, *why does she want me to think something happened between us—when nothing had?* He rolled over and with squinting eyes peered at her face.

"You don't remember me, do you?" she asked.

"Sure I do…it's just that my brain's killing me," he said.

"I'm not surprised. Do you drink like that every night of the week?"

"Only if I have to work the next day."

"Then, you remember last night?"

"That depends. Did you approve of me or not?"

"Very much so. It was wonderful."

"Then, yes, I remember everything."

"You're naughty. I'm sure we could do something to help jog your memory. Reruns can be very entertaining."

"I would love to, hon, but not right now. I'm just able to concentrate enough to keep my vital organs functioning. Maybe a little later? You wouldn't be handy in the kitchen, would you?"

"Don't tell me I've gone home with a chauvinist?"

"If I was a chauvinist, I would have assumed you could do it. Look, I don't mean to be rude or anything, but I need some food and some strong coffee. Can you fix me up or not?"

Though she complied with his plea and went to work in the kitchen, returning with two fried eggs, toast, and coffee, Trustrum felt that he just might be eating his last meal before execution. He had no idea what she was up to, but there was no doubt that she was one of them. *Is she here to kill me? Or is it just a matter of infiltration? Could the Coterie have decided to cash me in so soon? No, that wouldn't make sense. They wouldn't kill me this close to an exhibition—or would they?*

Slowly, painfully he raised himself to a sitting position. Maybe things would be clearer after he had eaten.

～～～～～～

"How's your swimming?" Trustrum asked as he removed the blue mainsail cover, readying *Tavernier* for a sail. His hangover was far from subsiding and sailing was not going to improve his condition. Nevertheless, he had convinced Susan that it was just what he needed. The truth of the matter was that he did need to get out on the water; however, his reasons had nothing to do with his aching head.

"I can swim. Why, are you expecting to sink?"

"You never can tell. It's important to know the abilities of one's passengers. Ever been sailing?"

"Not sailing. My few water experiences have been on powerboats."

"Well then, today is your lucky day," he said.

Trustrum released the remaining mooring lines and engaged the clutch. He skillfully motored out of the slip, taking heed of both the light wind and current, and he made his way down the familiar distance of Mill Creek into the Magothy River. It was still early morning, and there were few boats on the water. Workboats, out for crabs, had long departed the area, searching other waters, and would not return for another three to five hours, unless there was a change in weather and they were forced in earlier than usual.

When he was a safe distance from land, Trustrum pointed *Tavernier's* bow into the eye of the wind and quickly went to work at raising the sails. First, standing on deck beside the mast, he hauled on the halyard that controlled the mainsail. The wind, about five to ten knots, made the great sail move like an oversize bed sheet drying on a clothesline in the wind; the sail twisted and snapped like a whip. Once done, he quickly surveyed his surroundings, confirming that all was still safe. Then he moved to the jib and raised it as fast as he could high on the forestay. The process took him no more than three minutes, after which he returned to the cockpit where Susan had been sitting and watching. He took control of the helm and steered *Tavernier* off the wind, starting the first tack toward their destination—Dobbins Island.

It was a perfect day for sailing, with gentle winds and a bright orange sun that burned off the few cloud strands that had been lingering in the clear blue sky. Trustrum looked at Susan, who had the same expression he had seen many times before when introducing someone to sailing for the first time. He was amused at the irony that had it not been for the Coterie sending her, he probably would have missed sailing on this day. When all was ready, he turned the ignition key to off. Instantly, the engine silenced, revealing the magic of wind and sail.

"Far out!" Susan exclaimed. She moved forward to experience the moment from the bow as *Tavernier* carved through the dark green waters of the Magothy River. "Are we going out on the Bay?" she shouted back to Trustrum.

"No. Just to Dobbins Island...there," he said, pointing to a small, uninhabited island not more than one mile away. "We'll lay anchor in a little cove on the north side."

It took about twenty minutes to reach the cove. When the depth sounder indicated twelve feet of water, he turned *Tavernier* into the wind, bringing her to a stop. He dropped the anchor so that she lay about fifty feet from the island's closest stretch of land. Ordinarily, he would have anchored closer to shore, but today, he was not planning to have a picnic.

"What now?" Susan asked, her tone flirtatious and suggestive.

"We swim."

"Are you kidding?"

"Best thing for a hangover," Trustrum announced. He hung a ladder over the starboard side, and then bolted its top to the aluminum toe-rail.

"I can think of something better to do," Susan said, continuing her front. "Besides, I don't have a bathing suit."

"Neither do I," he responded. He quickly took off all his clothes and jumped over the side. When he resurfaced, he yelled, "It's wonderful! Come on!"

Susan laughed and shook her head back and forth, her

arms akimbo. Then she took off her clothes—but not as fast as Trustrum had—and stood for a moment on deck naked for the entire world to see. *She's beautiful. Too bad she's one of them,* Trustrum thought. She daintily stepped over the lifeline and leapt into the water with a little splash. She barely went under and screamed when she resurfaced.

"This is ice! You're crazy, Trustrum!"

"You'll get used to it—swim!"

They swam and splashed about, playing like children. Trustrum gradually directed them away from *Tavernier.* When they were about fifteen feet from the ladder, he allowed her to catch him.

"You're right. This feels wonderful," she said, wrapping her arms around him, and giving him a long, lingering kiss.

Then, in a calm direct voice, still locked in a full embrace, Trustrum said, "Susan, tell me who you are, or I'm going to drown you."

She took his words as a joke and laughed, throwing her head back. "I'm at your mercy. What do you want to know? Where I was born, where I went to school, or what I'd like to be doing to you in that warm boat."

"Who do you work for?"

She cocked her head back questioningly and said, "I'm in advertising. I freelance. Why?"

In a louder voice, Trustrum said, "Stop your games, Susan—if that's really your name—or you're going under!"

She started to push away from him, but he held her firmly.

"What are you doing?" she cried.

"How did you know where I live, Susan?"

"You told me! Before you passed out! Let me go!" She started to panic and forcefully pushed away with her legs.

"Right after I told you my name, I suppose."

Susan tried sprinting to the boat, but their time treading water had already tired her. Trustrum, on the other hand, was not in the least affected by the cold or the energy needed to keep his head above water. He was an expert swimmer, having competed on teams since he was a child. He charged toward her freestyle and, like in water polo, literally swam over her, pushing her under and causing her to choke on mouthfuls of the brackish water. By the time she recovered her breath, Trustrum was waiting by the ladder.

"You're not getting back on this boat until you tell me the truth," he said.

Gasping for air, she pleaded, "Please…Stop…I don't know what you're talking about…please!!"

Using his leg, he stopped her from reaching the safety of the ladder. She turned to look at Dobbins Island, which Trustrum knew lay too far away for her to swim to. He could tell from the way she moved that she was exhausted and uncertain of what to do.

"This is the deal, Susan. Either you tell me the truth or you drown."

"They'll kill me. Please!"

"I'm sure they'll understand. It's not like they covered drowning in spy school."

"Please!"

"Don't expect any pity from me, Susan. Now, talk!"

"I can't keep…this up…." Susan went under, but Trustrum did not assist her—he had a feeling that she would resurface. She did. "You're…you're…killing me!" she gasped. "Please!"

Trustrum climbed up the ladder and raced to bring it on board before she reached it; Susan lashed at the water in anger. Then, her facial expression turned to genuine fear. She was quickly losing the strength to keep her head above water. For a moment, Trustrum's compassion set in, until he reminded himself that she was nothing more than a female Baines.

"Just give me some names, *Susan*," he shouted, while slipping into his shorts and shirt though he was still dripping wet, "That's all I need to know." There was no doubt about it that she was in dire straits. Why she did not just turn over on her back and float, Trustrum could not tell—perhaps panic was blurring her ability to think straight.

"Pritchard…Baines…that's all I know," she shouted.

At hearing their names, Trustrum picked up the long boat-hook pole and held it for her to grab the handle. Then he slid the hook end through one of the rungs of the toe-rail so that he was able to free his hands, and Susan would still be supported. He re-attached the ladder over *Tavernier's* side and helped her to climb aboard. She sat on the edge of the cockpit on the raised coaming, gasping for air.

"So, why did they send you?" Trustrum flung a towel at her. It hit her in the face and upper body. She grabbed it and used it to cover herself.

"You…were being…rewarded," she answered, still breathing heavily.

"With you?"

"Yes."

"What are you, a hooker?"

"No. I'm an agent for the Coterie."

"Spare me. Either you're a hooker or you're supposed to be doing something else for them. So, what is it?"

"I was expected to keep tabs on you. With the exhibition coming up, they were afraid you were starting to stress out. They thought I would be good for you."

"You people are too much!" Trustrum said, then he paused. "So, how does someone get a job like yours? Don't tell me you answered an ad in the paper?"

Susan stared at Trustrum with cold eyes. He watched

her as she sat slightly bent over with her arms leaning against her legs, still trying to catch her breath. It was then that he realized she did not look beautiful to him at all. In fact, he thought, she was actually...evil looking—ugly.

He turned his attention from her to his boat. He thought of the Coterie and how they had ruined his life. Then, he started to laugh.

"What's so funny?"

"I guess they didn't mention to you that they bugged my boat?"

Trustrum watched Susan turn pale; it made him laugh harder. "You're history, lady!" Then, in a sudden burst of rage, Trustrum raised his foot and kicked Susan overboard. She landed headfirst in the water with a loud splash.

When she resurfaced, the towel she had been holding was floating next to her. Trustrum loudly said, "You go back to the Coterie and tell them that I've had enough of this."

"You're the one who said they can hear us. Tell them yourself."

"I've done everything you've asked of me. I deserve better!" he shouted.

"Deserve! Now you think the Coterie owes you something?" Susan snapped back.

Trustrum ignored her and continued addressing whomever was listening with the bug, "And I don't need a hooker or a baby-sitter!"

"Who do you think you are!" Susan yelled as loud as she could. Then, they were both silent.

Trustrum stared at her for a moment, without moving or saying a word. He watched Susan sculling in the water, breathing heavily. He was furious, and he had had enough of her. Finally, he realized that there was nothing left for him to do, so Trustrum went to the bow and weighed anchor.

"What are you doing? You have to take me back. You

will take me back with you, won't you? Trustrum? You can't leave me out here to drown! The Coterie, Trustrum, don't forget the Coterie. Baines will make you pay for this!"

Speaking loudly so that the electronic eavesdroppers were certain to know that he was addressing them, he said, "Your Susan will be on Dobbins Island—if she makes the swim. You'll recognize her as the naked one frolicking around in the brush." Finished with the anchor, he returned to the cockpit—Susan had followed him, swimming in the water below. He readied to turn the engine over and coldly said, "I'd move away from the boat if I were you. The propeller will tear you up."

"Trustrum Crook! You have to throw me a lifejacket—and some clothes to wear!"

"Lady, you came here to hang me out to dry. You're on your own. You'd better start working your way to that island before the tide changes, or you'll wind up floating in the middle of the Bay—facedown."

~~~~~~~

By the time Trustrum arrived at home, Pritchard was waiting inside for him. Trustrum felt as though he were a schoolboy who knew he had done wrong and now must face his parents—but he anticipated more than a mere slap on the wrist for his punishment. *Baines is going to love this,* he thought. He was sick to his stomach with nervousness.

"What are we going to do with you, Trustrum? Of all the artists of the Coterie, you are by far the most difficult."

"I don't want any more of your people in my life! I just want to be left alone!"

"Don't be so melodramatic. You were doing so well there for a while, but I understand that Mr. Coulbourne is beginning to have his doubts about you. You're just lucky the exhibition is coming up. Otherwise, Mr. Baines would be here instead of me. We were simply trying to help you during these stressful times before the showing."

"You just don't hear me, do you, Pritchard? I don't want any more of you goons in my life!"

"Fine. Whatever you say, Trustrum. But, you should at least consider hiring a maid. This place is a mess."

"I said no!"

"Okay, okay," Pritchard said quickly, raising his hands up, palms out, as if to fend off Trustrum's words.

"When will you take me to New York? I want to get this thing over with," Trustrum said—his words controlled and soft.

"Anytime you're ready. We can access the gallery in two weeks. In the meantime, there's still much to do. If you're finished here, you might as well get a jump on it. It would certainly make life easier for Mr. Underwood."

"That's a good idea. Maybe things will move along a little faster."

"That's our thinking."

"I'll have everything ready by Monday, next week. I want to do this and make it successful for everybody, then I'm through with the Coterie—you hear me?"

"Whatever you say, Trustrum."

"What about undercover Suzy?"

"What about her?"

"Did you guys send somebody for her, or are you just going to leave her out there?"

"See, you really do care. We've already dealt with it."

"And what about me?"

"Don't worry. The Coterie doesn't want their star artist looking roughed up the night of the big show." Pritchard paused, then he said, "But the morning after is a different story."

Chapter Ten
Fly-by-Night

Once referring to a type of large sail used on square-rigged ships when running with light winds, fly-by-nights were known as particularly easy sails to manage—making them an excellent choice to use in the dark of night.

Unbeknownst to the art world, the Coterie had made Trustrum Crook into a first-rate fly-by-night—of the more familiar derogatory kind.

⌇⌇⌇⌇⌇⌇⌇

Interviews and press conferences filled much of Trustrum's time leading up to the exhibition. Underwood kept things moving and well organized. He even followed through with having a coffee-table book printed with photographs of Trustrum's objets d'art, which was sent to a special list of collectors all around the world. One of Trustrum's obligations the night of the exhibition would be two hours of signing the thing.

To Trustrum, exhibition night reminded him of what he had seen on television when Hollywood premiered movies. The upper crust of society wanted to be seen with the latest fad—him. By the time he made it from the limousine into the gallery and walked past the gauntlet of photographers and interested onlookers, he was nearly blinded from the flashing lights. Pritchard, Baines, and an attractive woman whom he had never met before nor had ever spoken a word to escorted him. The woman seemed to appear from nowhere, hung on his arm for a while for all to see as they marched into the art arena, and then disappeared as soon as they were inside.

"I'm sure my date was hired, but how about all of my adoring fans? Did the Coterie pay them to gawk at me too?" he asked Pritchard when they had a moment to themselves.

"Just the girl. Besides, I wouldn't go as far as to say *adoring*—more like *intrigued*. It doesn't take much to happen for a crowd to form on New York sidewalks."

It was a gala affair with Trustrum as the man-of-the-hour. And for a short time, he nearly started to believe that he was deserving of such praise and admiration. As planned by the Coterie, every one of his creations had sold long before the evening's events. This was for effect— everything was to improve Trustrum's standing as a famous artist. He had to hand it to Coulbourne—the concept worked. Trustrum had been made into the artist whose expensive creations collectors sought.

"Starting to fall for this stuff, aren't you, Crook?" came a voice from behind that Trustrum recognized as belonging to Baines. Trustrum turned. "You're nothing, Crook. You're nothing and nobody. How's that make you feel?"

"I've got a roomful of people saying otherwise."

"They say so, because we told them to. And tomorrow, we'll tell them to say the same thing about another nobody." Baines softly laughed.

"You had a horrible childhood, didn't you," Trustrum said. "Let me guess. You never played well with others."

"That's right, Crook. Keep it up. Enjoy your moment— short as it will be."

Pritchard approached them, having finished discussing a publicity issue with Underwood on the other side of the room, and tried to intervene. "Gentlemen. How are things this evening?"

"Just fine, Mr. Pritchard," Baines quickly said. "In fact, I was getting ready to tell our esteemed friend here that Mr. Coulbourne is waiting to speak to him in the back."

"Sounds good to me," Trustrum said. He expected to be told that the nightmare was over; that he had fulfilled his work with the Coterie; that he could return to his old life and to Sarah.

The three men filed through a door and down a narrow hallway to a back conference room, where Coulbourne sat drinking a glass of champagne. A packet of documents was on the table.

"Trustrum, my boy. Come join me in a celebratory drink," he said, raising his glass as if making a toast.

"It would be my pleasure, Mr. Coulbourne," Trustrum said, picking up a waiting glass of bubbly and taking a sip. Then he sat down while Baines and Pritchard remained standing by the door.

"Well, Trustrum, here we are at last. The big day! You must be delighted."

"I'm glad that it's over. It will be wonderful to return to my old life."

Coulbourne ignored his statement, though he continued to smile. "How's your hotel room? Have everything you need?"

"Yes sir. First rate."

"Good, good. We like to keep our artists happy." He pushed the documents that lay before him toward Trustrum.

"Another life insurance policy?" Trustrum asked. He was confused.

"Basically, the same one. Just an increase in our protection."

"Why is this necessary?"

"Trustrum, as of tonight, you are a world famous—and more importantly—a financially successful artist. The

Coterie must protect its investment, and our insurable interest in you has grown considerably. Imagine, my boy, every one of your creations has sold for well above top dollar. By tomorrow, every high caliber collector in the world will desperately crave your work. The Coterie couldn't afford anything happening to you now."

"Of course they sold for top dollar—they were bought as *planned* by your people. And now, they can turn their investments over, make their high profits, and everybody's happy." Trustrum studied the insurance papers and read the increased amount. "This is for ten million dollars! You told me that after tonight I was through with the Coterie!"

"Good heavens, man! Are you an idiot? Do you really think we would invest as much as we have in you only to watch you walk away from it all? Either you work for the Coterie or we assist you in retiring from this world completely."

Trustrum was devastated. He had foolishly allowed himself to believe that his association with the Coterie was at an end.

Coulbourne continued, "You won't be required to keep as strenuous a schedule as you have this past year—say, four works per quarter? We don't want to flood the market and lower your selling power, do we?"

"Selling power? This is no longer just about you making money. This is about my life—my family. I can't do this! I won't do this!"

"You can and you will," Coulbourne firmly corrected. He turned to Baines and Pritchard and nodded. "Sign the papers and go be eccentric for your fans. You're beginning to give me a headache."

Trustrum looked over his shoulder and saw Baines standing close by. "Just sign it, Crook. We're all growing tired of your insubordination."

Trustrum picked up the pen that lay beside the

insurance policy and signed each page where marked. When he was done, he gently put the pen down and stood up without a word. He was in shock. Pritchard took hold of his upper arm and escorted him back to the festivities and the hordes of over-jeweled, richly-dressed people; it had become standing room only while they had been away. Not only were Coterie members present, but it seemed to Trustrum that half of the population of New York City was there as well. He spent the rest of the evening shaking hands and autographing books. Outwardly, he was charming. Inside, he was dying.

"We'll take you back to Maryland tomorrow, Trustrum. It's almost over. You're doing fine," Pritchard said.

Trustrum did not respond. It wasn't almost over. It might never be over. The night that was supposed to be the high point of his career as an artist had turned out to be the lowest point of his life. Now, he knew, there was no escape.

Chapter Eleven
Half Seas Over

Three sheets to the wind, splice the main brace, sun over the yardarm, half slewed, bottle up, groggy, Harry Freemans, loggerheads, suck the monkey—all from the sea, all related to the function of inebriation—often a miserable sailor's only means of forgetting his misfortunes.

The old standby no longer worked, Trustrum Crook needed to retake control of his life.

~~~~~~~~~

Before Trustrum knew it, seven months had slipped by. Fearing the worst the Coterie had to offer, he spent his days submissively creating useless objects—each costing more than most people earned in a decade. But instead of drinking his nights away as he had done before the exhibition, Trustrum would often drive to Cambridge to be with Sarah. It was not unusual for him to drive one and a half hours just to visit with her for ten or fifteen minutes. Then, there were visits when they were together for two days at a time—but never at his home or on the boat. They stayed in motels, with Trustrum pretending that the reason for their excursions was to learn more about the area. But the real reason was privacy. He needed to be able to speak with Sarah without having to worry that he might slip up and say the wrong thing. It was not the life he wished to have for himself or his daughter, but at least they were together often, which gave them a chance to renew their close relationship.

When not with Sarah, and not working on his latest project for the Coterie, Trustrum escaped his worries by improving his physical condition. His exercise regimen consisted of swimming laps at a nearby community pool or long, open-water distances in the Magothy River; lifting weights at home; and occasionally running outdoors on back roads in the early evening.

Trustrum was thirty-seven years old, and he was in good health to begin with, so it had taken just a little more than three months until he had molded himself into prime condition. The Coterie was pleased to see that Trustrum had ceased to overindulge in alcohol. They believed that he had finally accepted the destiny they had forced upon him—but that was not the case at all. Although he had no idea how he would get himself out of his situation, he had never given up on the idea of escaping from the Coterie. And he knew that whatever was to eventually follow, he would have an improved chance of surviving if he was fit.

Trustrum continued to fulfill the Coterie's mandated quota, creating more elaborate and more expensive objets d'art. He had become the fad-of-the-year in the world of elitist collectors, and the demand for his work grew each month. Of course, the rest of the world still had no idea that the reason nobody seemed to be able to get enough of his rare and unique work was because only members of the Coterie had the opportunity to buy it. To the world outside of the syndicate, Trustrum's latest creation seemed always to have been just purchased by someone else. And, eccentric artist that he was, he refused special orders and payments in advance, making it impossible for outsiders to secure a purchase. The exclusive art of Trustrum Crook quickly became known as something unavailable for most people.

There were more magazines and newspaper articles about him, which helped to maintain the public's interest level around the world. The publicity machine had long kicked in and had a life of its own. Now, journalists outside of the Coterie's control were interested in this new artistic phenomenon.

As the interviews put him increasingly in the public eye, Trustrum became more and more withdrawn. And though Coulbourne was probably right in saying that many others would envy his position as a famous artist, Trustrum took little solace in the old man's words. He craved the freedom the Coterie had stolen from him. He longed to wake up and not be concerned if Baines would see the need to remind him of the Coterie's protocol with another thrashing. He was tired of his secret life as a pampered slave. And he wished more than anything that he could somehow bring Jacqueline back.

Trustrum refused to consider hoping to share his life with someone. It would be horrendous to bring another person into his world. So, except for Sarah and his daily exercise routine—and his new side hobby of searching for the location of the Coterie's bugs in his home—when not working in his studio, he spent his time sailing. He had sailed little the year before, since the schedule that the Coterie had required him to follow had been too strenuous. Now, a little more than half a year since his first exhibition, much was still expected of him, but the demands were significantly more tolerable. He feared, however, that his sailing experiences would never be the same again, that he would never be able to drop everything to enjoy a glorious day. He would not be able to sail away for two, three, or even eight days at a time like he had done in the past when jewelry appraisals were slow and the climate was breezy and warm.

Sometimes he felt as though he were simply acting like a spoiled child, and he would remind himself that things weren't so bad, dare he say, even good…*no, you don't have it good, damn it…you're not in control of your own life!*

Despite his luxuries, Trustrum felt as though his life was binding and monotonous. Then, one day, a visitor came calling at his front door.

He had been working in the studio—creating another useless reliquary in solid gold with inlaid silver highlights—when he heard the doorbell ring. The front door was mostly glass, so he saw her before he opened it. Whoever she was, she was lovely: about 5'5", she was slender with fair skin and curly red hair. Her face reminded him of a china doll with big, round, green eyes and a pretty smile. From the luggage she carried with her, she appeared as though she were planning to stay awhile.

He opened the door. "May I help you?" he asked.

"Hi. I'm Megan Davidson—for the interview?" she said, her tone beginning with energetic confidence though quickly waning to uncertainty.

"And what exactly were you interviewing for?" he asked.

"Is Mr. Crook at home?"

"My name is Crook, but am I the Crook you're looking for?"

"Is there another?"

"There are many, I'm sure, but I'm the only one around here that I know of."

She put down her bags and fumbled with a paper. "A Mr. *Trusdum* Crook."

"That's Trustrum Crook, but I'm afraid I don't know anything about an interview."

"I spoke with your agent, a Mr. Pritchard."

"Oh, I see. That's different. Where did you come from?"

"Indianapolis," she said. Her eyes gave away her fatigue. "May I come in until we sort this out? It's been quite an ordeal getting here."

"I'm sorry. Please do. Let me help with your luggage. Can I get you a glass of cold spring water?"

"Thank you. That would be wonderful."

He showed her into the living room and fetched the drink

from the cooler in the kitchen. "You'll excuse me while I find out what's going on. Please wait here."

Trustrum walked back to the kitchen to make a private call, but just before he reached for the phone, it rang. He picked up the receiver in the middle of the first ring.

"Cute," Trustrum spoke into the mouthpiece.

"I thought I'd save you the trouble of dialing," Pritchard said.

"Next time, don't trouble yourself. I like to dial. It makes me feel like my house isn't bugged."

"But it is, and I listen to everything you say. At least, somebody here does."

"Why didn't you tell me you were sending her over?"

"You would've put up a fight, and quite frankly, I didn't feel like dealing with it."

"Well, Mr. Pritchard, I'm putting up a fight now! What do I have to do to get through to you people? I don't want one of your goons living under my roof—male or female."

"Trustrum, she's not one of our people. She doesn't know a thing about the Coterie. So, unless you want her knocked off, don't say a thing to her about it. I contacted a professional agency. She's a trained, live-in domestic."

"I especially don't want anyone else who's innocent getting tangled up in this—not because of me."

"Too late. If she doesn't work out with you, we'll send her to one of the other artist—perhaps one not as caring as you. And let me tell you, we've got some real winners in our ranks. You won't be protecting her if you let her go, you'll probably be indirectly causing her harm. Besides, no one's entirely innocent, Trustrum. You really should pickup a Bible once in a while."

"Like you do. Listen, you can't put this on me!"

"Sorry. It already is on you, pal."

There was a long silence. Trustrum could not

decide what to do, then he said, "Why didn't you find someone local?"

"Control. This way she has no friends or relatives she can rely on," Pritchard said. "You really are an ingrate. You should be thanking me."

"For what?"

"I did pick a pretty one, didn't I?" Pritchard laughed. Trustrum slammed the receiver down into the cradle and returned to the living room to find the young woman sitting on the couch waiting for him.

"You heard any of that?"

"You did get a little loud at the end. Look, I can see you weren't expecting me, and I don't want to cause any trouble."

"You're not causing trouble. It's just that our dear Mr. Pritchard has a way of not telling me what he's scheming, until it's happening—it's disconcerting."

"I guess it would be," she agreed. "How is he connected to you anyway?"

"Some days I'm not too sure, to tell you the truth. So…he told me you're here as some sort of housekeeper— is that right?"

"Yes. The arrangement was that I spend this weekend here to see if we're compatible."

"Compatible? This is sounding more like an arranged marriage than a housekeeping job."

"You don't have to worry about that, Mr. Crook. Marriage is the last thing on my mind."

"There you go—we already have one thing in common. Look, I'm in the middle of something downstairs in my studio. Why don't you settle in the guest room—top of the stairs, turn right. I'll carry your bags up in a minute, and we can talk about dinner when I'm through working."

"How long do you expect to be?"

"Two, maybe three hours," he said.

"Do you have food in the house?"

"Uh...I'd say mostly fruits and some veggies. I think there's half a quart of chocolate soy milk still safe to drink."

"Vegetarian?"

"Semi."

"What's that mean?"

"It means I stray with no guilt."

"How about straying tonight?"

"Not a problem."

"The cab passed a grocery store on the way here."

"You can't really be up for cooking tonight. Why don't we go out or have a pizza delivered?"

"No, it's fine. I want to," Megan said.

"Then I want a Thanksgiving dinner with all the fixings," Trustrum said in jest.

"Be careful what you wish for, Mr. Crook. You just might get it."

"Please call me *Trustrum*."

"I'll need some money, and I guess I'll have to borrow your car...Trustrum."

"Oh, sure," Trustrum said. He turned and quickly walked to the kitchen where he found his wallet on the counter. He pulled out four twenties and handed them to Megan, who had followed him. "I can't remember where I put my keys down yesterday, so let me give you the spare to the car," he continued, rooting around in the catchall drawer. He handed her the extra key. "Look at this, you haven't been here thirty minutes, and I'm already giving you money and a car," he said. "Wait a minute, one more thing. Follow me." Trustrum, with Megan again following, went down a flight of steps to the family room and headed to the backdoor.

"That's an unusual doorstop," she said, nodding to the

wood and metal object lying on the floor.

"It's an old piece of rigging called a deadeye. Looks like a skull, doesn't it?"

"Yes, it sort of does. Are you into sailing?"

"Oh yeah." They continued outside onto the patio. Trustrum walked over to a decorative rock on the ground next to a cluster of boxwood bushes. He lifted up one end of the rock and with the other hand pulled out a set of keys. He turned, now facing Megan and said while handing it to her, "Money, car, and home in under thirty-five minutes. You definitely have some kind of talent."

~~~~~~~~

Three and a half hours later, a sweet aroma filled the house, eventually drifting into the studio. When finished with his work for the day, Trustrum retreated to the kitchen.

"Smells wonderful," he said.

"Your cat thinks so," Megan said. She reached down to pet Marquise, who was following her around the room. "What's your name, honey?"

"Marquise," Trustrum answered.

"That's a pretty name for a pretty kitty."

"So, what do we have here—turkey—you cooked a turkey?"

"Not a whole one. Just a breast."

"Oh. So, we have turkey, sweet potatoes, green bean casserole, *and* stuffing *and* rolls you *did* make a Thanksgiving dinner!"

Ten minutes later, they were seated before a handsomely set dining-room table. During the meal, the conversation revolved around Megan's trip from Indianapolis to Annapolis by train and taxicab, and Trustrum's work as an artist. Trustrum had opened a bottle of Chardonnay, which they shared. After dinner, since

Trustrum insisted on helping, they worked together to clean up the kitchen and finally settled outside on the patio. They drank the last of the wine while sitting together on a wooden swing.

"So, Megan Davidson, tell me. Why would you possibly want to work as my housekeeper—and so far from home?"

"Is there something wrong with that?"

"Nothing at all. But you must agree that you're coming a long way to fill a position you appear to be well overqualified for."

"I'm starting over, Trustrum. It's the same old story: divorce, no money, no credit after eleven years with Mr. Right—or so I thought he was." Trustrum could easily see the sadness in her expression even though it was dark outside and the porch light was not strong.

"What's your story?" she asked.

"Who's interviewing who here?" Trustrum asked.

"Formalities ended after the third glass of vino, Mr. Crook." Megan reached under the swing and picked up the empty bottle from the floor, where Trustrum had placed it standing upright. "Do we dare drink another one?"

"Why not?" Trustrum answered, taking the bottle. He stood up from his chair and went into the house. Five minutes later, he returned with an uncorked, full bottle and two new glasses, one of which he handed to Megan. He said, "We're going to regret this tomorrow morning."

Megan raised her glass toward Trustrum. Pouring from the new bottle, he filled her glass nearly to the rim. "I've just spent the last twelve years trying to live up to...well, let's just say, I'm due for some changes—I'll take my chances," Megan said. Trustrum returned to his place on the swing, after filling his own glass and putting the bottle within arm's reach on the floor, checking that it was safe from being knocked over.

"So, you were going to tell me your story, Trustrum."

"Was I?"

"It's your turn."

"Not much to tell you. My life has evolved into two things: my little girl, Sarah, and my work as an artist. Outside of that, nothing else exists for me. Who has time for anything else?"

"Sounds lonely."

"Actually, it's not so bad."

Neither said anything for what felt like a long time. Then Megan broke the silence, "So, if you're willing, I can start right away."

"Fine. We'll put you on the payroll immediately, but I won't need you to start until the end of April."

"You're going to pay me for three months of nothing?"

"Take it or leave it."

"I don't get it. Mr. Pritchard said you needed someone right away."

"I don't have to tell you that I didn't expect anyone knocking on my door today."

"That's for sure."

"I need a little time to get things in order before you move in."

"I can understand that."

"But I also like knowing that in—what is it really, two-and-a-half months—I'll have you here running the house. I assume Pritchard and you have already come to terms on compensation?"

"Yes."

"So what do you say we leave it open for some time during the last week in April? Just show up and be ready to take over," Trustrum asked.

"Okay, I guess. I just thought you needed someone right away."

"Don't try to understand eccentric artists, Megan. You'll never do it."

Megan laughed. "Don't misunderstand me. I'm not complaining. Who wouldn't want an extended paid holiday?"

"Then it's a deal," Trustrum stated.

"As easy as that?"

"We're set—except for the handshake." They smiled at each other and shook hands—their eyes met. Megan leaned forward first, but Trustrum was quick to follow. They kissed. Trustrum stopped first and moved his head back a few inches, then they gently came together and kissed again, but for a longer time. Megan abruptly pulled away but remained facing Trustrum. Both blurted out apologies— their words overlapped. They laughed.

"I suppose the wine's at work again."

"Yeah," Trustrum quietly said, uncertain what else to say.

"Well, I guess we'd better call it a night," Megan said.

"Yeah," Trustrum agreed. Megan stood up and handed him her empty glass.

"What was it you said earlier about the wine?" Trustrum had a blank expression. Megan continued, " Something about morning regrets?"

"Oh yes. Wine and women."

She smiled and said, "Good night." Then, Megan went into the house to her room.

Trustrum remained where he was sitting on the swing— thinking of Jacqueline.

153

Chapter Twelve
Scandalize

Shortening sail is one way of regaining control of a ship that is overpowered by winds—doing so posthaste is referred to as scandalizing.

Trustrum Crook was at the brink—something had to give.

~~~~~~~~

Trustrum needed a diversion. He needed stability. He needed to ground himself. He needed to return to his roots by immersing himself into the industry that had always been there for him like a friend. This is what filled Trustrum's thoughts as he stormed through the house that sunny afternoon—two days after Megan had headed back to Indianapolis.

The house was already secure, so Trustrum left by the garage, which upon closing automatically joined the loop of the security system. Twenty minutes later he arrived in downtown Annapolis and found a rare parking space on State Circle, almost in front of his destination—Harris's Pawn and Curios.

When he went to enter the little shop, the front door stuck in the lower corner, causing Trustrum to have to yank it extra hard to force it open. The tiny, high-pitched bell fastened to the top of the door bounced wildly, announcing that someone had come in. But Trustrum noticed that Bob Harris did not look up to see who it was. Instead, he stood behind one of his glass showcases, examining a jewel with his loupe, while a man, apparently a customer, watched his every move.

Just seeing Bob, with his bushy walrus mustache and his long, unkempt ponytail, made Trustrum feel better. It was reassuring to know that some things had not changed.

Trustrum stood back, not wanting to interrupt, and saw that Bob was holding a pink sapphire and diamond ring in his hand. When he was finished examining the ring, Bob look up. He was startled to see Trustrum.

"Hey, Trustrum!" Bob said. The customer turned and looked to see whom Bob had addressed. "Here you go, sir. This man is one of the best in the area when it comes to appraising jewelry. Trustrum, look at this ring. I'm not going to say a thing. You tell him what it is."

"It'd be my—"

"He wants me to buy it. But I'm not going to say anything. You tell him what you think. It'll be just what I said."

"Sure, my—"

"He thinks it's a ruby. But you tell him what it is. I'm not going to say a thing about it until after you tell him."

Trustrum took the ring and pulled out his own loupe from his pocket. Leaning forward over a showcase to take advantage of one of the spotlights, he took his time examining the ring.

Bob walked toward the back of the store and as he did said, "It's not what he thinks it is, but I'm not going to say anything until you tell him."

Trustrum lowered both hands. He returned the loupe to his sport-coat pocket and rested his left hand, which held the ring, on the showcase. "What Bob's getting at in essence is semantics. The best way I've found to explain it over the years is this: Sapphires come in every color of the rainbow. Few people realize it, but rubies are simply red sapphires. Since pink sapphires are less expensive than rubies, there exists an eternal dilemma. When is the lower-valued pink sapphire dark enough to be considered the more costly ruby?"

"When?" the man asked.

"The stone is always a pink sapphire when the jeweler is buying it, and it's always a ruby when he's selling it."

Not finding the humor in what Trustrum had said, the man continued, "It was sold to me as a ruby. It's not?"

"Like I said, it's just semantics. I wouldn't consider it a ruby, but at this stage of the game, what it's called won't change its quality—it is what it is and it's worth what it's worth."

Bob walked back to where the customer and Trustrum were standing and resumed his place behind the showcase. Instead of handing the ring to the customer, Trustrum handed it back to Bob.

"How much is it worth?" the customer asked.

"Listen to me," Bob said. "Tell me what you want for it."

"I paid three thousand dollars for it."

"I don't care about that. Buying and selling are two different things. What do you want to sell it for today—right now? I'll give you a check. You can go to the bank and cash it."

"I thought two thousand."

"Oh no," Bob said. His voice was loud and quick. "You can take it around and come back later, if you like. You won't get more anyplace else, but you're way off with two thousand."

"How much, then?"

Trustrum remained silent and watched.

"No. I won't say until you shop around, then come back. Then, you'll see I give the highest price in town."

"I don't want to go through this again. How much will you give me for it?"

Bob looked at it again. Then he said, "Four hundred. That's it. Take it or leave it."

The customer's expression showed his disappointment. Then, hesitantly, he said, "I'll take it."

Bob went to the back of the store, taking the ring with him, drafted the man's check, and paid him. After the customer had left to the sound of the tiny bell, Bob laughed.

"Good going, Trustrum. I'll turn this ruby ring over easily for twenty-five hundred."

"Maybe so, but I meant what I said, it's not a ruby. I wasn't lying to the guy. That's a pink sapphire."

"What are you talking about? If that's not a ruby—"

"Forget the corundum, already." Trustrum pointed to a ring not so prominently displayed toward the back of the case. "What's the story on the eight-grainer?" Trustrum asked. At twenty-five points a grain, Bob did not hesitate to pull the two-carat, round, brilliant-cut diamond set in a six-prong platinum mounting from the showcase and hand it to Trustrum.

"There's a beauty," Bob said. The tag read thirty thousand, which meant, right off the top, Bob would sell it for fifteen to anybody walking into his shop. Trustrum could never understand why Bob felt the need to lower himself professionally by participating in the automatic-discount racket—but then, he had always been more surprised that customers fell for it.

Pawnbrokers and many jewelers offer around ten percent of what would be the item's *true* retail price. Trustrum Crook loved estate jewelry for its workmanship and history, but also because it was where a real expert shined brightest. It held the greatest potential for some of the most profitable deals for jeweler and savvy customer alike. Trustrum figured that Bob had paid only fifteen hundred dollars for it.

"When did you get it in?"

"Time was up yesterday. I put it on the floor just this morning."

"Do you think the person who sold it to you intended to come back for it?"

"They always intend to come back and get it, Trustrum," he said with a laugh. "She's history with this ring. If she comes back now, she can buy another one from me."

"Always the sentimentalist, Bob."

"This is no charity I'm running here. The soup kitchen is down the street."

"Let me have it for three thousand. That should give you keystone," Trustrum said. Keystone is industry code for a two-time markup, while triple-key refers to a three-time markup.

"You're out of your mind, Trustrum. You are a crook. I can't afford to give this to you."

"Save the theatrics, Bob. What's your price?"

"Six thousand, and it's yours."

"Bob, you're killing me, here. Four thousand," Trustrum responded.

"Five thousand. That's as low as I go."

"Pay you next week? Come on, do it. That's got to be a quick thirty-five-hundred-dollar profit, and you didn't have to blink an eye."

"I wish I was making that kind of money."

"Do it," Trustrum repeated.

"Okay, okay…oh, here, you might as well take this," he said. He reached into a drawer in the back of one of the showcases and pulled out an envelope that was stuffed with documents. "It's the original appraisal that goes with the ring. The lady brought it with her. Let me get the memo book. You have to sign for it."

"Since when is my word not good enough?"

"Your word is just fine, Trustrum. What's wrong with your John Hancock?"

"I'm telling you, Bob, this business is really starting to lose its charm. Whatever happened to the days when a handshake was enough? Where's the romance gone?"

"Couldn't tell you, Trustrum." Bob finished filling out the memo sheet and shoved both memo book and pen toward Trustrum and said, "Sign."

~~~~~~~~

Trustrum Crook was thrilled to be in his element: the wheeling and dealing; the chase for the elusive profit; the knowing, when all others around him did not—including Bob Harris. Trustrum had realized when examining the old appraisal papers belonging to his latest purchase that the color of the diamond had been listed wrong—in his favor. Since Bob had purchased the diamond ring undoubtedly based on the incorrect, lower grading—and lesser value— Trustrum found himself holding a real bargain.

As he hurried to his car, having left Harris's shop, he was excited, for he knew just the person he could sell his newfound treasure to. He hopped into the Beemer and within ten minutes, found another parking space on the other side of town just off Spa Road.

"Hi, Mildred," Trustrum said as he strolled into the little boutique known to all in Annapolis as Millie's Lingerie.

"Why, if it isn't Trustrum Crook, the outlaw of jewels," she responded. "You haven't been around in a long while. Where've you been hiding yourself?" she asked, having just finished selling something to two young women who made their way out the door.

"I'm sorry to tell you, Millie. I just haven't been in the market for buying woman's lingerie, lately."

"Well, that's too bad, dear. Come here and give me a hug," she said as she pressed her large bosom against his chest, nearly crushing him with a strong bear hug. "I read about Jacqueline. I'm so sorry, Trustrum."

"Thanks."

"How are you really doing?"

"I'm fine, Millie. Really."

"Sure you are. So, what brings you in, Trustrum?"

"Millie, this one you're going to have to sit down for."

"Ooh, do you have a goodie for me?"

"You're going to love this so much, you'll want to pay me twice."

"Honey, there's but one thing I'd consider paying twice for, except I'm not desperate enough to do it—yet," she said and then let out a shriek. "Oh, the things I say sometimes!" Trustrum followed her to the back of the store. She sat at her desk, which was covered with papers and a pile of bras and matching panties, which had obviously just been delivered and were being priced for sale. "What did you bring me?"

Trustrum sat down in the chair across from her, then reached into his jacket pocket and presented the diamond ring to her.

"Now, that's a rock!" she loudly exclaimed. Actually, nearly everything Trustrum had ever heard her say was loud. "What are the specs?" Millie, a connoisseur of fine jewelry, knew diamonds intimately.

"Two carats, VVS2 clarity, G color. I figure a conservative retail replacement cost at twenty-five thousand. Normal wholesale cost to a jeweler would be about sixteen. Millie, you can add this lovely bauble to your collection for only eleven thousand."

"Why only eleven?"

"Because I know you won't do twelve."

"Cute. Really, Trustrum, why so cheap?"

"Two reasons. First, I just picked it up. If you buy it today, it'll be a quick turnover. If you don't, then I'll sell it for more somewhere else. The longer it takes to sell, the more I'll need to get for it. Second, I bought it from a guy who you'd think after all his years in the trade would know what he's doing—especially since he holds himself up to the public as an expert on gems—but he doesn't. Millie, you have a better eye for stones than he does."

"Mine comes naturally."

"Well, it's not my responsibility to train the guy at his job."

"Ninety-five hundred and you've got yourself a deal," she said. Over the years, she had grown to trust Trustrum. Still, she felt obligated to respond with a token counter-offer.

"Deal," Trustrum said.

"Of course, I don't have that kind of cash lying around here. Can we make the exchange next week?" she asked.

"No problem, Millie. How about Tuesday?" he asked. He stood up and headed for the door.

"That's fine—hey! Don't you want to keep this thing until I pay you?"

"You hang onto it."

"Are you sure, Trustrum?"

"Sure, I'm sure. I'm old school, Millie."

~~~~~~~

Trustrum left Millie's lingerie shop feeling good about himself for the first time since the Coterie had taken control of his life. He got into his car and just started driving. He made his way along the narrow streets of Annapolis, eventually accessing a ramp that put him onto route 50 east. By the time he passed over the Chesapeake Bay Bridge to Maryland's Eastern Shore, the emotional high he had felt from going back to his old life had vanished. The longer he drove, the more depressed he became. He followed the highway through Easton, then Cambridge, and then Salisbury—he barely noticed passing through any of the towns, stopping only for red traffic lights. His thoughts were so distant, so caught up with the Coterie, that he had not even considered visiting Sarah when passing through Cambridge. When he finally stopped the car and turned off the engine three hours later, he was at the end of a dead-end road. Beyond was a strip of beach and the crashing waves of the vast Atlantic Ocean.

Trustrum got out of his car and walked onto the beach. As the sun disappeared inland, he followed the shoreline, walking close enough to the waves so that his feet would sometimes get splashed. Without a real destination, he headed toward the Ocean City skyline as darkness overtook his world.

Chapter Thirteen

Sally

To sally a boat is to rock her back and forth in an effort to break free from having run aground.

Trustrum Crook was more than ready to sally his life.

~~~~~~~~

From the outside looking in through the glass front door, it appeared to Trustrum that no one was in his home. He unlocked and opened the door and went inside. He stepped over to the alarm keypad on the wall and was surprised to see that it had not been activated. He turned, intending to go upstairs, when Pritchard, who had quietly come down from the bedroom, startled him.

"Pritchard! What happened to you?" Trustrum exclaimed. Pritchard's face was bruised and swollen and his left eye was blood red.

"I'll tell you what happened to me. You! You happened to me, Trustrum. For some stupid reason, I talked Mr. Coulbourne out of having you killed. Are you out of your mind? What possessed you to leave town like that?"

"I needed to get away."

"You've been gone for a week, damn it. Where were you?"

"Don't give me that. You knew I was in Ocean City—my car is wired. I know it, and you know I know it. So, stop playing games."

"This is no game, Trustrum. We thought you understood

that," Pritchard said. Trustrum did not respond. Pritchard became enraged, "Look at me!"

"I don't get it. Why'd they pounce on you?"

"Someone had to pay for your actions, and I'm your agent."

Trustrum laughed out loud. "Hey, I like this. I go AWOL, and you get your face bashed in."

"You son of a—"

"Ah, ah, ah. We must think of protocol."

"What are you doing, Trustrum? Don't you realize how close you are to crossing the line?"

"Come on, Pritchard. You're one of them. What do you want me to do, pat you on the head? Sorry they rearranged your face, but it goes with the territory."

"And it goes with yours too. You've pushed the Coterie for the last time. One more stunt like this, and it's over for you."

"Let me tell you fellows something. I've decided that I don't care anymore. The Coterie has me—fine! But I'm taking my life back. I'll make your expensive toys, but no more telling me which end is up. You hear me? I demand to have my life back!" Trustrum shouted. Then, with a lower but still firm tone he said, "And I want you out of my home." Pritchard was tongue-tied. Trustrum continued, "Did you bring the supplies I ordered?"

"Eh? Oh, yeah."

"Of course you did, because I'm the money-maker the Coterie needs."

"You listen here, Crook. You've got a lot of insurance money riding on your head. Don't you forget it!"

"You won't kill me. I'm worth too much to the Coterie."

"You think you're worth more than ten million dollars, Trustrum?"

"That's a drop in the bucket compared to what my art will sell for over the long run."

Pritchard laughed. "*Your* art—who are you kidding? You're nothing without the Coterie, you fool."

"Get out! Get out!" Trustrum grabbed Pritchard, who was caught off guard, and pushed him out the front door. "I've had it with you!"

~~~~~~~~

To Trustrum's surprise, the Coterie let him alone. Five days went by and no one made contact with him. He continued to work on the next reliquary, which he anticipated would take about a week's worth of fourteen-hour days. When the sixth day arrived, after completing yet another grueling marathon workday, he decided to take a run. He knew the fresh, night air would help him to sleep, and if he was going to finish his work on schedule, he would need his rest.

Trustrum decided on a five-mile course he had run many times before and set out at a brisk pace. It was mostly flat terrain, lying next to water and wooded areas, and as he followed the winding back roads, he found himself alone in the darkness that had fallen since having left his home. He allowed his mind to wander while he jogged along. Years of running roadside had given him the ability to mentally drift away and still be aware of his surroundings—especially, oncoming cars. The road curved down a gradual slope and was lined on the sides with untamed brush and trees.

Suddenly, from out of the overgrown foliage, only three feet away, directly pointing perpendicular to the road and Trustrum's path, a car turned on its lights—blinding high beams—and darted out onto the road. There was no time for Trustrum to think—instinctive reaction and adrenaline took control. He dove with all his might into the brush and landed in a patch of tall, thorny bushes. He wrestled his way out of the brush and scraped his hands and legs on razor-sharp gravel that sporadically covered the area in patches. The car sped down the road a short distance and then screeched to a stop, spinning in a one-hundred-and-eighty-degree turn. Seeing the vehicle now coming back, Trustrum quickly gathered his composure—faster than he otherwise would have with such a spill.

In a flash, Trustrum was up and running; this time, into the wooded area. Tree branches tore at his clothing, and brambles cut his legs. Still, he kept running. He could hear men yelling, but the words were unclear. Next, he heard gunshots: four pounding blasts! They were very clear.

The patch of forest soon ended by a creek. Trustrum lunged off the bank and landed waste deep in the cold, black water. His feet plunged into the soft miry bottom up to his knees. He dolphin-dived into the darkness, kicking up sludge and turbid water. He swam harder than he had ever in his life, but crossing the narrow waterway felt to Trustrum as if he were crossing the English Channel.

When he finally made it to the other side, Trustrum scurried up the bank into the yard of a waterfront home. He wasted no time distancing himself from the creek, running around to the front of the house and onto the street. His lungs burned and his body felt heavy, but Trustrum pushed himself to keep moving.

~~~~~~~~~

Trustrum stood in front of his home carefully surveying the situation. Deciding that nothing appeared to be out of the ordinary, he approached the front door and gently opened it, trying to be as quiet at possible. He paused before entering and listened, but heard nothing. Then, he proceeded inside and deactivated the alarm system. The few lights on each floor that were rigged with timers dimly lit the house. Marquise greeted him as she usually did with a loud meow. *You're a good sign,* he thought, as he knelt down in the foyer and stroked her back and scratched under her chin. He locked the door and reset the alarm. That way if there was someone in his house, at least when he made a break for it, the authorities would be alerted. Limping, he checked all three floors, and each room and closet and crawlspace he could think of. He even raised the door to the attic and shined a light around the dark angular room—all seemed as it should, he was alone.

The adrenaline rush that Trustrum had experienced earlier had long since subsided, and his injuries screamed for attention. His legs and arms and hands were badly abraded. His knees were terribly cut up and embedded with sharp stones and dirt from the roadside. His face and neck were scratched from the thorny brush and tree branches. He looked at himself in the mirror. He looked disheveled and beat up, and he felt worse.

Trustrum had placed his cordless phone beside the bathtub before getting in for a long soak. After he had become acclimated to the hot soapy water, which burned every wound and soothed every muscle, Trustrum called Pritchard, using the number on which he could be contacted twenty-four hours a day.

"What is going on, Pritchard?"

"What are you talking about?"

"I'm talking about the car that nearly killed me—twice!"

"Well, Trustrum, what can I tell you that I haven't said already. Maybe now—"

"If you think this changes anything, you're wrong. I'll go to the police. I swear I will!" *Wait, what am I saying?* But before Trustrum could take back his misspoken threats, the line went dead.

~~~~~~~~

Over the next two days, Trustrum was tormented with fear. He repeatedly called Pritchard's direct line, but there was no answer. Trustrum would work for an hour or two and then try calling again, hanging up only after he had allowed the phone to ring ten, twelve, sometimes fifteen times. He tried to convince himself that Pritchard was refusing his calls simply to teach him a lesson, and that in the end all would be fine; but deep down, he was frightened. *Could this really be it? Did I go too far? Could the Coterie just walk away after all?* his thoughts were on the danger he was in. As he hand-engraved ornate designs on the side of a solid-gold box, he suddenly slipped with the graver, leaving a large gash. Now, enraged, he picked up the rectangular-shaped container and threw it against the wall. It bent a corner as it crashed with a loud clanking against the floor. When all was still and the room was quiet, Trustrum turned off the light and sat motionless in the dark studio.

He started when the phone rang. He was ecstatic. *They've called,* he thought as he raced to turn on the light and pick up the receiver.

"Hello? Pritchard?"

"I was calling for Mr. Crook. He is at this number?" the unfamiliar voice inquired.

"I'm Trustrum Crook. Who's calling?"

"Trustrum, hi. It's John Allen, Allen and Associates. Sorry to be calling so late. I didn't expect to get anybody. I was going to leave a message."

"Yes…of course. How are you, Mr. Allen?" Trustrum asked, his heart pounding.

"Fine, thanks. Listen, I know we had to reschedule your jewelry appraisal program once or twice over the past couple of years. I'm really sorry that happened, but I'm sure you can appreciate how things go sometimes in business. One day you're up, and you make plans. The next thing you know, something happens that disrupts everything."

"Sure. I know exactly what you mean."

"We still would like to use your services. It's been so long, I guess I ought to first ask if you're still doing that sort of thing?"

Trustrum hesitated, not certain how he should answer. As it stood, the Coterie forbade him spending time doing anything outside of creating their precious garbage. But as far as he knew, the Coterie was either through with him, which meant he would need an income; or the Coterie was going to put him into an early grave, which, he rationalized, meant that John Allen of Allen and Associates would simply get a little of his own medicine.

"How's sometime in September look for you?" Trustrum asked.

"That would be great. What day?"

"I'm totally open. You figure out what's good for you, and it'll be fine with me."

"You can't beat that. But you're sure any day in September is available?"

"Let me put it to you this way: they'll have to kill me to keep me away."

~~~~~~~~

With the warm, sunny weather over the past weeks and since running had become a dangerous form of exercise, Trustrum had taken up swimming in Mill Creek, where *Tavernier* was docked. Sometimes he would rise early in the morning or he would take a break in the middle of the day and swim against the outbound current for whatever distance suited him, and then he would roll over and float on his back, drifting leisurely with the morning sun in his face, until he came to the place where he had started.

One afternoon, he walked along the pier and stopped beside *Tavernier*. Using the mooring lines, he pulled her closer to the finger pier and climbed aboard. He unlocked and opened the companionway hatch and went below, where he changed into his swimsuit and began a routine of stretches in an effort to work out the tightness in his muscles. Then he went topside and jumped into the water.

Trustrum moved swiftly at first, swimming freestyle, trying to warm up. He took a moment to allow his body to adjust to the cold temperature and rolled over onto his back. Just then, Jack, the marina caretaker, came into view.

"Trustrum Crook, you're crazy to be swimming in that cold water."

"It's not so bad if you wear one of these wet suits, Jack. You should try it. It's invigorating."

"No, thank you. I'll stick to my tub. Get a cramp in there and you can use the toilet seat to pull yourself out. Ain't no toilet seats next to that drink."

"Thank heaven for small favors. See you later, Jack," Trustrum said, laughing for the first time in days. He rolled onto his front and commenced swimming. His body was sore, and he felt nervous and uneasy. The swim was the best thing for him to get both his body and his mind back into shape. Every four or five strokes, he would lift his head to check that he was swimming a straight course. When he came to a certain bend in the creek, he relaxed, floating on his back, and slowly drifted with the current in the direction of *Tavernier*.

Suddenly he felt a slight bump on his calf. For a moment, he wondered what it was—a turtle, a fish, a waterlogged stick? Then he felt something—or someone— grabbing his leg. Before he could gather his wits, Trustrum was pulled underwater. He held his breath until his body screamed for air. Then he sucked the murky water into his lungs. *What's keeping me down?* He panicked and kicked frantically. The cloudy waters, combined with bubbles from his thrashing, prevented him from seeing anything. Choking, Trustrum clawed and punched at the water, trying to reach the surface before blacking out, he thought, *Which way is up…I'm drowning!*

"Trustrum? Trustrum? Come on, man, don't let go," said

a voice in the darkness. As Trustrum awoke, he found himself throwing up water from his lungs as he lay in a dinghy. He felt a stabbing pain in his gut along with nausea. Jack knelt over him and supported his head to the side.

"What...happened?" Trustrum forced out in between coughing and choking spasms.

"If I didn't know better, I'd swear there were two scuba guys out there holding you under!" Jack declared.

Chapter Fourteen
Slipping the Cable

Slipping the cable has two very different meanings. The good news is that it refers to cutting the rode when losing an anchor is less important than a quick departure.

The bad news, for Trustrum Crook, is that slipping the cable also refers to a sailor who dies.

After recovering, Trustrum raced home and headed straight for the phone. Anger was not his motivation, but fear. He grabbed the phone and dialed Pritchard's number—the one that had more than once been referred to as Trustrum's lifeline. A computerized voice said: "We're sorry, the number you have reached has been disconnected. No further information is available about this number." Stunned and in shock, he dropped the phone.

Now, there was no doubt in Trustrum's mind—the Coterie would be coming for him, if they were not already on their way. He knew he could not run forever, and that, in the end, he would have to confront them—one-way or the other. What to do? He needed time to think.

With a burst of energy, Trustrum Crook ran to his bedroom closet and pulled out the metal container that held his important documents. He located his will and a personal life insurance policy in the amount of three hundred thousand dollars. With them in hand, he dashed downstairs and laid them on the table in the foyer. Then, he searched for Marquise and found her sleeping on the couch in the family room. He scooped her up in his arms and headed out the door to the Reynolds's house.

He pounded on the front door five times, then another five times. Finally, Mrs. Reynolds came to the door and opened it. "Hello, Trustrum. Is something wrong?" she asked.

"Yes. I need a big favor." Trustrum held Marquise out to her. Mrs. Reynolds took the seal point as Trustrum continued. "I have to leave town on an emergency."

"Oh, I hope its nothing serious."

"Me too. Listen. Some people may be coming and going at my place. I'm afraid she might get out."

"Of course, Trustrum." Mrs. Reynolds, now cradling Marquise, looked at her and said, "We'll take good care of your kitty." She followed her words with affectionate kissing noises.

"The thing is, I'm not sure how long I'll be away."

"Go on and do what you have to do, Trustrum. Don't worry about Marquise."

"Sorry to throw her on you this way."

"She'll be just fine here as long as it takes."

"Thanks a million. I do have to run." Trustrum said. He turned and darted full speed back to his home. There, he picked up the documents he had left in the foyer and set the alarm. After securely locking up, he jumped into his 330Ci, which had been sitting in the driveway. He started to back out of the driveway when he remembered the bug and tracking device. He jammed on the brakes and got out of the car. Having weeks before located where the Coterie had hidden the device, Trustrum lay on the macadam driveway and slid underneath the front end. He took out his sailor's knife, which he usually carried with him, and worked loose the rectangular box and trailing antenna wire. The system was not tied into the car's electrical system, so Trustrum felt that it was safe to assume it would continue to function on its own battery power source even after he had freed it from its hiding place. He tossed it into the bushes in front of his house.

Trustrum climbed back into his car and headed to Cambridge to see Sarah—perhaps for the last time. As he drove across the Chesapeake Bridge, he looked at the great expanse of water below. Up to this point, panic had controlled his actions: his only concern was making certain that Sarah and Michelle had the necessary documents to inherit his estate once the Coterie had done the inevitable. But now, high on the bridge that allowed him to look out over the Chesapeake Bay, he decided that he would make a run for it in *Tavernier*. He knew that sailing away was only a temporary solution, but it would buy him some time, and maybe he could come up with a plan to save himself. First, however, he needed his little girl and ex-wife to disappear.

Michelle made no attempt to hide her disapproval with Trustrum's unexpected visit. When she opened the door and saw him, her half-smile turned instantly to a frown.

"What are you doing here?" she asked.

"Not today, please. I came to see Sarah for a moment and to give you these," he said, handing her the papers.

"What are they?"

"Everything you need in the event of my sudden demise," he answered. "My life insurance policy, the deed to my house, the title to my car, and my will. I have it in a trust that goes to Sarah with you controlling everything."

"What's going—"

Trustrum interrupted her. "Sarah and you need to go to one of your relatives," he said in a low voice. "This is no joke. I've gotten myself into some big trouble. I need to lay low for a while, until I come up with an idea to make things right again. You need to take our little girl and get the hell out of here."

"Trustrum—"

"Not tomorrow. Not in one hour. Grab your keys, some clothes, and some toys for Sarah, and leave now. Please," he pleaded.

"Look, I don't know what it is you've gotten yourself into, but it has nothing to do with Sarah, and it certainly doesn't have anything to do with me. I don't even want to know what it is."

"There's no getting around it, Michelle. Because I love Sarah, they can get to me through her…and you."

She started to say something, and he put a finger to his lips. "Don't say anything else," he whispered. "I'm begging you. For once in you life, please listen to me."

"All right, that's it! You're out of your mind. This is ridiculous."

"We're wasting time. Where's Sarah?"

"I don't want to bother her now. She's taking a nap."

"She can nap in the car. Let's go."

"No, Trustrum!" Michelle shouted at him, which caused both of them to pause. Michelle studied Trustrum's expression and considered what he had said. She realized that she had never seen him so frightened.

"Okay, okay," she said, as though she were exhausted. She left him standing at the front door and ran upstairs to pack a bag without another word. Trustrum waited just a moment, then followed her into the house, went up the stairs into Sarah's room, and picked her up from her bed where she was sleeping.

"Daddy? What's going on?"

"Mommy and you are going for a ride in the car. You can sleep in the back seat."

Sarah hugged him and tucked her head onto his shoulder as he carried her to the car. After strapping her in with a seatbelt, he examined the vehicle from top to bottom—from what he could tell, there were no unwanted electrical devices.

"Wait—what do we have here?" Trustrum said. He lay

on the street and inched his way under the car. Reaching up, he worked his right hand into the engine. He used his left hand to take his sailor's knife from his pants pocket, flicked it open one-handed, and reached up into the engine. A minute or two later the device came free. He yanked the rest of the wiring out as he rolled out from under the car. Michelle came out of the house just as he was standing up. She carried a single large travel bag and two dolls for Sarah. Trustrum held up the device.

Michelle abruptly stopped, still holding the bag and dolls, and began to cry. "Oh my God. Oh my God. Trustrum!"

"Knock it off. You can't fall apart on me."

"What's going on? Who are these people?"

Trustrum threw the electronic device across the yard. It bounced off Sarah's swing-set. It did not appear to break, but it was far enough away, so it could not pick up their words. "Look, just calm down," he said. He hugged Michelle and whispered in her ear, "That may just be a tracking device. There may still be a bug in the car. So don't say anything you wouldn't want the rest of the world to hear when you're around it. Go to your friend's house—the one in Delaware. Stay there until I call. Now, go."

~~~~~~~

Trustrum knew that it was foolish to return to his home, but he had not been thinking clearly when he left, and in the rush, he had overlooked the little money he had saved over the past months to be used for such an occasion. Worse, he had completely forgotten to grab his credit and debit cards. There was no getting around it, he had to return to his home.

The sky was filled with clouds—making it darker than it ordinarily would be for early evening—and the wind was picking up. Trustrum turned on the radio. "...bay and surrounding waterways are under a small craft warning.

Stay tuned for more information as it comes in about this Nor'easter, which could prove to be quite a storm for the Chesapeake area and northern East-Coast states." The forecast over, the radio announcer rambled off the rest of the day's local news, but Trustrum did not pay any attention to what was said. His thoughts were on his plan and the heavy rain that had started to pelt against his car.

The Chesapeake was a body of water known for squalls that caught many a sailor by surprise. Trustrum had experienced his share of storms on the Bay, but few sailors, if any, would voluntarily head out in such weather. If his sailing friends knew that he intended to embark on a voyage in such a violent storm, they would think he was mad. Still, he would gladly face the worst the bay had to offer rather than to duel with the Coterie. He would use the storm as cover and escape in the night—but to where?

Because of the blinding rain, it took Trustrum twice as long to get home as usual. When he was within walking distance to his house, he pulled over and parked. Lightning flashed and thunder clapped as the rain continued to fall. He got out of his car and started to walk—but not directly to his home. Instead, he scouted the neighboring streets, looking for any vehicles that might belong to the Coterie.

"Baines, you lazy dog," Trustrum said aloud as he stood in the rain only one block away from the entrance to his community. A black Lincoln Towncar with New York plates sat curbside.

He walked over to the car and looked inside. It was empty. Baines had probably already broken into his home and was waiting for him to return. The tracking device the Coterie had attached to Trustrum's BMW, which he had left in the bushes in front of his house, had indicated to the thugs that he had not driven away. Trustrum smiled, thinking that Baines must have been disappointed not to find him at home.

Before walking away from the car, he felt the hood; it

177

was cold. He took this as a good sign, for it meant that Baines, whether alone or with others, would have had a chance to become bored and inattentive. He knelt down next to each of the tires and cut off the stem from each one with his knife, then watched the air quickly leak out until the car rested on its metal rims.

Determined to have the benefit of surprise on his side, Trustrum returned to his car and waited. Somehow he drifted to sleep—a loud crack of thunder startled him awake. He looked at his watch—2:27 AM Five hours had passed. His clothes were still wet, and he shivered from the cold. He pulled himself together, and with all his courage, started to slowly walk toward his home. *Time to make my move,* he thought. *Even Baines will be tired by now. His senses will be dull. Now is my opportunity,* he continued, attempting to convince himself that he would have the upper hand.

He climbed a tree standing near the outside of the fence that surrounded the entire community. He slid out on a branch that hung over the fence and jumped to the ground. With the rain and lightning and thunder all around him, he neared the house, observing that it was completely dark. This confirmed that someone was waiting inside for him; his lights were on timers, so someone would have had to turn them off. Trustrum decided to enter the house through the family room on the terrace level using the patio door.

As he carefully turned the cylinder of the first, second, then third deadbolt, he was glad for the noises of the storm. The door handle lock stuck, and he had to wait for a loud burst of thunder before opening it with a forceful click. From where he stood outside, the sound had been masked, but he had no way of knowing if it had been noticed from the inside. He gently opened the door, when to his surprise, the alarm keypad blinked its light and made the soft chirping noise that indicated the alarm had been activated. He had not considered the possibility that they would have turned it on after having gone inside. Stunned by this unexpected development, Trustrum froze momentarily and listened to five beeps as someone elsewhere in the house punched a keypad with the code numbers that relayed to the security company that all was well—no intruders.

Trustrum charged into the room and up the stairs to the first floor. He had intended to continue up the stairs to the top floor, in an effort to reach his bedroom where he had hidden his money and bankcards; but he abruptly stopped. In the darkness, he saw the outline of a large man—Baines!

"It's over, Crook. I told you this day would come."

Trustrum barreled up the remaining few stairs that separated them and dove as hard as he could, aiming his shoulder into Baines's shins while wrapping his arms around his lower legs; Baines fell backward against the wall. Wasting no time, Trustrum jumped to his feet and pummeled Baines's face and gut. Baines swung at him and struck Trustrum in the head with a handgun. Trustrum fell down the short flight of stairs back into the family room.

"Come on, Crook. You can't be that easy." Baines moved down the stairs and proceeded to kick Trustrum again and again as he lay on the floor. But then, apparently underestimating Trustrum, Baines dropped his guard for just a moment. Trustrum saw his chance and kicked out with his right leg, landing a hard blow to Baines's gut. Baines keeled over with his wind knocked out.

Taking advantage of this opportunity, Trustrum, who was breathing heavily, wobbled to his feet, stepped forward, and struck Baines with his best punch—Baines fell to the ground. Trustrum realized he could not take a chance on going upstairs. He had no idea if Baines had brought his associates with him. Money and bankcards or not, it was time to leave. Trustrum had almost reached the door leading outside to the patio when he glanced back. Another flash of lightning revealed that Baines had regained his composure and was close behind.

"You're mine, Crook!" Baines shouted as he lunged toward Trustrum.

Trustrum dodged to the side, trying to avoid the large man as he flew through the air. Trustrum fell back against the wall and collapsed to the floor next to the deadeye doorstop. At the same time, Baines crashed into the wall and also landed on the floor. But where Trustrum had hit the wall with his back, Baines had rammed it hard with his head and now lay on the floor dazed. Without thinking, Trustrum stood up, grabbed the heavy deadeye, and began clubbing Baines on the head again and again.

Trustrum stepped back, put down the deadeye, and stared at Baines, who did not move. In the darkness, Trustrum was not sure if the man was even breathing. "Hey…you're not dead…Baines?" But there was no reply. Trustrum panicked; the thought of killing—even Baines, the man who had come to kill *him*—made Trustrum sick.

In his agitated state, Trustrum forgot the possibility of someone upstairs and ran all the way up to his bedroom, going straight to the bookshelf. He pulled out the book in which he had hidden the money and cards—but when he fanned through the pages, Trustrum discovered that they were missing. "Damn you, Pritchard!" he shouted. Then, he remembered having used the debit card recently and that he had not yet returned it to its hiding place. Perhaps Pritchard had not found it.

He moved quickly to the closet and rummaged through the pockets of one of his jackets. "Yes!" he cried after finding it. He wasted no more time and hurried back down the three flights, returning to the terrace level to leave. As he passed the door of his studio he thought of the solid-gold box on which he had last been working.

He went into his studio and picked up the objet d'art from the floor where it had landed when he had thrown it earlier. He examined it, noting the large gash, the dents, and that it was slightly misshapen—but it was still gold nonetheless, so he took it. He returned to the family room where Baines lay and found his handgun—a fully loaded .45ACP 1911. Trustrum went through Baines's jacket and found two full clips for the automatic weapon. Then, without a word, Trustrum stepped over the motionless body and left his house, closing the door behind him.

The wind blew the trees fiercely as the rain beat down. Trustrum had been soaked since before entering his house, so walking to the marina in the pouring rain made no difference. There were about fifty boats docked. The wind was causing the halyards to bang against each boat's mast, creating tinny, clanking sounds, which Trustrum had always thought eerie and lonely. The lights were on in the tugboat, *Rebecca May*; Trustrum could see Jack inside, wearing heavy-weather gear. *Rebecca May's* engines were cranking away loudly, as if Jack was making ready to head out.

"Jack! Jack! What are you doing?" he shouted over the noise. Jack came out on deck and leaned over the rail.

"What's that, Trustrum?"

"What are you doing?"

"Heading out. This storm's nothing for *Rebecca May*. They're saying it's moving out to sea anyway. I'm bound for the C and D Canal. Got a job in the morning," Jack shouted. "You just checking *Tavernier*?"

"I'm going out, too."

"In *Tavernier*? At night in this kind of weather? You're crazy!"

"No choice! Jack, I need a favor."

"Name it."

Trustrum motioned for Jack to wait, and he ran to *Tavernier*. Trustrum climbed aboard, opened the port lazarette, and went below. Three minutes later, he climbed out carrying the bug and tracking device. He jumped onto the pier and ran back to *Rebecca May*. When he was about twenty feet away, he laid it down on the pier and walked up to Jack.

"It would help me to no end if you would take that thing over there north with you. Maybe drop it overboard when you reach the middle of the C and D."

"What is it?"

"A listening and tracking device."

"I *knew* I saw two scuba guys that day you nearly drowned. What kind of trouble are you in? FBI after you?"

"No, I wish they were. It's nothing to do with the law. In fact, it's very much the opposite."

"Man! Sure, throw it in the back near the engine. That'll give them something to listen to for a while."

"I owe you twice now, Jack." Jack winked and nodded his head.

There was no time to lose. After giving Jack the electronic device, Trustrum went into action and quickly readied *Tavernier* for storm conditions, while allowing the engine to warm up. From the bow, Trustrum surveyed the situation and realized it would not be wise to try to leave under such conditions without help. Just when he thought to go for Jack, Trustrum turned to see Jack loosening the port stern mooring line.

"Now, you owe me three times," Jack shouted over the raging storm.

~~~~~~~

Having not heard from Baines for hours, Pritchard, Steeg, and Abrams left the motel where they had waited as ordered. Baines had wanted Trustrum all for himself, and despite Mr. Coulbourne's possible disapproval, the assassination squad's leader had made them stand down while he attempted to execute what should have been an easy assignment.

They moved cautiously through Trustrum's house. Guns drawn and ready to spring into action, they spread out and searched every room. They were looking for Baines and Trustrum Crook.

It was Pritchard who found Baines lying passed out on the floor of the family room. Having confirmed the house as otherwise empty, they turned on the lights.

"You—find the cat," Pritchard ordered Abrams. "You"—he pointed to Steeg—"go to the marina and see if he's there."

"You don't think he'd try sailing in weather like this, do you?" Steeg asked.

"He's a scared man on the run. There's no telling what he might try to do. But if I know Trustrum Crook like I think I do, he'd choose a storm over us any day. Now, go!" Steeg hurried outside, jumped into the Lincoln, and screeched the tires as he speeded to the marina. Fifteen minutes later, he returned with the news.

"You were right. His boat's gone. He's got to be out of his mind." Steeg had brought in the suitcase that contained the tracking system, and began to set it up.

"I can't find any cat around here," said Abrams.

In an outburst of anger and frustration, Pritchard kicked Baines, who was now semiconscious, but still outstretched on the floor. "If we lose him now, he could go into hiding, and we won't have a chance of finding him for who knows how long. This is it, gentlemen. We need to locate him—now or never." Pritchard spoke in a strong, authoritative voice. Baines was slowly returning to consciousness, but anyone could see that he would need a doctor. The Coterie was contacted, and Mr. Coulbourne made the necessary arrangements. Baines would be reprimanded for his failure.

Pritchard paced back and forth as Steeg continued to fiddle with the tracking system. This was Pritchard's chance to shine. If he came through with finding Trustrum—with

183

cleaning up Baines's mess—he could well be promoted. He snickered at the thought of Baines as his subordinate. Pritchard had dreamt of this day for many years.

"What's taking so long?" Pritchard asked.

"There's interference from the storm, sir."

"Make it work! We've got to get moving."

Abrams said, "Sir, we should have no difficulty catching up with him by land."

"I realize—"

"Got it, sir!"

"Good! Where's he heading?" Pritchard asked.

"North. Toward Baltimore."

"Throw Baines in the trunk. We don't have time for him now," Pritchard ordered. The trunk of the Lincoln was large enough; he rationalized, that Baines would be just as uncomfortable in it as he would be anywhere, and they needed space in the back seat for Steeg to operate the tracking device. Abrams drove while Pritchard sat in the front passenger's seat. He was in charge now.

～～～～～～～

Heading toward the other end of the Bay, Trustrum fought to stay awake as he sailed *Tavernier* toward Tangier Island, a small, isolated island, which stood miles from the Eastern Shore to the east and farther still from the mainland to the west. For years, the home of watermen, it had been colonized during the Elizabethan era, resulting in a people who, four hundred years later, had their own unique accent. This would be his refuge. He could stay on the island for as long as he needed, until he developed a plan—if he could just make his way through the storm.

～～～～～～～

Chapter Fifteen
Hove-to

At times when it is important for a sailboat to remain nearly stationary without the use of an anchor—and the reasons for this are many; for instance, to allow time to decipher the best course to travel—a sailboat can hove-to, which means to stall it, using the sails and rudder.

Trustrum Crook needed to hove-to so that he might have time to determine his own best course to travel.

~~~~~~~~

Few of the inhabitants of Tangier Island had noticed *Tavernier* before Trustrum had completed the task of laying anchor in the late morning after the storm. Almost twenty-four hours later, they still had not seen any signs of life aboard the mysterious sloop. As usual, the men of the island made their way to their boats and readied to head out for another day's crab harvest hours before the sun would rise.

"Let me go out and see if anybody's there, Dad," begged Aaron Stuller. He was a strapping eighteen-year-old and the eldest boy of Albert and Stacey Stuller's three children.

"Of course, there's somebody aboard, Aaron. That boat didn't get here by itself," his father said.

"Let me go check it out. Maybe there's something wrong."

"I'm sure they're just tired. It must have taken quite a lot to make it through such weather. Hand me that pot over there," Albert said, hurrying to finish with the morning chores of organizing the boat so that they could head out and begin another grueling day on the waters of the Chesapeake Bay. They had over one hundred pots to pull up and re-bait before they could call it a day; he was anxious to get started.

"Then, can I go?" Aaron persisted, moving to get out of the work-boat in hopes of rowing a nearby dinghy over to the *Tavernier*.

"Enough. We have to head out. If no one's moving about when we come in, we'll see."

By the time the sun was shining, they had traveled far from the island and checked many of the pots. As expected, the catch was sparse. Albert's son had never known crabbing as his father once lived it, in its glory days, when pots were pulled up brimming with crabs. Now, the days were long with little to show for their efforts. Finally, they finished with the last pot and turned their boat for home.

"Do you think anybody's come out yet, Dad?" Aaron asked with the excitement of a child on Christmas morning. Tourists visited the island nearly every day of the year, rain or shine—*come-heres* was what the islanders nicknamed them. They came on large party boats by the hundreds as well as on privately owned boats like *Tavernier*. But this was different. The *Tavernier* had blown in at the tail end of a horrific storm, had laid anchor before anyone had noticed, and then, her crew had disappeared without a trace. It was all Aaron could do to contain his excitement. When the end-of-the-day's work was completed, which included thoroughly washing down the boat, Albert consented to Aaron's wish of visiting *Tavernier*. Together, they climbed into the dinghy that had been tied to the pier and rowed over to her. The gossip from the folks who had been watching from the pier was that no one on the island had seen any movement on her since she arrived.

"Ahoy, *Tavernier*. Anybody aboard?" called Albert. He

paused, waiting for a response, but there was none. With a closed fist, he knocked his knuckles against the hull. "Hello? Anybody aboard the *Tavernier*?" This time, Albert and Aaron heard someone moving inside. The wooden slats of the companionway hatch were dismantled, one at a time, and out stepped Trustrum Crook, looking like a man who had just awakened from a long sleep.

"We were starting to think something was wrong," Aaron said. "Have you been asleep the whole time?"

"How long have I been here?" Trustrum asked, his thoughts groggy.

"A whole day and night," Albert said.

"Must have looked like a ghost ship."

"We were starting to wonder," Albert said. "Got caught in the storm, huh?"

"Man, that was rough sailing. I don't want to do that again too soon. Did it do any damage here?" Trustrum asked.

"Not really. We expect bad weather around here, so we're more or less prepared for it," Aaron said.

"I'm starving. Any suggestion where I can get some good eats?"

"There's really only one restaurant on the island, and it closed when the last load of tourists returned to the mainland for the day. You're welcome to come to dinner at our home," Albert offered. "By the way, my name is Albert Stuller. This is my son, Aaron."

"Nice to meet you. I could use a home-cooked meal. I'll be happy to accept your invitation," Trustrum said. "Let me lock her up, and we can go."

"You're on Tangier Island. There's no need for locks once the come-heres leave," Aaron said.

"The mainland's got nothing on this island," Trustrum said. He climbed over the lifeline into the small dinghy with his new island friends. Ten minutes later, the three men were walking along one of the many five-foot-wide paths toward the Stuller home—no wide streets and no cars on Tangier Island.

Trustrum felt at home the minute he saw the simple Cape Cod and went inside. The rooms were small but not cramped. Trustrum found the atmosphere cozy and inviting. Stacey Stuller, Albert's wife, seemed overjoyed to have a houseguest, and she hurried to add one more place setting to the table. The house was filled with the delectable aroma of dinner cooking. Trustrum looked around him as everyone, including the two younger girls, went about their individual tasks before dinner. He could think of no better place to be—if only Sarah was with him.

Stacey gave Trustrum, as guest, the chair at the end of the table where she usually sat opposite Albert. They bowed their heads in prayer, giving thanks for being together and for their new friend having made it through the fierce storm.

"This is real watermen cooking, Trustrum," Aaron said, handing him a platter of crab cakes. "You won't find this on the mainland."

"Dad says momma's the best cook on the island," Carrie Stuller said, a pretty girl of seventeen, who was the second oldest.

"I was going to say that," piped up Chrissy Stuller, the youngest at four-and-a-half years old.

"Now, Chrissy, mind your manners in front of Mr. Crook," corrected Stacey, as she passed a large bowl of mashed potatoes. Turning toward her guest, she asked, "Trustrum, what on earth were you doing on the bay in the middle of that storm?"

"Mostly just trying not to drown."

"Where were you coming from?" Albert asked.

"Annapolis."

"You could have put-in at hundreds of places between Annapolis and here," Aaron stated.

"Maybe so, but then I wouldn't be eating the best crab cakes I have ever had in my entire life." Trustrum grinned. Albert and Stacey laughed, and the girls giggled.

"I would love a few more slices of tomato," Trustrum added.

"Momma grew them in the garden," Carrie said.

"Well, they're delicious. Everything is."

"It's our pleasure, Trustrum. How long are you planning to stay on the island?" Stacey asked.

"I'm not sure yet. I didn't head out with any real plans. I do that sometimes—just take off and plunk around the bay. I'm in no rush, I'll tell you that."

"In the middle of a storm?" Carrie innocently asked. Everyone stopped eating and looked at Trustrum, who looked back at them with a blank expression.

Finally, he said, "There wouldn't be an ATM around here, would there?" The Stullers continued with their dinner as before.

"No, but there's one in Crisfield," Aaron said. Crisfield, the so-called capital of crabs, was a waterside town on a lower peninsula of the Eastern Shore.

"We've been shorthanded on the boat, Trustrum. We could use you on the water, if you're interested," Albert said.

"I couldn't promise how long I'd stick with it."

"Understand."

"Then, okay. It'd be my pleasure."

"Ever been crabbing?" Aaron asked.

"Once. A long time ago."

"Then, you ought to know that pleasure has little to do with it."

"You'll have to wake up at four in the morning," Carrie said.

"I was going to say that!" Chrissy said.

They sat on the porch for the rest of the late afternoon and early evening, talking and watching the girls play. Trustrum realized while sitting with them that it was the first time since becoming entangled with the Coterie that he genuinely felt at ease. He thought about Sarah and silently prayed that she was safe. He missed her and wished that she were with him, playing with the Stuller children. Well fed and relaxed, Trustrum grew tired. At seven, he returned to *Tavernier* and fell soundly asleep; his four AM wake-up call would come before he knew it.

Albert steered the workboat, *Stacey II*, next to *Tavernier*, and Trustrum hopped aboard. It was still dark, but the small harbor glowed from the lights of the many crabbers heading out for a long day's work. By five in the morning, the three men were hard at work. Albert skillfully maneuvered the boat alongside the floating pot markers. Although the water was covered with the bullet-shaped floats, each crabber had his own registered color code. Aaron snatched up their markers with a long hook. Each marker, bobbing on the surface, was connected by rope to the crab pot, which rested on the sandy bottom of the bay. Crab pots are traditionally square cages made from mesh wire resembling chicken wire. Trustrum's job was to share the load with Aaron. Together, they would pull up the pots, using a lifting machine that took away much of the strain. Nevertheless, Trustrum found it to be exhausting, backbreaking labor.

Four hours into the day and while en route to the second line of pots, they took a break to eat the sandwiches that Stacey had prepared for them.

"Think you could do this every day, Trustrum?" Aaron

asked, pouring coffee from a thermos.

"I was just thinking how I wouldn't mind this life-style, but I don't know if my back could take it."

"It's a good life—hard—but good. Used to make some money at it, too. But crabs ain't what they used to be. Crabbers have to work many times harder today for far less. Aaron, here, will probably have to head for the mainland one of these days. Get a job on a farm or drive a truck."

"I'm not farming, and I'm not driving a truck. I'll tell you that, right now."

"Son, I keep telling you, pretty soon you won't have a choice."

"I thought laws had been put in place to help the crabs bounce back," Trustrum said.

Both Aaron and Albert laughed. "When was the last time a politician stuck his nose into anything that amounted to any good?" Albert said.

"The two biggest changes they've made are the two biggest jokes around here," Aaron said. "They made it so crabbers can't crab past two every day, and not at all on Wednesdays."

"Why doesn't cutting back help?"

"I don't know one crabber who isn't done for the day by one o'clock—every day. And what if we can't go out on Wednesdays. The crabs don't know it's Wednesday. They still climb into the pots no matter what day of the week it is. All the politicians did was give us Wednesdays off and heavier pots to pull up on Thursdays," Albert said.

"Course, twice as much ain't what it used to be, either," Aaron said.

"The cultured pearl industry has had some trouble over the years, too," Trustrum said.

"Really?" Albert asked.

191

"Yeah, some kind of blight. But it's supposed to be on the rebound."

"What's caused it?" Aaron asked.

"Pollution, global warming, ships releasing contaminated ballast water—who knows. It's probably a little of everything."

"Do you work with pearls, Trustrum?" Aaron asked.

"I'm a jewelry appraiser. I work with all kinds of gemstones."

"That sounds like a neat job."

"I love it."

"I love my work too, Trustrum," Albert said. "but I don't know how long it's going to last. I'm afraid you're looking at the last of a breed."

Trustrum thought that in his own way, he too was the last of a breed—that is, if the Coterie had anything to say about it.

~~~~~~~~

The last crab pot was re-baited with a frozen, raw chicken leg and dropped overboard. In all, they had collected only four bushels of crabs. Albert put the engine full-throttle as he planed back toward Tangier Island. He had told Trustrum he hoped to be one of the first to arrive so that they would not have to wait long to unload. He would sell their catch through the cooperative; a large boat that bought the catch of many watermen and ferried it to Crisfield, where it would be sold to dealers and transported up and down the East Coast.

Trustrum, smelling of his work, returned to *Tavernier* and showered, then, lay down for a nap before heading to the Stuller home. It had been agreed that meals were part of his pay. During the dinner conversation, he said, "I need to go to Crisfield to get some money from an ATM and make a phone call."

Aaron laughed. "Trustrum, we live on an island, not in the outback. We have a phone."

"I don't want to take any chances of being traced—" As soon as he said it, Trustrum realized that he made a mistake. He was tired, and he had not thought before replying. Trying to recover, he said, "I'm kidding, of course." No one laughed, but Aaron grinned.

"What kind of trouble are you in exactly, Trustrum?" Albert finally asked.

"I was just pulling your leg, Albert. I'm not in any trouble…really."

Changing the conversation, Stacey asked, "Are you married, Trustrum?"

"Divorced."

"Oh, that's too bad," she said. "Any children?"

"One. Her name is Sarah. She's six years old. Here's a picture of her," he said. He took her picture out of his wallet and handed it to Stacey.

"Isn't she a cutie? Look at her, Albert. Look, girls," she said, holding it so that her husband and the two girls could see.

Carrie and Chrissy looked carefully at the photograph. Albert gave it a cursory glance and asked, "Exactly what do you do in the jewelry business?"

"Mostly appraising so that people can properly insure their jewelry. I also do a little manufacturing, that sort of thing."

"Momma, you should show your charm bracelet to Mr. Crook," Carrie said.

Chrissy was about to speak, but Trustrum quickly said, "Hey, Chrissy, were you going to say that?"

She blushed and said, "Yeah," as she covered her eyes with her arms. Stacey went to her bedroom and returned carrying her charm bracelet. She made light of it, but Trustrum could tell it was a prized and cherished possession. "It's just an old bracelet with a bunch of worthless charms." She handed it to Trustrum. He carefully examined it, then placed it on the table, and looked at each charm.

"Charm bracelets are back in style, Stacey. I think everyone is tired of seeing them just lying around in their jewelry boxes. Now, women are wearing them again. I think it's wonderful. A beautiful way to preserve memories."

"If I wore mine, I'd end up sending one of my babies to the doctor. It's so clumsy," she said, taking it back and lovingly draping it over her wrist. It was her entire life documented in gold shapes dangling from a garibaldi-link bracelet with a pressure box clasp and figure eight safety hasp. There was a charm from when she had been graduated from high school, one for each child, an Empire State Building, an Eiffel Tower, and of course, a three-dimensional crab. All in all, the bracelet spanned over twenty years of Stacey's life.

"You should wear it, Stacey," Trustrum said.

"I'd look silly. Nobody wears these things on this old island."

"I'm telling you, you'd be on the cutting edge of fashion, if you did."

"You'd be the talk of Tangier Island, momma," Carrie said.

Trustrum spent a little more than a week working on the bay. Every day was the same—on the water from early morning to early afternoon, clean-up and a nap from about two o'clock until five o'clock, then dinner and socializing with the Stullers, until it was time for bed, which was no later than nine. He missed Sarah. He wished she were with him. He knew she would have liked playing with Carrie and Chrissy. What was he going to do about the Coterie?

The engine roared as the three men plowed through the water on their way to Crisfield. Albert had ordered some new pots from a mainland supplier, and they were ready for pick-up. Aaron was just happy to be going to the mainland for any reason. Trustrum was anxious to finally get to call his answering machine and make contact with his real life.

"Now, run this by me again," Albert said.

"It's April 23, right?"

"Right."

"Then it's a holiday, because on April 23, 1564, William Shakespeare was born.

"Huh," Albert grunted.

"By the way, it's the day he died, too—fifty-two years later, in 1616.

"Dad, Trustrum says he's got one for every day of the year," Aaron said.

"Don't be giving Aaron any more bad ideas. It's hard enough getting him out of bed in the morning, as it is."

Trustrum took the bow line as they approached the quay; Aaron manned the stern, and Albert expertly maneuvered the boat with its starboard side to the cement wall. They tied off the mooring lines, and then each man went off in a different direction. Trustrum headed straight to a bank. It was the Crisfield branch of the bank he used in Annapolis.

"What do you mean: the account is closed!" Trustrum loudly said to the teller. "That's my private account, and it had thousands of dollars in it as of two weeks ago!"

"What is the problem here, Ms. Phillips?" inquired a snooty little man who appeared to be in charge.

"Mr. Neal, this man—"

"My name is Trustrum Crook. I've been a client of this bank for over twenty years."

"We have not existed that long, Mr. Crook."

"Well, the bank that I originally gave my money to—that your bank bought out—did. I didn't change anything. You guys did. The point is, my money is missing!"

"I'm afraid I don't remember seeing you in here before."

"You will note on your computer screen there, that I opened my account in your Annapolis branch. I thought I was in luck, finding you in Crisfield."

"We now have branches virtually all over the state," he said.

"Good for you, but I still can't seem to get my hands on my money. So the fact that you're in every part of the state really doesn't do me any good, now does it?"

"Our records show that the account was closed five days ago. Let me call the Annapolis branch where it was handled for details."

Trustrum, exasperated and feeling as though the Coterie was closing in on him, turned without another word and walked out of the bank. He found a pay phone and called home, using his toll-free business line, to access the messages on his answering machine.

"Hi, Trustrum. This is John Allen, here, from Allen and Associates. We've come up with a date when we'd like to do the appraisal program. Give us a call so we can discuss it. Thanks."

"Trustrum? This is Adriana Silva... Trustrum... Something terrible has happened... It's Sebastiao. He has died, Trustrum. His heart gave out...He was—" Suddenly, someone picked up the phone at his home, interrupting the message.

"Crook, know who this is? You better listen to me and listen good. I'm tired of playing around with you."

"Baines? You're alive!" Trustrum's emotions were mixed. He was relieved that he was not a murderer, but he was more frightened now than ever.

"Swallow your false sentiments, Crook. I'm here, and Mr. Pritchard's here. So are a couple other old friends, but we're not going to be here for long. You see, Mr. Coulbourne has ordered that as of the time we make contact with you—meaning as of this moment—you have exactly forty-eight hours to turn yourself in. I want to be absolutely clear with you, Crook. If you decide to go to the cops or should you decide to do something really stupid like not showing up, then we'll be visiting Michelle and your sweet little Sarah."

"You don't know where they are."

"They're back home, Crook."

"What? You leave them out of this, Baines!"

Baines laughed at Trustrum. "Who are you trying to impress? Listen to me! I have one concern, and that's you. It's your time to go, Crook—so, what's it going to be? Either way, you're history. What you need to decide is whether or not you're going to take your precious little Sarah down with you. But, it is over for you, Crook. Mark my words."

"I swear, I'll—"

"You'll nothing but shut up! Now, this is it: be here, at your home, within forty-eight hours—you got it? That's five PM on April 25. Be here by then, and Sarah doesn't know we exist. Otherwise, it's over for the kid. Understand? Understand! Say it!"

"I understand."

~~~~~~~

Shaken, Trustrum returned to *Stacey II* to find Albert and Aaron ready to go. He hoped they could not see how upset he was.

"How'd you make out with the bank?" asked Albert.

"My account's been closed."

"Closed?"

"I've made a mess of everything."

Albert gave Trustrum a long look but said nothing more. Trustrum and Aaron untied the mooring lines, and Albert directed *Stacey II* out onto the Chesapeake Bay, heading back to Tangier Island. Aaron sat alone at the stern, just looking at the water and sky. Trustrum stood next to Albert at the helm.

"Anything else happen back there?" Albert asked.

"Yes. I accessed my home phone machine. A close friend of mine has died."

"Oh, no. What happened?"

"Heart attack."

"Was he an old man?"

"Early seventies…His wife left the message. I had promised him awhile back that I would look out for her if something like this happened. Now, I can't even take care of myself."

"How did you know him?"

"He was my mentor. His name was Sebastiao Silva. He taught me everything I know about bench-work, sculpting jewelry—just about everything, it seems."

"Well, I know that it's not much, but at least he was able to leave you his legacy. In a small way, he's still with you. Don't misunderstand me. I'm not making light of his passing, but it is a part of the big picture. And he had a long life."

"Sure."

"At least, he had a legacy to give you. With crabs the way they are, my legacy is worthless to Aaron…He'd be foolish to go into this line of work today…it's as if I had dangled the secret of life in front of him only to snatch it back—and let me tell you, this truly was once the greatest way to live your life…You should remember and take comfort in that you hold Mr. Silva's legacy."

"That's nice, Albert. It's a nice thought."

Aaron joined his father at the helm. Trustrum, needing to be alone, took a place on a pile of canvas that was bunched up in the back corner of *Stacey II*. His thoughts raced back and forth: *Poor Adriana, I have to call her somehow…Baines, that bastard…What if the Coterie traced the call?…What if they now know I'm in Crisfield?…Is it safe to call Adriana?…Why did Michelle take Sarah home?*

He was sick with worry. *I have to go back, there's no question about it. But then I'm a dead man. So much for Silva leaving him a legacy….*

Suddenly Trustrum sat up straight. *Legacy—yes, that's it!* Quickly he began to formulate a plan. *It would only work, though, if Adriana was involved…I wonder if she's up to it? Even if she is, could I swing it before the forty-eight-hour deadline expired?…Could I make it work?*

Unaware that Albert and Aaron were watching him, Trustrum stood and paced back and forth on the deck, thinking, planning. Finally, he came back to the present and found the two men staring at him.

"I think I've got it—the answer to my problem, that is. But I'll need your help."

"Name it," Albert said, still having no idea what was the problem.

"Well, for one thing, you could turn this boat around. I suddenly need to make a couple of calls."

Albert did not hesitate. He spun the helm, making as tight a 180-degree turn as *Stacey II* could handle, and headed back to Crisfield under full steam.

"Take the helm," Albert shouted to Trustrum over the

noise of the roaring twin engines. He took his wallet out of one of his back pockets and pulled out a plastic card. "I suppose you'll be needing my emergency phone card." He handed it to Trustrum.

"Thank you."

"What else, Trustrum?"

"Depends on how things go on the phone, I guess. Wait. Actually, you could do one more thing, right now."

"What's that?"

"Pray."

Chapter Sixteen
Williamson Turn

In the early 1940s, John A. Williamson developed a maneuver to quickly turn a boat so that it headed exactly reverse of her original course. The ability to do this was especially helpful in recovering a man overboard.

Trustrum Crook was hoping to do just that and save...himself.

~~~~~~~~

It was simple for Trustrum to locate Claire Perkins's telephone number through information. The hard part was making Mrs. Perkins understand what he needed her to do without telling her the truth.

"Why don't you call Adriana on her own phone?"

"Because I think there's something wrong with it."

"Well, hang up and I'll call her to see if it's working."

"No, you don't understand. This is Trustrum Crook—"

"I know who you are, Trustrum. I just don't—"

"Please just do me this little favor...please."

"Oh, all right," Mrs. Perkins said.

"Mrs. Perkins!"

"What now?"

"It's really important that you don't say that there's a phone call for her, and whatever you do, please do not mention my name. Understand?"

"No, I don't understand. What am I supposed to tell her the reason is for her to come to my house?"

"Just say that there's something at your home that you have to show her, and that it's very important that she comes over right away."

"Oh, for heaven's sakes. Hold on," Mrs. Perkins said. She put down the phone, but Trustrum could still hear her complaining out loud to herself. Ten minutes later, he heard the faint murmur of two people talking in the background. Then he heard someone pick up the phone.

"Hello?"

"Adriana, is that you?"

"This is Adriana."

"It's Trustrum Crook."

"Trustrum?"

"Yes, it's me."

"Why are you calling me on Claire's phone?"

"I know this is a bit unorthodox, but I'm not messing around. This is serious."

"Go on."

"It's difficult to explain the details over the phone, Adriana. You need to just listen to me for a minute."

"All right."

"Now you have to stay calm, but the reason I did this with Mrs. Perkins is that there's a strong chance that your phone is tapped."

"What?"

"Adriana, do you trust me?"

"Of course I do," Adriana said without hesitating.

"Do you still want to live in Brazil?"

"Yes, if there was any way I could afford to. But, Trustrum, even after selling the house, there would be little in equity left over. We had to take a second mortgage on it a few years back to make ends meet. I would be afraid of running out of money once I was there. At least here, a woman has a better chance of making a living."

"What if I told you I could see that you had all the money you would ever need?"

"Why are you talking nonsense, Trustrum? Are you okay?"

"Just listen to what I'm saying. I'm in trouble, Adriana. I need you and—" Trustrum stopped talking mid sentence. He now felt awkward referring to his deceased friend simply as *Silva*—and *Sebastiao* was definitely out of the question—especially when speaking with Adriana. Neither name alone carried the respect his mentor deserved. "I need you and Mr. Silva to help me."

"What are you talking about? Didn't you get the message I left at your home?"

"Yes, I got it."

"Then you understand that Sebastiao has died?"

"Yes, but he can still help both of us. Only, it's important that you understand that there's risk involved—a great risk."

"How do you mean?"

"There are some really bad people who aren't too happy with me."

"Oh, Trustrum. Does it have to do with that jewelry-artist thing you've been into?"

"Yes."

"Oh, Sebastiao had his doubts about it. He said it happened too fast."

"I guess you could say that I made a pact with the devil—but I had no choice. It was either agree to be involved or die."

"This is really too much for me, Trustrum."

"I know. I swear there was nothing I could do to stay out of this."

"So, what's changed?"

"What do you mean: what's changed?"

"What's changed that you think now you can get out of it without them killing you? Who are these people?" she asked in a whisper.

"It's not safe for you to know."

"Oh, Trustrum, how did you get yourself into this mess?"

"I don't know. Just my luck, I guess. Someone once told me that it's the nature of the trade. Look, Adriana, I know I'm asking a lot of you—more than I have a right to—but I have nowhere else to turn. And to be perfectly honest with you, if you hope to ever live in Brazil through my help, this is as much your last chance as it is mine."

"And what about Sarah and her mother? Are they in any danger?"

"If I don't pull this off, I'll either have to turn myself over to them, which means I'm a dead man, or they'll go after Sarah."

She was silent for a moment, then said, "Then there's no choice. Okay, I'll do what I can, but I don't see how Sebastiao can help us now."

"I'll explain everything when we're together. You do understand, we're dealing with killers?"

"Trustrum, I've survived wars, revolution, and a life with Sebastiao Silva—I can handle this." They both laughed, but Trustrum noticed that his hands were shaking.

"Since you called my house last week, I wouldn't be surprised if they're watching your home hoping I'll surface. If this is going to even come close to having a chance at succeeding, we need to move right away," Trustrum said.

"Do you really think they've been listening to my phone conversations, or are you just becoming paranoid?"

"I think there's enough of a chance that I wasn't willing to risk it. In fact, from this point forward, I believe it would be prudent to act as if we know that it is. Adriana, these guys are thorough, and they have a lot at stake."

"Enough to kill you though?"

"It's all about money to them—plain and simple. Nothing else matters, and what they want me for concerns a *lot* of money."

"Oh, Trustrum."

"Look, I'm pretty sure they would have had to plant any bugs from inside the house. Would they have had any opportunities to get in?"

"I don't see when. I'm home all the time."

"What about when you go to the grocery store?"

"My neighbor has been shopping for me since Sebastiao died."

"Mrs. Perkins?"

"No, on the other side. Mrs. Koenig."

"Oh, sure," Trustrum said. "But you called me before the funeral, didn't you?"

"Yes, of course."

"Then they could have had someone in your place during the service."

"No they couldn't. A friend from work stayed at my house while I was away. The people at the funeral home had warned me about burglars. Apparently, it's a common practice for them to check the obituaries to find homes to rob. Can you imagine that. What kind of person could do such a thing?"

"There are all kinds of lowlifes out there, Adriana. Listen, even though it sounds like your house is okay, I still say we proceed as if it's bugged."

"I agree," Adriana said.

"Can you be ready to leave at any time?"

"Trustrum, are you talking about sending me to Brazil right away?"

"If everything goes as planned, I'm thinking you could be on a plane by tomorrow night."

"Oh, my."

"You'll have to travel light, right?"

"I'll put together two small travel bags. I can be ready to leave any time....You know something? When Sebastiao and I had to leave Brazil, we barely had an hour to grab some of our things. We lost everything that day—except for some diamonds Sebastiao had managed to hold on to. Here, it's happening all over again."

"I know. But after this is over and you're safe in Brazil, I promise to take care of packing up everything you own and sending it to you. I'll even help with selling the house. Whatever it takes, Adriana."

"I certainly didn't think my day would turn out like this when I woke up this morning," she said. "Well, okay, let's do it."

"Timing is everything. So we need to put aside our emotions for now. Can you do that?"

"Yes, I can do that."

"Good. Now, remember the trip the three of us took last summer?"

"Of course."

"Don't say it. I'm certain we're safe on Claire's line, but since you'll understand what I'm telling you without coming right out and saying it, and our lives are at risk....you do understand that your life will be just as much at risk as mine is?"

"Go on, Trustrum. Where should meet?"

"Remember that blue thing Mr. Silva looked at for the longest time. We had to drag him away from it—remember?"

"Yes. I do." She laughed, but it sounded to Trustrum as though there were also tears.

"I'll see you there tomorrow at noon. And one more thing—"

"Yes?"

"Did you ever finish Mr. Silva's scrapbook."

"The scrapbook? Why would we need that?"

<center>~~~~~~~</center>

Trustrum hung up the telephone and took a deep breath before making a second call, which was to William Weinstein. Trustrum would not need to involve him as much as Adriana, and so he chose not to tell him as many details for now.

"William, it's Trustrum Crook."

"Trustrum? Nice to hear from you, lad. How is everything going with you?"

"To tell you the truth, William, not so good. I need a big favor from you to maybe turn things around."

"Something on memo?"

"Not like that, William. I need a ride."

"A ride? As in my car?"

"Exactly. I need to take advantage of our friendship, so this is the deal: don't ask questions, understand that what I'm asking you to do is more important than anything has ever been in my life, and that I need you to meet me at Union Station in DC at eleven AM, promptly, bring at least two thousand dollars and make sure the gas tank is full. Got it?"

"Are you out of your mind? What's going on?"

"William! You're already breaking the first rule. Now, please do this for me. I'm talking life or death here."

"Really?"

"Really."

"Okay, Trustrum. Boy, you really do live on the edge. If it was anybody else, I'd think this was a prank call."

"This is no prank, William."

"No prank, huh?"

"I need you, pal."

"Union Station—eleven AM—tomorrow—two thousand bucks, right?"

"You got it."

"If it was anybody else…"

〜〜〜〜〜〜〜

Trustrum spent a restless night tossing and turning in *Tavernier's* V-berth. The next morning, Albert and Aaron motored *Stacey II* alongside *Tavernier*, where Trustrum stood waiting on deck. He had put Baines's handgun into the solid gold box, which he in turn had put into a duffel bag that had been stowed aboard ship. With the bag in hand, he hopped aboard *Stacey II*, and they were off. It was 7:30 AM; they would have more than enough time to reach Washington DC before Trustrum's scheduled rendezvous with William Weinstein. The sun shone as it slowly climbed in the cloudless sky. The air was calm, and the water showed not the least ripple. *Stacey II* had no problem quickly planing across the smooth surface at top speed.

"When are you planning to tell us what's going on, Trustrum?" Aaron asked.

"When it's all over."

"What about *Tavernier*?"

"I'll come back for her. But if two months goes by and I haven't returned, she's yours, Aaron."

"Oh man, thanks. I'll take good care of her."

"Don't get your hopes up too high, I'm going to do my best to survive this."

"Yeah, Aaron, she's only yours if Trustrum doesn't make it out of this mess he's in," Albert pointed out.

"Sorry, Trustrum. Didn't mean it that way."

"I know you didn't."

"Since you *will be* returning for her, can I stay on her until you come back?"

"There you go. That's a fine idea—as long as your father agrees to it." Albert nodded his head in approval.

From the Chesapeake Bay, they rounded the tip of Point Lookout and headed up the Potomac River toward the District of Columbia. Trustrum's stomach tightened as they approached his drop-off point and docked.

"Here's a few dollars. I'm sorry there's not more to give you," Albert said, handing Trustrum what was probably his life's savings.

Trustrum shook his head. "You've already done more than enough for me, Albert. I'm already forever in your debt. Someone's picking me up downtown; he'll have money. You keep this," Trustrum said, handing the money back. Then, Trustrum turned toward Aaron and shook his hand. He turned back to Albert and shook his. It was low tide, so he had to climb up out of *Stacey II* to the higher-standing pier. He made sure of his footing before taking the duffel bag from Aaron, who handed it up from the boat. Trustrum flung the duffel bag over his shoulder and thanked them, again.

Trustrum did not hesitate after that. He turned and walked briskly away from the water's edge toward downtown Washington, DC. Carrying the duffel bag, he made his way to Union Station. He stayed outside when he got there, standing next to a rare patch of tall trees and watched for William's car. Traffic was heavy. Perhaps there was a parade or a protest or a special convention going on that he was not aware of, he thought. He feared that he would not find his friend.

Twenty minutes after the time William was supposed to have arrived, Trustrum started to panic. Without William—without Adriana—there was no plan. He could not afford for anything to go wrong. *This isn't going to work,* he thought. "This isn't going to work!" he said aloud.

"What's not going to work?" he heard someone say, startling him. He quickly turned to see William standing with his hands sunk deep into his pants pockets.

"What are you doing sneaking up on me like that!"

"You're like a cat on a hot tin roof, Trustrum. Get a hold of yourself. What's not going to work?" William asked again.

"There's no time. Where's your car?"

"I've been sitting over there waiting for you for the past half hour. I finally saw you standing here."

"Come on, we have to hurry. We're picking up someone at the Natural History Museum."

"You're dragging me to the Smithsonian?"

"Just to meet someone."

"Then where are we going?"

"New York City."

"What!"

~~~~~~~~~

Trustrum left William in the car double parked, and hurried into the Natural History Museum. He had to stand in line for several of what seemed like the longest minutes of his life in order to purchase an admission ticket, and then finally he was in. He headed straight to the place where he hoped Adriana would be waiting for him. The blue thing he had referred to on the phone was the Hope Diamond exhibit. As usual, there was a crowd of people around the square window behind which sat the most famous of all diamonds in the world. But he did not see Adriana. He looked around the room, which was filled with showcases of some of the rarest gemstones ever discovered, and spotted her off to the side, standing next to two bulging, soft-sided traveling bags. He walked up to her, and without a word, they embraced for a long moment.

Finally, Trustrum said, "I'm so sorry about Mr. Silva. I loved him."

"He loved you, too, Trustrum."

"I know. Well, I suppose we should get going."

"Trustrum, when I was going back home after I had spoken with you at Claire's, I saw two men waiting out front of my house."

"What did you do?"

"At first nothing. But the more I thought about how brazen they were—just sitting in their car out in the open like that—I got angry. So when I was ready to leave to meet you, I did what any woman living alone would do—I called the police."

Trustrum laughed. "Simple but brilliant," he said.

"Effective, too. It gave me enough time to slip out the back door and get away through the alley. I left my car parked out front and used the Metro to come downtown."

"Chalk one up for mass transportation. I get the feeling I did the right thing by using Claire's phone to call you." Trustrum picked up Adriana's bags, and they walked out of the museum and down the block to the car. William got out of the car when he saw them approaching and helped Trustrum load the bags into the trunk.

"Heavy. You carried them all the way down here yourself?" William asked. Adriana smiled and nodded.

"William Weinstein, this is Adriana Silva. Adriana, this is William Weinstein." The two shook hands and said hello.

Trustrum continued, "Where's the scrapbook?"

Adriana bent down and pulled the oversize book out from one of the bags. "Here."

"Perfect." Trustrum said, taking the book. Then, having slipped it under his arm, he helped Adriana into the back seat, and then he took the front passenger's seat. "You know where to go, buddy," he said to William, who started the car and began to work his way through the busy streets of Washington, DC.

Thirty minutes later, they were on route 95 north. Trustrum looked at William, who concentrated on the road as he drove well over the speed limit, then at Adriana in the back seat, who had closed her eyes and seemed to be asleep. *I've got to be out of my mind, involving these two wonderful—and innocent—people in this mess. What was I thinking I would accomplish with two senior citizens up against the Coterie?* he thought.

A few times during the trip, Trustrum thought about calling the plan off. He wanted to tell William just to pull over at the next rest stop and drop him off—but he could not bring himself to do it. The point of no return had passed—besides, he was not ready to die.

Trustrum sat looking out the window, thinking of his situation. Eventually, William interrupted his thoughts. "Well, Trustrum, we passed Baltimore, and you tell us nothing. Now, we pass Philadelphia, and still, you tell us nothing. We'll be in New York shortly. Don't you think it's time to tell us what's going on?"

Trustrum looked at Adriana, who opened her eyes at hearing William's words. Trustrum recounted the main events of the past twenty-three months that had led to his present circumstances. Adriana had been told a brief summary on the telephone, but now she listened as Trustrum described each detail.

"Oy vay, some ganavim!" William blurted out.

"What?" Trustrum asked.

"Thieves! Ganavim!" William shook his fist above his head, causing the gold in his bloodstone ring to sparkle.

"Don't forget murderers," Trustrum said.

"Well, that's the thing. You're telling me these people are expecting you to give yourself over to them, so they can kill you. And your way of handling this is to drive to New York with us? Trustrum, in case you haven't noticed, we're a pretty lame group—no offense meant, Adriana," William said, glancing at her through the rearview mirror.

"None taken," Adriana said.

"If you two are finished, we need to focus. Adriana, what can you tell me about some of these photographs of Mr. Silva—and this newspaper article." He handed her a few of the photos and the cutout article he had pulled from the collection.

There was a photo of Mr. Silva when he was young and one when he was old—in both he worked at a jeweler's bench. A local weekly newspaper had written the article about him when he had set up a small repair shop in Amherst, Massachusetts, in the early eighties, after first immigrating to the United States. Then, there were pictures of his large jewelry manufacturing business in Brazil.

"He was so proud of that business. He started it himself and worked it until the day we had to escape from the country. There were forty-three employees at that time," Adriana said.

William, still watching the road as he continued north toward their destination, said, "That must have been some operation."

"Yes, it was. He had to be good as an artist, a businessman, and a leader of people to run that factory. He always said that there was no other business in the world that needed so many different skills and talents as the jewelry business."

"Well, Mr. Silva is about to receive the recognition he deserves," Trustrum said.

"What do you mean?" she asked.

"I'll tell you what I want to know first," William interrupted. "Trustrum, what's in your bag?"

Trustrum smiled, and as he pulled the gold box from the duffel bag, he said, "I can answer both of your questions at the same time. This is Mr. Silva's latest work." He held up the shiny gold rectangle. "It stands unfinished, as well as damaged. It will be the most desirable and valuable of all his creations, because it is the last thing he was working on. In fact, he died while making it."

During the rest of the drive into New York City, Trustrum described his plan to William and Adriana. William frowned but said nothing. Adriana listened intently, also remaining silent. Trustrum was relieved that neither objected nor said he was crazy.

William exited from Interstate 95, paid the toll and took route 495 toward New York City. He paid another toll at the Lincoln Tunnel, after they waited for fifteen minutes in line, then crossed under the Hudson River into Manhattan. Trustrum directed William to park the car in a multiple-level parking lot in the West Forties, and they walked to a diner where they sat in a booth. William and Adriana ordered food, but Trustrum had no interest in eating; he only ordered black coffee. As they waited for the waitress to bring them their orders, Trustrum borrowed William's credit card and went to the pay phone. By the time he returned fifteen minutes later, William and Adriana had nearly finished their meals; Trustrum sipped his cold coffee.

"I wrote down your flight information on this napkin. The ticket is paid for. If things go as planned, I'll take you to Kennedy Airport and see you off. Are you okay with these?"

"I'm fine with it," she said.

"Just think, Adriana. You'll be in Brazil with your family

214

before you know it," William said.

"You're very kind to pay for my ticket, Mr. Weinstein," she said.

"Don't thank me, Trustrum will be paying me back. I guarantee you that."

"Speaking of which," Trustrum said, "where's the cash I asked you to bring?"

William reached into his breast pocket and pulled out his billfold. He took out a wad of bills and handed it to Trustrum. "Two thousand—eighteen Franklins and ten Jacksons, as ordered."

Trustrum took one hundred dollars in twenty-dollar bills, folded it up, and slipped it into his pants pocket. He gave Adriana the rest. "This should see you through until I send more. But, if I don't return for you within three hours, I need you, William, to drive her back to Washington. Maybe you could look in on her every now and then just to see that she's all right."

"No problem, Trustrum," William answered.

Trustrum took out the expensive box from the duffel bag. He opened it, quickly pulled out Baines's automatic pistol, and just as quickly, tucked it into his inside jacket pocket. Before looking up, he returned the box to the duffel bag and handed it to William. "Whatever you do, don't lose this." William nodded.

Trustrum took in a big breath, held it for a moment, and then exhaled. "Well, this is it." He looked at his wristwatch. "It'll all be over soon—one way or the other."

He stood up, shook William's hand and gave Adriana a kiss on the cheek. "So, we're clear that both of you just wait here until I come back. Right?"

"Sure," William said.

There won't be much time for talk then. Adriana, you'll come with me, of course. We'll make one stop before heading to the airport. And William, you've been a great friend, but your role in all this will be over…I guess you'll just head on home."

"But won't you need me to drive you somwhere after Adriana's plane leaves?"

"No need. I have a feeling someone will be along to give me a ride."

Chapter Seventeen
Dead Reckoning

Determining a ship's location without the help of the stars, relying solely on the comparison of time and distance to the trip's known starting location, is not always an easy thing to do.

Trustrum Crook desperately needed his own dead reckoning if he hoped to stay alive.

~~~~~~~~~

Trustrum hailed a taxi and gave the address for the offices of Paul C. Underwood and Associates. Traffic was moving at a quick pace; for once he wished it would slow down. But when the taxi arrived in front of the building, Trustrum did not hesitate. He paid the driver and swiftly moved across the wide sidewalk and through the front doors into the lobby.

He used the stairway to reach the third floor where Underwood's office was located. As he walked down the hallway he was relieved not to cross paths with anybody. It was Wednesday, an hour before lunch, and the other office doors were closed. He wondered if he could pull this off without alerting anyone else in the building. Trustrum opened the door to Underwood's office and stepped inside.

"Mr. Crook?" the receptionist asked. Trustrum turned away from her, and facing the door, he locked it. "What are you doing?"

"Hi, Carolyn. Where is he?"

"*Mr. Underwood* is in his office, but he's on the

phone…Mr. Crook, you can't go in there!"

Trustrum stormed into Underwood's office to find him sitting behind his desk reading a newspaper.

"What the—" Underwood barely had time to blurt out.

"Shut up and listen. Where's the bug?"

"The what?" He let the newspaper fall onto his desk and stood up. "Get the hell out of my office before I throw you out, Crook!"

Trustrum heard the sounds of Carolyn making a phone call. He could only assume that it was for help. He pulled the gun out from inside his jacket and pointed it directly at Underwood. Trustrum shouted, "Carolyn, put down the phone now, or you'll be to blame for the new hole in your boss's head." She slammed the receiver down. "Now, get in here."

But instead of obeying his command, Carolyn ran toward the door, trying to escape. Trustrum darted after her, grabbing a handful of her long mane before she had managed to unlock the deadbolt. She fell back onto the floor. Still controlling her by her hair, Trustrum raised his other arm and pointed the gun just in the nick of time at Underwood, who had charged out of his office into the reception room and was about to pounce on Trustrum.

"Get back!" Trustrum shouted. Underwood raised his hands and stepped backward, returning slowly to his office. Trustrum pulled Carolyn up and dragged her with him. Underwood moved behind his desk and sat down in his seat. Trustrum shoved Carolyn down onto the couch that stood next to the back wall. "Move and I shoot. I'm not kidding." She trembled with fear.

Trustrum stood close to Underwood, still pointing the gun at him. "I don't have time to repeat everything I say. Now, where's the bug."

"Go to hell."

Trustrum leapt at Underwood and pistol-whipped him,

until he slid to the floor, unconscious and bleeding. Finally, Trustrum stepped back and looked at Carolyn. "I don't want to do the same thing to you, but I will. I have nothing to lose, you see. So, just tell me where the bug is."

Crying, her hands covering her face, she shouted, "I don't know!"

"Don't lie to me. You know more about what's going on in this office than Underwood."

"How would I know what's going?" she asked, still crying.

"Because that's how it works in *every* office. The staff always knows more about what's going on than the boss does. So where is it?"

"There are two: one's on the inside of the lampshade on his desk, there's another one on the back of the picture on the reception room wall—the one of the antique cars."

"Don't move or I'll blow your head off," Trustrum said. He quickly stepped out to the reception room, found the first bug, and yanked it loose—the picture and frame to which it was attached fell to the floor, breaking into pieces when it landed. Then he returned to Underwood's office, felt for the second bug on the lampshade, and ripped it off. Once he had crushed them under his foot, he looked at Underwood, who appeared to be regaining consciousness. "Make the calls to the publicity crew. I need an emergency press conference scheduled at the normal place in two hours."

Underwood tried to laugh, but it came out as a stifled snicker. "You're dead, Crook."

"If you're not going to cooperate, then you're no use to me," Trustrum said and pointed the gun at Underwood's head.

"You're out of your league."

For a moment, Trustrum nearly thought he could do it, but a moment later, he came to his senses. Once again, he rapidly swung at Underwood, striking him with the pistol with each word. "I...don't...have...time...for...this!" Underwood fell out of his leather seat onto the floor unconscious. Carolyn stared at Underwood as he lay battered and bleeding on the Oriental rug. Trustrum turned to look at the petrified young woman.

"See this! Do you see this! Do you want me to do this to you? Huh? What's it going to be, Carolyn?"

"You'll never get away with it! They're probably on their way over here, right now," Carolyn screamed.

"That's why you're going to do it fast, starting right now!"

"Please! They'll punish me!"

"What would you rather deal with: *maybe* being punished by them or *definitely* being beaten to death by me? If you don't start calling this instant, I'm going to start bashing your brains in, until either you make the calls or they get here. Now, who are you going to bet on?"

"Okay, okay," she said. She wiped her eyes, took a deep breath, trying to calm down, and made the first of ten calls that started a chain reaction of phone calls and e-mails with an organized network of people who would make up Trustrum's press conference. Thirty minutes later, the Coterie's well-funded media circus had been activated. When she finished with her last call, she gently hung up the phone and looked at Trustrum.

"Now, just one more thing, and I'll be on my way. Take off his clothes."

"What?"

"Take off his clothes, now!"

Carolyn looked at the unconscious, rotund man as he lay on the floor. Trustrum pushed her toward him, and she knelt down and began the difficult task of disrobing the heavy, limp body. Meanwhile, Trustrum ripped out the telephone lines: first in Underwood's office, then in the reception room at Carolyn's station. He unlocked the front door leading to the hallway and carefully looked out to make certain no one was around. Then he closed the door and locked it again. When he returned to the office, Underwood lay naked on the floor.

"Grab his right arm," Trustrum instructed Carolyn, and the two of them dragged Underwood around the desk to the other side of the office where there was a little storage closet. Trustrum swung open the door. Cluttered, metal shelves—no windows—almost enough room for two people: it was perfect. Trustrum had Carolyn help push Underwood inside.

"Good. Now, your next," he said, slightly out of breath.

"I have to get in there with him?"

"C'mon, Carolyn. Don't mess with me." She cringed and stepped toward the dark closet. Trustrum put his hand on her arm, stopping her. "First, your clothes. Let's go. You're holding me up."

"Why do I have to take off my clothes?" she asked in a tone revealing her panic.

"No clothes, no phone—there's a pattern here, Carolyn. I'm trying to gain a little time, and you're not helping the cause. So, let's go and take it off...now!"

Carolyn muttered under her breath as she disrobed. When she finished, she stood in front of Trustrum with her left hand over her groin and her right arm across her breasts. Trustrum jerked his head to the side, indicating that she should move. She glared at him and stepped silently into the closet, carefully avoiding Underwood, who lay in a heap on the floor. Trustrum closed the closet door and wedged a metal, straight-backed chair between the floor and the doorknob. He heard Carolyn cursing him at the top of her lungs, but her exact words—muffled by the door—were unclear.

Before leaving, Trustrum scanned the office and considered his next move. He hated to do it because of the noise it would make, but he knew he had no choice. So, he picked up the computer, raised it over his head, and threw it to the floor. It broke into pieces with a crash. Then, he did the same, to the monitor. Trustrum cringed at the sound. He had not expected it to be *that* loud and worried if others in the building had heard. Nevertheless, he was glad he had done it, for if by chance the computer contained the only easily available list of the media contacts, Trustrum did not want the Coterie henchmen to lay their hands on it and cancel his interview. Then, he hid Baines's automatic pistol in Underwood's desk. He would have preferred to have kept it, just in case, but he could not think where in his plan he would have another opportunity to safely ditch it later on—besides, he might accidentally hurt somebody with the thing.

Before leaving, Trustrum surveyed Underwood's office and the reception room. Just when he had decided that he had done everything possible to slow down the Coterie's pursuit of him, a phone rang from behind Carolyn's desk. Startled, Trustrum immediately began to search for it. First, he confirmed that all of the phone wires had been pulled out of the wall and damaged beyond repair—still, the phone rang. Then, he realized what it was and reached into Carolyn's purse for her cell phone. Trustrum detached the phone's battery and put it and the phone into separate pockets of his sport coat.

Exhausted, Trustrum chose to use the elevator. *The Coterie goons seemed to always use the stairs in this place anyway,* he thought. Still, he was anxious as he waited for the car to arrive once he had pushed the button. However, fate was on his side—when the doors slid open, the elevator was empty.

Trustrum ran his shaking hands through his hair, which was wet with perspiration. The knot in his stomach tightened with each floor the elevator descended. When the door opened on the ground floor, he hesitated for a moment, then poked his head into the lobby and scanned the area—no one. Trustrum hurried through the vestibule,

222

out the large glass doors, and into the busy streets of New York City.

~~~~~~~~~

In the taxi, heading back to the diner where William and Adriana waited, Trustrum noticed the blood that had dried on his hands. He tried to rub it off with his shirttail, but it did not make much of a difference . The driver did not speak, but Trustrum was aware the man was watching him in the rearview mirror. Finally, the cab stopped in front of the diner. Trustrum handed the driver the fare and tip through the opening in the safety glass that separated them and got out. As he walked into the diner, Trustrum sunk his hands deep into his jacket pockets.

William and Adriana had moved to a booth in the far corner. William was facing the door and, seeing Trustrum enter, stood up. "What happened to you, Trustrum?" he asked. Adriana gasped and raised her hands to her mouth when she saw him. William did not wait for his friend to reply. He grabbed Trustrum by the arm and quickly escorted him to the men's room. Trustrum saw in the mirror why the taxicab driver and his friends reacted the way they had—not only were his hands bloody from striking Underwood, but his face and hair had been splattered and smeared with blood.

"What a mess," Trustrum said.

"What did you do to the guy, kill him?" asked William. As Trustrum began splashing water on his face, William wet paper towels and began scrubbing Trustrum's hair.

"I didn't kill him. But I gave him something to think about."

"You're lucky the police didn't see you. You need to stop this. It's insane."

"What are you talking about? I succeeded. The plan is on track."

223

"You've got to be out of your mind, Trustrum. I don't see how running around New York looking like Jack the Ripper is going to help us."

"Well, I hadn't planned on the blood, but I did get the job done."

"What did it take to get him to make the calls?"

"He wouldn't call anybody, but his sweet secretary was most obliging after she watched me crack his skull open. There, that looks much better."

William looked Trustrum over while Trustrum looked at himself in the mirror.

"You're sure you didn't kill anybody?"

"Not yet, but the day's not over."

"Oy vay. There's no getting it off your jacket," William said. "Wait, put this on." William took off his sport coat and handed it to Trustrum after he had taken off his own. Trustrum put on his friend's sport coat—it was a little big—and William began to stuff Trustrum's sport coat into the lavatory trash bin.

"What's this?" William asked, having felt something hard in one of the pockets.

"Oh yeah, it's a cell phone."

"Good thing I noticed it."

"Actually, that's the perfect place for it. It's not mine, and I don't want it."

"Sure?"

"Positive," Trustrum said.

William finished shoving Trustrum's jacket into the trash bin. Then he surveyed Trustrum's appearance. "Passable."

"Come on, we have to hurry," Trustrum said, and both men returned to the booth where Adriana waited. Her level of anxiety had obviously increased; Trustrum sat down across from her and took her shaking hands.

224

"Calm down—just calm down. We're on track. I think this is going to work."

~~~~~~~~~

Three Coterie associates that Trustrum had never met before were in a car heading to Underwood's office. One of them, named Montgomery, was on a cellular phone, checking in with Baines.

"What do you mean you're in a traffic jam? There's no answer at Underwood's, and I need you there now!" screamed Baines over his cellular phone as he, Pritchard, Steeg, and Abrams drove north on Interstate 95, past Baltimore. They had been notified when Trustrum had surfaced at Underwood's office, and had immediately started the journey back to New York City. "Listen to me, you imbecile. I don't care if you use the subway, or if you have to run all the way there. Just get to Underwood's and find that guy!"

~~~~~~~~~

"You're sure you don't want me to wait?" William asked. "I've come this far, Trustrum."

"I'm certain. There's no need risking more lives than is absolutely necessary."

"I just don't feel right leaving you two like this."

"William, it's true I'll be in danger until I leave on the plane," Adriana said. "But if the Coterie discovers you know about them, you'll be easy for them track down later on, whether I pull this off or not. Trustrum will look out for me. You've done your part. Now it's time for you to go home."

"She's right, William."

"Trustrum will see this through, and I'll be on my way to Brazil before you're halfway home."

William grasped their hands and squeezed them firmly.

"Good luck to both of you." Then, he slid out of the booth and stood up. He paused for just an instant, then he turned and walked away without another word. Trustrum and Adriana silently watched him cross the room of the diner and exit through the front entrance. Adriana, who had had to twist around in her seat in order to watch him leave, turned back to face Trustrum. "It feels as though we have reached the point of no return."

"We've been there all along, Adriana," he said. They spent the next thirty minutes reviewing how they were going to handle the press conference. Finally, when it was time, Trustrum paid the bill for the food, and they took a taxi to the hotel where the Coterie press conferences were routinely held.

As Trustrum helped Adriana out of the taxi, he was surprised at the number of people who were swarming into the hotel lobby. He had never seen so many people attend one of their meetings before. They walked into the lobby and found the concierge, who directed them down the hallway to the second large conference room on the right.

It was now ten minutes past the time Trustrum had scheduled the conference. The room was packed with journalists. *Could the Coterie have augmented the number of news people on their payroll?* He could see from the logos on the cameras and microphones that there were representatives attending from mainstream media as well, which had never happened before as far as Trustrum knew. *What is going on?*

"I had no idea there would be so many people, Trustrum," said Adriana, her voice revealing her fear.

"Maybe it's a slow news day or something. Hey, all the better for us," he said, and, carrying the leather bag, he pushed through the crowd with a surge of confidence. Adriana, carrying her two travel totes, was close at his heels as they made their way to the front podium. There was no time to lose. Trustrum knew it would not take the

Coterie long to find Underwood and Carolyn, and then, they would know where to find him.

Now in the front of the room, with Adriana by his side, Trustrum stepped onto the stage, then took out the unfinished gold box and placed it onto a side table in front of the audience. Next, he took out the photographs and news clippings of Mr. Silva. He paused a moment and looked at the now hushed crowd of journalists before speaking into the microphone.

"Ladies and gentlemen, thank you for coming here on such short notice. I recognize many of you from past gatherings. For those of you joining us for the first time, my name is Trustrum Crook. I have a prepared statement I wish to read to you. Then, I will answer questions. I must warn you now that this will be brief, since we have another appointment to make."

From his pants pocket, Trustrum pulled out a folded square of paper, opened it, and smoothed it out against the podium. Adriana, looking over his shoulder, observed that the crumpled paper was nothing more than an advertisement for a Laundromat.

"I, Trustrum Crook, am not the artisan that the public has been led to believe that I am," he began, as if reading from the paper. "Although I am an artisan, I am not the person responsible for the many wonderful works, such as this unfinished one, that have been exhibited and sold under my name." Trustrum paused. The room was silent. He and Adriana glanced at each other. Then, again addressing the crowd of newspaper and television and radio reporters, Trustrum continued.

"I was asked by the real artisan to act not just on his behalf as agent, but also, he urged me to pretend to be the very artisan. This was not meant to fool the public in order to cheat them. Whether I made the articles or another artisan made them does not change what they are: unique, one-of-a-kind objets d'art. Very special, gifted hands were required to create such works of art, and those hands belonged to Sebastiao Silva." Trustrum bent down and picked up the largest picture of the bunch and held it up for the crowd to see. "This is a picture of Mr. Silva…here, another showing him at work behind his workbench. Having come from Brazil as a political refugee, he feared notoriety. Although his talents as an artist could not be stifled, his fear of public recognition prevented him from claiming the praise he so deserved.

It is now with sadness that I tell you: Mr. Sebastiao Silva has died. He suffered a heart attack nearly two weeks ago. It was late at night, and he had been working on this reliquary before you. Note the gash and dent on the lid— Mr. Silva made them at the time he had the attack. His wife, Adriana, is the representative of his estate. She has decided to leave this, his last work, exactly the way it is— unfinished and scarred. We feel that this article is priceless. It will not be for sale at this time. However, Mrs. Silva does possess a number of works by Mr. Silva, which are in a safe place and will be sold at her and my discretion. Ladies and gentlemen, allow me to introduce to you, Mrs. Sebastiao Silva."

Strobes flashed. Trustrum stepped away from the podium, and Adriana stepped up. She looked weary and when she spoke, her words were soft. "My husband, Sebastiao was deeply moved by the interest collectors have shown in his work. He loved the jewelry business and put his heart into everything he touched, whether it was an important creation or something as simple as repair work. Thank you for helping to preserve his memory." She turned away, tears flowing down her cheeks. Trustrum stepped up to the podium again. "Adriana will return to her homeland, Brazil. I have been asked to continue as the agent, here, in America. I will put together a formal press release within the next week describing further details about Sebastiao Silva. In the meantime, I will try to answer just a few questions."

"How much do you expect the reliquary will sell for when it's finally put up for sale?" called out someone from the crowd of reporters.

"As I said before, it's priceless. A similar work by Mr. Silva recently sold for five hundred and twenty-seven thousand dollars. It would not surprise me if each of his creations tops the million-dollar mark."

"Exactly how large is this back inventory of Mr. Silva's work?" asked another voice from the crowd.

"The number of articles that remain to be sold and their whereabouts will remain confidential at this time for security reasons. However, I can tell you that over the next ten to fifteen years, we expect to sell two or three of Mr. Silva's creations each year. Art collectors need not worry."

"Do you anticipate fraud charges against you, Mr. Crook?" called out still another voice.

"There has been no fraud connected with Mr. Silva's art in any way. I need not tell you that we live in a time when technology threatens the most sophisticated security measures. We believed that the only way to protect Sebastiao Silva while he created his priceless art was to keep him out of the spotlight. I also want to remind you that the price of an artist's work usually increases considerably at the time of his or her death. We expect Mr. Silva's work not only to show such increases in value, but also, increases caused by the enhanced interest of collectors due to the unusual revelation you have just heard. My acting as the artist was never meant to deceive. I was merely a vehicle to protect Mr. and Mrs. Silva. Now, ladies and gentlemen, time has run out. Thank you for coming."

Trustrum escorted Adriana toward a side door away from the inquisitive mob, but only after reclaiming the solid gold reliquary.

With Baines and Pritchard in the back seat and Steeg and Abrams in the front, the black limousine was thirty miles south of Manhattan on Interstate 95 north. Baines was livid, screaming into his phone. "You idiots! There's no excuse, Montgomery."

"Yes sir," answered Montgomery, who was back in the car with the other two associates. It was slow going through the congested city streets.

"So, where is he?" Baines shouted.

"The girl said he made her organize a press conference at the usual place. We're on our way now."

"Good. We'll meet you at the hotel. Keep me informed and get him!" Baines shouted.

The Coterie men arrived at the hotel as the room was emptying. They pushed through the crowd, trying to find Trustrum. Montgomery rang Baines.

"Tell me you've got him," Baines answered.

"Sir, we reached the press conference too late. We discovered from one of our media contacts that he's with some lady named Adriana Silva. Both of them are supposed to be heading to Kennedy. Apparently, she's catching a flight to Brazil, if you can believe that."

"What I believe, Mr. Montgomery, is that you better not let that happen. Now, listen to me. We're heading straight to the airport. I don't care what it takes; just get there before we lose him."

"Yes, sir…Oh, Mr. Baines, there is one more thing."

"What?"

"The press conference. *This* you really won't believe…"

~~~~~~~~~

Trustrum and Adriana had walked out of the conference room with barely minutes to spare. He assumed that the Coterie would eventually catch up to him, he just did not want Adriana around when they did. He was anxious to get her checked in for her flight.

During the taxi ride to Kennedy Airport, Trustrum said, "You were wonderful, Adriana. They bought it. I think we have a chance."

"Then it's over, right?"

"For you it is, but I still have to contend with the Coterie. They may go ahead with their plans for me—just to save face." Adriana rested her head on Trustrum's shoulder for the rest of the ride to the airport. For now, there was nothing more to say.

As soon as they arrived at the airport, Trustrum helped Adriana check in. There was just a little over a half-hour before take-off by the time she had her boarding pass in hand. Trustrum encouraged Adriana to hurry—he wanted her safely beyond the X-ray point.

Before passing through, Adriana turned to him. "I will pray for you, Trustrum."

"Thank you. How about one for Sarah, too."

She smiled. "And for Sarah. But what about our lie, Trustrum?"

"What lie?"

"We stood in front of the whole world and said that Sebastiao made those things."

"Oh. Well, I was thinking about that—as far as I'm concerned, he did make them."

"What do you mean?"

"Mr. Silva taught me every skill I know when it comes to working gold and gemstones. In a way, I'm just an extension of him—sort of like his living legacy. That's more than Faberge could say, and everybody and his brother credits him for making those eggs."

"Faberge didn't make them?"

"He didn't even design most of them. He had a factory

full of designers and craftsmen."

"I always thought he had been the one."

"But that's my point—he *was*. It's just that his genius was in pulling it all together using the right people and then marketing the stuff. As far as I'm concerned, Mr. Silva had just as much if not more to do with making our objets d'art than Faberge had with his. So, let's not speak of it again—agreed?"

"Agreed."

They hugged, she kissed his cheek, and he kissed hers. "Take care, Trustrum."

"You, too."

She turned to leave, carrying the two travel bags, but stopped after a few steps and turned back to look at Trustrum. "Are you sure you know what you're doing?"

"I'm sure that I need you to go through that X-ray and catch your plane. Now go."

<hr>

After Adriana's plane departed, there was nothing left for Trustrum to do, but wait. No sense returning home to Annapolis, the Coterie would eventually catch up with him and just drag him back to New York City—if they did not kill him first. No, the Coterie, in its infinite wisdom, would have to figure out that he was at Kennedy. They would find him waiting in the airport lounge—drinking in the airport lounge, that is. When he found a bar to his liking, he walked in and ordered a drink. He reached into his pocket to pay, but discovered that along the way, he had lost the little change that was left after three long New York cab rides. His lack of money was not a dilemma; however, since he did not plan to leave the bar until the Coterie found him. "If they want to kill me, they'll just have to pay my bar tab," he said to himself.

As he slowly drugged himself one drink at a time, he

laughed at the irony of having a priceless work of art made out of gold—its scrap-gold value alone worth a fortune—sitting right next to him on the floor, when he did not even have enough money to pay for one of his drinks, let alone the tab he was building.

"What are you laughing at, Crook?" came the deep, throaty voice Trustrum knew belonged to Baines.

Trustrum, now drunk, swiveled around on the barstool. "Baines! Pritchard! Associate guys! It's so good to see you fellows! I've missed you," he said. His words were heavily slurred, and he wavered even as he sat.

"Let's go, Crook. And keep it down."

"He's not going anywhere until the tab is paid," demanded the bartender, having seen the men take hold of Trustrum by the arms and start to lead him toward the door.

"That's right, and I'm broke. So, I guess I'll have to stay. Barroom sanctuary! Barroom sanctuary!"

As Pritchard and Steeg dragged Trustrum out of the bar, Abrams paid his sixty-three-dollar bar tab. They accompanied him out of the airport, and then pushed him into the back seat of the limousine waiting at the curb. Trustrum resigned himself to the fact that whatever happened was now out of his hands.

"Hey, you guys," he said, stumbling over his words, "do me just one favor, will you? If you're going to kill me, do it before I sober up. The hangover with this one's going to be killer enough."

Chapter Eighteen
Fiddler's Green

The old seaman's heaven, where everything a seaman lacked while months—perhaps, even years—at sea was plentiful: green grass, happy fiddle music, women, and drink.

Trustrum Crook had always thought the image of a Fiddler's Green appealing—if only he did not have to die to get there.

~~~~~~~~

Trustrum cooperated; there was no sense in struggling. He was at the mercy of the Coterie, and there was no other way around it. The limousine with the darkened windows transported them back to the Coterie headquarters. The ride seemed endless, and fear caused him to sober up along the way. He noticed on the elevator ride from the parking garage to the top floor of the building that he was surprisingly alert. Baines stood behind him in the elevator car; during the limousine ride, Trustrum had looked at him and smirked at seeing the bandages wrapped around his head.

Steeg and Abrams shoved Trustrum out of the elevator and pushed him into the wall across the corridor. Then they dragged him down the hall toward the room in which he would learn of his fate. Pritchard opened the door of the conference room. Trustrum was forced inside and made to sit in a chair.

"Mr. Crook, you have been extremely difficult these past years—very difficult," Coulbourne said. He was seated behind his desk. Steeg and Abrams remained standing by

Trustrum's chair. Pritchard was off to one side; Baines stood opposite him.

"I'm sorry I've been a problem for you, but I never did want to be part of this."

"Shut up, Mr. Crook! " Coulbourne yelled. It was the first time Trustrum had ever heard him raise his voice. *That's not a good sign,* Trustrum thought. Regaining his composure, Coulbourne continued. "You have managed to design and actualize an ingenious financial situation. On that, I congratulate you. Dead-artist prices with an endless supply of salable product—I like it—I like it a lot. Of course, we couldn't repeat this with other Coterie artists—it would be too obvious for us to replicate it. But you'll be glad to know that I've decided to allow it with you."

"Then you're not going to kill me?"

"For the time being—no. And we're going to give you the freedom that you think you so badly need. In return, you will supply us with two works every year—using your Silva charade."

"Only two?"

"Anymore and it wouldn't work. Now, would it? How many things could your Mr. Silva possibly have had just lying around. Realistically, the intrinsic costs alone would have been prohibitive. I figure we could allow an average of two to enter the market each year and string it out for about five, maybe ten years."

Trustrum thought about Coulbourne's words, then remembered the ten-million-dollar life insurance policy the Coterie held on him. "Are you telling me that I'll only be useful to you for five or ten more years?"

"You've proven you're resourceful, Mr. Crook. I'm sure you can think of something to replace the Silva project, once it is exhausted. I have confidence that you will come up with something that we can use you for; the Coterie does not like losing good people when we find them."

"Then nothing's really changed. I'm still your slave until the day I die."

"You see, this is one of those times when perspective makes all the difference. Think about it this way, Mr. Crook. Everybody works and makes a certain amount of money. Then, based on the amount they make, they must give a percentage of it to Uncle Sam. That is the price of living in this wonderful country and taking advantage of all its glorious opportunities. Now in your case, in addition to your obligation to Uncle Sam, you have an obligation to Uncle Coulbourne. Go on with your life, have your precious freedom, but…in order to have such an opportunity, you have to pay a tax each year to the Coterie by creating two objets d'art. Simply think of it as the price of doing business."

"Otherwise you'll leave me alone?"

"Just like the IRS, Trustrum—we'll keep close tabs on you, but as long as you pay us, we'll leave you alone."

"I will be getting rid of the bugs."

"As long as you supply us with two works each year, I don't care what you do."

"Since we're cleaning things up; what about the price you have on my head?"

"You mean the insurance policy?"

"Yes."

"Of course, we will retain it. You'll have to die someday, Mr. Crook," he said, grinning. Then, he added, "Fortunately for you, it appears this time, we both win. Because, I assure you—and do mark my words—I will never be the one to lose."

~~~~~~~~

As the limousine carried Trustrum home, he considered what he had done and began to feel remorse. Trustrum reflected on the ramifications of having passed the credit to

Mr. Silva. Before now, everything he had done stemmed from survival instincts alone. His only motive had been survival for himself, Sarah, and his friends. Ethical? Moral? He shook his head. He wanted to believe that there was no comparing what he had done to what other people have done throughout history and will continue to do in the future—and most times out of nothing more than greed. From dollar diplomacy to…well, just about every business out there has its own game running, he thought, and he of all people knew that the jewelry industry probably topped the list.

He knew he was rationalizing, but what choice did he have? He realized that there was no getting around it; he would just have to live with it—but could he?

It did not take Trustrum Crook long to make up his mind: he *could* live with it.

~~~~~~~~

The limousine stopped in front of Trustrum's house. There was no communication from Abrams, who drove, or Steeg, in the passenger seat; they simply waited for him to get out. His feet had barely touched the ground and the door closed, when the car sped away, tires screeching. Trustrum stood for a moment, first watching the car drive away, then looking at his home. He went to the front door— it was unlocked. He quietly opened it and stepped inside. Could Baines have beaten him home, planning to finally have his revenge?

"Hello?" he called out, but no answer. "Hello?" he called again. Then with a burst, Marquise came bounding down the steps, loudly calling out in her Siamese voice. "Hey, girl. How did you get home?"

"Trustrum! I didn't hear you come in." Megan stood at the top of the stairs.

"I just arrived. What are you doing here?"

"What am I doing here? Where have you been?"

"Wait a minute. I'm asking the questions. Why are you here?"

"Are you kidding me? We agreed that I would move in and start as housekeeper sometime during the last week in April. Well, here it is and here I am."

"I'm sorry. You're right."

"I nearly gave up waiting for you, but then I remembered about the backdoor key you hide under the rock."

"And I guess the alarm system wasn't on."

"Yeah, and a good thing too. I had forgotten all about it until I had come inside," she laughed. "A lot of good it did you, huh?"

"I guess it would work better if I turned it on every once in a while."

"The neighbors brought the cat over when they saw I was here. I hope you're not angry that I came in and took over like I did, but I thought that's what you had intended for me to do."

"It's okay, Megan, really. I'm sorry I put you in that position. I've been overwhelmed with things lately, and I simply forgot when you were coming."

"You seem hesitant about all this. You're not going to renege on our agreement, are you? You realize I've given up my apartment and moved all the way out here and—"

"No, no, no. Everything's fine. I just ran into some trouble, but it's done with now—" Trustrum abruptly stopped talking. Then he said, "Don't move." He quickly went to each floor to the places he knew some of the Coterie's bugs were hidden. He tore them loose one at a time and carried them downstairs to the garage, where he crushed them into bits and pieces under the heel of his shoe before throwing them into the trash can. Megan had stayed in the kitchen and could not tell what Trustrum was doing from the little she had viewed of his actions.

Returning to the kitchen, Trustrum laughed when he saw Megan's quizzical expression. "Don't ask," he said.

"Whatever you say. What about the press conference?"

"Huh?"

"Am I allowed to ask about that?"

"You saw the press conference?"

"It was on the TV. Of course I saw it."

"Man, that's not going to help my appraising business."

"Are you kidding? The way people are today, I bet the phone will be ringing off the hook."

Trustrum sat down at the dining-room table and looked around his home. He could not wait for Sarah to be there with him, he thought.

"You look like you could use a good meal," Megan said. "How about I cook you something special?"

"Thanks, but I think I'll just go upstairs and soak in the tub for a while."

"Before you do that, you might want to return this message. A Mr. Allen from Allen and Associates called. He said he needed to talk with you...something about an unanticipated scheduling conflict that's come up. Says he'll have to reschedule some program you were going to put on for his clients."

Trustrum sighed, feeling a warm glow inside. "It's great to be back home. I have to tell you, Megan, after what I've been through, I feel like a million—make that ten million—dollars."

"I doubt I'll ever know how ten million dollars feels."

"Come on. You know what I mean. It's like I could take on just about anybody or anything right now—and win."

"Is that right," Megan said. "Then, it's your turn not to move. Stay right there." She turned away from Trustrum and went to the sideboard. On it was a large stack of mail—obviously accumulated over a number of weeks. "You might want to consider having the post office hold your mail the next time you go away for a while. Your mailbox was bursting at the seams."

"Actually, there had been someone picking it up, but something happened unexpectedly, and they stopped doing it. I guess I can count on you for that from now on, can't I?"

She picked up an envelope from the top of the pile and stepped back toward Trustrum. "I was going to wait to give this to you, but since you're feeling invincible, maybe now is a better time."

As he reached for the envelope she held out to him, Trustrum said, "Whatever it is, it can't compare to what I've just survived."

Then he read the return address, and Megan watched as Trustrum's smile turned to a frown. "Oh, no!" he moaned. "Not the IRS!"

Trustrum tossed the envelope on the table, stood, and headed toward the door.

"Where are you going?" Megan asked.

"There's someone I have to see, right away."

"What about your bath?"

"It can wait."

An hour later Trustrum was parking his car in front of Sarah's house in Cambridge. She was in the front yard, surrounded by a white picket fence, playing with three neighborhood children, when she saw Trustrum getting out of his car.

"Daddy!" she shouted and ran toward him. Trustrum quickly crossed the road and knelt down to meet her just inside the gate, and they hugged each other. "Oh, Daddy, I've missed you."

"I've missed you, too, baby."

"Why do you have to work so much?"

"Sometimes there's just no getting around it, sweetheart."

"Well, I wish you could be with me more."

"Is that what you wish, huh?"

"Yeah."

"You mean, out of all the wishes in the world, the best you can come up with is spending more time with your daddy?"

"That's my wish."

"Then wishes do come true."

"Really?"

"Yes, because I quit my job. From now on, I'm sticking to appraising, just like before."

"And we can go sailing together?"

"Of course, we'll go sailing—lots and lots."

"Oh, I can't wait!" Sarah said, hugging Trustrum tightly. But then she abruptly pulled away and looked at him straight in the eye, making a stern face. "And no more talking about that necklace—just sailing."

Trustrum laughed and pulled Sarah in for another embrace.

"I promise—just sailing."

Acknowledgements

Special thanks go to:

Patrick Murray Young, who so imaginatively captured the essence of my story in his painting.

Buck and Deborah Webb for their friendship and caring support.

Cathy Calhoun of Calhoun Jewelers, who is always generous with her guidance and jewelry expertise.

Chip Craig for spending countless hours discussing this work and sharing his ideas about its marketing.

Sanford Rubin and Edwin Rubin of Treasure Chest Fine Jewelry, Fred T. White of Michelle Lee Jewelers, and Paul and Jan Metzner of Jewelry by P.M. Creations—long time colleagues and friends who have supported me professionally, personally, and in this work.

the many friends and appraisal clients who over the years have shared their thoughts on this work.

Dann Shannon and my friends at Trimble & Durst.

Would you like us to notify you when new Crook Book titles are published?

Let us add you to our confidential mailing list. We will be glad to contact you about them as well as other titles by our authors as they become available.

Send your name and postal address or your email address to:

Trimble & Durst, LLC
PO Box 1054
Bel Air MD 21014

Or email us at:
books@trimbledurst.com

Visit us on the web at
www.trimbledurst.com

Coming soon:

Second in the *Crook Book* Series
BLOODSTONE

Wholesalers on the road, carrying suitcases full of jewelry inventory, are being robbed and murdered at an alarmingly increased rate. In and around Washington and Baltimore matters worsen so that jewelry appraisers—mistaken as wholesalers—are added to the growing list of victims. While FBI and police agencies are consumed with preventing terrorist attacks, Colombian gangs, known for their crimes against American jewelers, are working overtime—until even Trustrum Crook finds himself struggling to survive.

Third in the *Crook Book* Series
OLDEST PROFESSION

"I'm telling you, what everybody thinks is the oldest profession puts the cart before the horse...because whoever the very first person in history was to do this thing surely had to have done it for jewelry. That's why I always say, the jewelry trade is ahead of prostitution—though not by far," said Trustrum Crook.

ccccccc